THE SWORDSMAN

A MEDIEVAL ROMANCE

BY KATHRYN LE VEQUE

THE BLACKCHURCH GUILD:
SHADOW KNIGHTS SERIES

KATHRYN LE VEQUE
NOVELS

WWW.KATHRYNLEVEQUE.COM

ARE YOU SIGNED UP FOR KATHRYN'S BLOG?

You'll get the latest news and information on exclusive giveaways, exclusive excerpts, coming releases, sales, free books, cover reveals and more.

Kathryn's blog followers get it all first. No spam, no junk.

Get the latest info from the reigning Queen of English Medieval Romance!

Sign Up Here

kathrynleveque.com

England's most elite training guild.

Knights of the highest order.

Numquam dedite. Never surrender.

THE HISTORY OF THE BLACKCHURCH GUILD

St. Giles de Bottreaux was a knight who had been disgraced for using unconventional tactics. Having served the Duke of Normandy, he was present at the Battle of Hastings. Unfortunately, he caught wind of a Norman lord who was about to betray the duke, and he tortured the lord to gain valuable information about the Saxon resistance.

He was vilified for it.

St. Giles was released from the duke's service because the rebel Norman was both a rich man and a distant cousin of the duke's. With no means of income, St. Giles and his brother, St. Lyon, wandered England, unable to find a suitable position. In desperation, they were forced to become part of a Saxon pirate group out of Watermouth, Devon.

Realizing that piracy was lucrative and putting their knightly skills to good use, the brothers quickly rose in the ranks and ended up commanding their own ships. St. Giles eventually formed his own pirate crew with the help of his brother, men known as Triton's Hellions. Their ships were the *Argos*, the *Mt. Pelion*, the *Pagasa*, and the *Athena*. St. Giles' specialty was in recruiting disgraced knights and giving them a new and rich career. Those knights began training other knights for a life of piracy at an abandoned church on the shores of Lake Cocytus in the Exmoor Forest. The place was called "Blackchurch" because it was a black, burned-out shell of a former sanctuary.

But such a place, hidden from the world, was a perfect staging ground for a warriors' guild.

More trained men meant more ships and more wealth. The pirate ships sailed the known world, bringing back men as well as treasure. As the years passed, those same ships brought diverse warriors from all over the world to the shores of Devon. While St. Giles settled in to manage their growing empire in the Exmoor Forest, St. Lyon assumed the pirate enterprise. All of the trained warriors he brought to Blackchurch combined with other elite trainers to create the most complex and comprehensive battle training system in the world.

England, who had always dismissed Blackchurch as a pirate training ground, gradually became aware of the quality of those who had completed the course. They were the best-educated warriors in the world. The Earl of Wessex was the first to come to St. Giles and ask him for some of the fine men he'd trained. Soon, fully trained knights with good reputations began asking for admission to the training grounds to learn the "Blackchurch way" of life and warfare. It became lucrative and prestigious. St. Giles' grandson, St. Andrew de Bottreaux, was granted the title Earl of Exmoor by Henry I because St. Andrew gifted the king with an elite group of specialized knights who saved the king on more than one occasion. Soon, the Crown got behind this extraordinary training ground.

Blackchurch's reputation was cemented.

These days, Blackchurch is far less about piracy and far more about training the most coveted and skilled warriors the world has ever seen. Men and women are accepted as long as they are qualified and can pass the entrance test. Every trainer has a specialty—new classes of recruits are formed monthly from qualified applicants from all over the world, and each group of recruits spends at least six months with every trainer. To pay for their training, they either pay the fee once they pass the entrance test or they pledge a portion of their salary once they graduate and find a position. Training is harsh and intense. It is expected that even out of the vetted recruits, most will fail. Those few who succeed become forever known as Shadow Knights, a coveted title denoting their superior status.

As graduates say, you simply don't survive Blackchurch.

You *become* Blackchurch.

THE FAMILY TREE OF DE BOTTREAUX AND THE TRAINERS OF BLACKCHURCH

De Bottreaux tree (Lords of Exmoor, who run Blackchurch):

St. Giles b. 1040 – was part of the conquest of 1066, died 1100. Brother, St. Lyon, served with him as a pirate, and it is St. Lyon's descendants who continue to run the pirate conglomerate known as Triton's Hellions. Now run by St. Abelard de Bottreaux.

St. Simon b. 1070 – d. 1135

St. Andrew b. 1094 – d. 1160

St. Paul b. 1119 – d. 1195

St. Denis b. 1147

St. Denis has two sons—St. Gerard (died 1212) and St. Sebastian, a.k.a. "Sebo," b. 1171 and 1173 respectively. Both trained at Kenilworth and Warwick Castle. Veterans of the Third Crusade.

Current list of trainers (moniker is listed after ancestry):

Tay Munro (Scottish/Greek) – the Leviathan – teaches endurance, physical fitness, structure, and discipline. He's the boot camp, the gateway to the rest of the training.

Sinclair "Sin" de Reyne (Norman) – the Swordsman – sword training, warfare, military history, how to command an army, etc.

Fox de Merest (Norman/Saxon) – the Protector – teaches men how to defend and kill using daggers and other weapons. He's the "MacGyver" of Blackchurch. His class is about defense and thinking outside of the box.

Payne Matheson (Scottish) – the Tempest – Teaches offense. Instructs men on how to size up enemies and figure out their weaknesses. How to fight battles from the ground up.

Kristian Heldane (Dane) – the Viking – He is sea-bound. Everything he does is on water—fighting on water, instruction on boats, etc.

Creston de Royans (Norman) – the Avenger – Interrogation, treatment of the enemy, anything underhanded. How to handle torture and difficult conditions. (Sometimes works in tandem with the Conquistador)

Aamir ibn Rashid (Egyptian) – the North Star – Military history (global) and tactics from other armies. Understanding different cultures and how that dictates their fighting techniques.

Cruz Mediana de Aragón (Spanish) – the Conquistador – Conquest and diplomacy, politics, and art of negotiation. Bribes, coercion, and leverage. (Sometimes works in tandem with the Avenger)

Ming Tang – (Chinese) – the Dragon – Former Shaolin monk. Name means "bright water." Fighting kung fu, using hands, feet, and staff only. Fighting with the mind and not a weapon. Meditation for a warrior to calm the mind and the spirit.

Bowen de Bermingham (Norman/Irish) – the Titan – Warrior etiquette and responsibilities, discipline, hand-to-hand combat, using the landscape/land to one's advantage, living off the land, concealment, stealth. Sometimes works in tandem with the Leviathan and the Tempest.

Assistants (second-level trainers assisting the first level):

Axton Summerlin (The Protector and The Swordsman) A trainer eventually known as **The Kraken**.

Anteaus de Bourne (The Swordsman and The Tempest) A trainer eventually known as **The Eagle**.

Rhodes St. James (The Leviathan, The Viking, The Avenger) A trainer eventually known as **The Centurion**.

Location Map for The Blackchurch Guild

Exmoor Forest, Devon, England

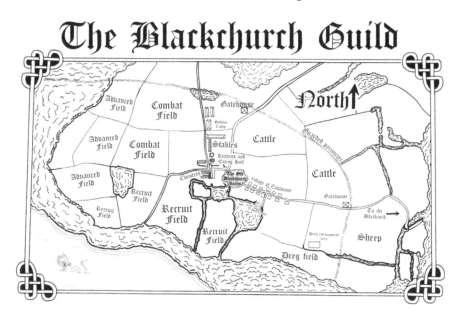

They call him The Swordsman...

Part of the powerful de Reyne family, Sin is a black sheep. A man with a mysterious past and a family he doesn't speak of, he is one of the elite trainers at the Blackchurch Guild, the premier knight training school in England. They call Sin "the Swordsman" because of his skill with a blade, but that skill is about to be put to the test.

So is his heart.

Elisiana Maria Isabella Fernandez y de Verra is a young lady with a problem. Hailing from a very strict family with a Spanish father and a Norman mother, she's had her entire life planned for her, including an impending betrothal that will strengthen family ties. Unable to live a life in chains any longer, Elisiana makes the bold move of running away from home to start a new life. That new life brings her straight into Sin's path.

No one knows much about the new serving wench at the favored tavern of the Blackchurch trainers, but they do know she's very pretty. Having just returned from a lengthy battle assignment north of Paris, Sin is returning to his training position when he meets the young woman with dark hair and flashing, pale eyes. She has spirit, and they manage to strike up a friendship. But friendship turns to something else, and just as Sin is starting to feel something for her, all hell breaks loose—Elisiana's brother locates her and the truth of her identity comes out.

Elisiana is not only of noble blood, but she's also promised to another man.

Now, the Swordsman must make a choice—return to Blackchurch and forget the fiery lass? Or will the man with the mysterious past finally reveal his true self and fight for what he wants?

Who he wants.

Join Sin, Elisiana, the Blackchurch knights, and two factions of pirates as the battle for Elisiana's freedom begins. It's a wild ride through tradition, piracy, blood, battle, and the power of love in this epic Historical Romance adventure.

Numquam dedite. Never surrender.

That's Blackchurch's motto. For the love of Elisiana, it becomes Sin's battle cry.

AUTHOR'S NOTE

The Swordsman has arrived!

I've really loved writing about the Blackchurch Guild simply because it's so different from the usual family sagas. These guys aren't family, but in a sense, they're closer than family because they choose to be loyal to one another. Blood doesn't force them to. It's strictly by choice. Maybe that makes the bonds stronger.

How do these guys differ from the Executioner Knights, my other "band of brothers" series? There's a lot of difference, actually. The Executioner Knights are all men from great families, all bonded together at the highest echelon of service because of family ties and training. The Blackchurch trainers are bonded purely by their seamless service to Blackchurch, and I love how devoted they are to each other, which is never more evident than it is in this book. These aren't cousins or guys who have fought together in the Levant. These are simply the best of the best who ended up at Blackchurch, training the best of the best, and they are by far the most diverse group I have. We have men born in China, Egypt, and Madrid to name a few. But they celebrate those differences, and I really love that.

On to the tale...

Take note of a few things here. One of them is the mention of the "Great Sea." That is the Mediterranean. It has been called many things over the centuries, but around this time, "Great Sea" was one of them. We've also got a few appearances by pirates in this book and I wanted to mention, most notably, they discuss cannons. Gunpowder had been around for centuries and although it's documented that cannons really didn't come to England until the early fourteenth century, it's quite possible that pirates (or any seafarers) had them far earlier. These were the men (and women) who were sailing all of the known seas and beyond, so it's quite possible they knew about cannons and gunpowder well before documented examples. I've gone on that premise and taken some creative liberties.

So, what Easter eggs do we have in this book? Little nuggets you might recognize? I can tell you that we've got an appearance by a character you met in *The Dark Spawn*. Anteaus de Bourne, the youngest de Bourne brother (brothers to Corisande de Bourne de Velt) makes an appearance in this book. It's nice to see him spread his wings a little in his quest to become a Blackchurch knight, so keep an eye out for him. Also, even though all of the Blackchurch trainers make an appearance, you get to know a couple of them a little better, as they play strong secondary roles. Best of all, you get to meet the pirate branch of the Blackchurch family and they're a hoot!

Speaking of pirates, one thing you may notice if you've read any of the Pirates of Britannia connected world books (the connected world formed with author Eliza Knight several years ago) is the names of the Spanish (Castile) pirates. It's the same as it is in the Pirates of Britannia world. This story is set about two hundred years before that connected world, but you'll see the origins of the Spanish pirates. It's been a lot of fun to revisit the high seas and the life of a pirate (albeit briefly), and I really love, in particular, the leader of the Castilian pirates. Very elegant, but very deadly!

With all that out of the way, the usual pronunciation guide and things to note:

Note: All of the de Bottreaux men (Lords of Exmoor) have first names that start with "St." (Saint). When speaking informally or referring to each other, they drop the "St." You will see this in dialogue, and it is not a mistake—that's how they are traditionally addressed.

De Bottreaux—duh buh-TROW

Elisiana—ee-LEE-see-AH-nuh

Aristeo—uh-riss-TAY-oh

St. Denis—if you're French or know French, then you already know this, but to the Americans or others who might read it as Saint Dennis (where the "S" is not silent), it's actually pronounced San Duni or Deni. The "S" is silent.

And with that, there's nothing more I can say except buckle up—it's going to be a bumpy (but fun) ride!

Happy Reading!

Hugs,

Kathryn

PROLOGUE

Year of Our Lord 1221
Fremington Castle
England

"AND THEN I shoved her face into a capon pie!"

The table erupted into laughter. Such was the result of Aristeo de Verra's stories because he told them so brilliantly, true or not, and they always had a moral where the man—or woman—of his choice got their comeuppance. In this case, however, he was telling the story of his first meeting with a woman his father very much wanted him to marry, and Aristeo evidently shoved a pie in her face.

But everyone was laughing about it.

"*Mi hijo*, nay!" Adriano Celestino Fernandez y de Verra, head of the House of de Verra and the hereditary holder of the title *Conde de Pontevedra*, clapped a hand to his forehead in dismay. "Tell me you did not do this terrible thing!"

Aristeo, a genuinely handsome young man with a winning smile who had inherited the title of Lord Fremington from his mother's side of the family, was laughing so hard that he was crying. "Of course I did," he said. "It was coming out of her nose. She blew her nose and pie sprayed all over the table."

He made a gesture of pie shooting out of nostrils and the crowd at the table roared. All but Adriano, his father, and perhaps Elisiana, his younger sister by two years. Neither one of them were smiling— Adriano because he truly wanted this marriage to the House of de Mora and Elisiana because she didn't find her brother funny at all.

The man was a barbarian.

But no one else seemed to think so. Even Adriano got over his outrage when Aristeo went to his father and hugged the man, kissing him on the top of his head. Aristeo's kisses to his father were like holy water from a priest—they absolved everything. Adriano shook his head at his naughty son, but he was smiling at him, and Aristeo knew there would be no punishment. As he went back to his seat, he collected another cup of wine.

"She was too ugly for me, Papa," he said. "I cannot marry a woman who makes me want to gouge my eyes out, can I? Would you truly condemn me to such a match?"

Adriano sighed heavily and shrugged, asking for more wine from a passing servant. It was a lost cause, he could see, but he worried that his eldest was setting a bad example for his two younger sons, Diaz and Esteban. They had listened to Aristeo's story with glee and even now were trying to shoot food out of their nostrils in demonstration. Adriano let it go on because tonight, it was only family. His children, his wife, his wife's brother, and his family, plus Adriano's mother and father all the way from Pontevedra. Abuelo and Abuela liked nothing better than to see how lively and joyful their grandchildren had become.

Even if it was at someone else's expense.

But, then again, this entire meal was at someone else's great expense.

Elisiana's.

She'd been forced to attend, just like she'd been forced to entertain her mother's visiting relatives since their arrival. That included her uncle's new wife's son, who was a knight serving the Earl of Lincoln. His name was Adolph, of all things, because his father's family came from Saxony. He was tall, very fair, with a big nose and a wide forehead. He wasn't unkind or appalling, but more like a slice of white-flour bread soaking in a bowl of milk. He was bland, mushy, and pale.

There was no excitement.

In fact, there wasn't anything about Adolph de Rade that Elisiana found attractive or even interesting, and she deeply resented her parents trying to throw her at the man. At twenty years and one, she was considered old for an unmarried woman and knew very well that her parents were in an increasing state of panic over it, a problem that seemed to be solved when her uncle married the widowed Lady de Rade and the woman came with an unmarried son.

And here they were.

But Elisiana had a plan.

She was always the girl with the plan, always the girl who looked at life as if she actually had a choice in it. As the only daughter of a very traditional family, the reality was that her choices in life were few. She was expected to do as her parents told her and a little more than that, but the unfortunate fact was that Elisiana was not a young woman inclined to be a subject to her parents' whims. Her mother was a relatively meek woman who did what her husband told her and Adriano believed that all women needed a man to guide them.

That was where Elisiana parted with her father.

From the day she learned to walk, Luciana had been the independent sort. She never needed help, and never wanted help, and even if she did happen to somehow require it, she wouldn't ask. She figured it out herself. Headstrong and stubborn, her parents had reluctantly sent her to foster when she was about ten years of age, which was far too old for a young woman who had been raised in a household where she essentially did what she wanted. Her parents had given her too much freedom and perhaps even too much encouragement to think for herself, which came back to haunt them when they sent her away to foster.

It had been a rude shock to Elisiana to realize that not all young women were encouraged to think for themselves.

Fostering at Pevensey Castle with the House of de Valcourt, Elisiana entered a strange new world. Lady de Valcourt was very skilled and taught her charges all the things that young ladies needed to know—dancing, music, singing, painting, and other cultured subjects. She also taught reading and, in particular, had a love of romance poetry, something Elisiana also loved. In fact, she excelled at it because the idea of romance got into her head. Instead of writing poetry, she started sketching out young women in scandalous clothing because she felt that was more passionate and beautiful that a bunch of words tied together. A talented artist, she used charcoal to draw and became very good at it, but after being caught drawing female breasts early on, she learned to do them in secret.

Soon enough, the other young ladies wanted naughty pictures, too.

They wanted pictures of young women with big bosoms who sat at the edge of the pond and saw their reflection in the water. Or they wanted pictures of young women and their suitors, which was more popular. Elisiana found herself drawing different suitors for different girls, and they all paid her quite handsomely for it. She even drew pictures of suitors kissing the women on their breasts because one afternoon, she'd seen a soldier do it to a serving wench and that experience had titillated her.

The naughtier, the better.

News of her talent spread. Ladies in the village had heard about her dubious talentand they too began to pay her for beautiful pictures of beautiful women doing naughty things. Sometimes it was nothing more than a head, long hair, a winsome expression, and a torso with the woman's hand holding her bare breast. She'd draw that particular picture for the wife of the richest merchant in town, who showed it to her friends. After that, Elisiana had more commissions than she could handle, all the while completing them under the nose of Lady de Valcourt, who was delightfully oblivious to what her young charge was doing.

But the ignorance didn't last forever.

Unfortunately, she and her naughty sketches were discovered and, after lectures from the local priest as well as Lady de Valcourt, it was decided that Elisiana was incorrigible and she was sent home in disgrace. Very rich, but in disgrace. Her father, however, fully blamed Lady de Valcourt for exposing his virginal daughter to such experiences that caused her to draw those images. Never had he blamed Elisiana, though he should have. She'd been completely at fault, and upon returning home to Fremington, she'd resumed her sketches and sold them, in secret, through a woman in town who sold imported goods.

The ladies of Fremington and surrounding villages had their fantasies fed, at least for a while, until Elisiana was discovered again. Her mother begged her to stop and her father refused to buy her art supplies, but she bought them herself, and in secret, to continue her craft. After years of doing it, she'd become extremely proficient at it.

She was the rage of Devon.

And her parents knew it. She'd heard them speak of it, speaking of how a husband would settle her down and give her an outlet for her "impure tendencies." That was exactly why Adolph was here, to take her as his wife and force her to focus on him and forget about everything that made her happy and creative. Elisiana was a free spirit, probably too much of one, but the truth was that she wasn't going to let a husband curb her talent.

More than that, she wasn't going to stand for a forced marriage.

She wanted out.

"And you, Lady Elisiana?" Adolph said to her, jolting her from her thoughts. "Surely you would not smash a suitor's face into a capon pie. It seems rather extreme to me."

Elisiana looked over at him, seeing that he was genuinely trying to be polite and bring her into the conversation, but all she could see was a tool by which her parents trying to assert control. The man didn't know he was a pawn, but he certainly wasn't resistant the way she was. All evening, she'd been watching her uncle's new wife whisper to him and his eyes would always focus on her. That told her she was the subject of such conversation.

But, already, he was in over his head.

"It depends on the situation, my lord," she replied steadily. "If he deserved it, I would not hesitate to punish him."

Adolph smiled, amused. "What would be so egregious that it would warrant your punishment?"

Elisiana shrugged. "That is difficult to say," she said. "If I feel threatened or insulted, mayhap that would invite such a reaction. I think anyone would react in such a manner if they felt threatened or insulted. My brother, of course, was neither threatened nor insulted. Aristeo is an excellent knight and I do not think he is afraid of anything. He did not more as a joke, though I do not think the lady saw much humor in his actions."

Adolph nodded. "True," he said, glancing at Aristeo down the table. "Jokes can be taken too far."

"I would agree."

"Lisi," Adriano spoke up, looking at his daughter. "Now that the meal is over, why not take Sir Adolph out into the garden? The moon is full tonight. It should be a lovely walk."

Elisiana resisted the urge to roll her eyes at her father. The man would have been less obvious had he stood on the table and shouted.

My foolish daughter needs a husband!

Give the man any more wine and he just might do it. Elisiana smiled thinly at him before turning her attention to Adolph.

"I am certain my lord would not be interested in a garden," she said. "Only women appreciate such things."

Adolph was already on his feet. "It would be nice to take in the fresh air, my lady," he said. "May I escort you?"

So much for trying to discourage the man. Rising to her feet, Elisiana had to pass by her father in order to make her way out of the hall, and she made sure to pinch him, hard, on the back of his right arm. Adriano yelped, pretending he'd merely dropped a spoon into his lap when those at the table turned to him curiously. Meanwhile, Elisiana had made her way to the doorway of the small hall at Fremington's big keep. The chamber was actually a solar, but it was so large that the family used it for intimate dining when they only had family meals or no more than twenty guests to entertain.

Elisiana led Adolph into the grand entry, which was a wide chamber with a low ceiling. Iron sconces lined the walls, each with a fat-burning torch. It created a good deal of light, but it also smelled and smoked because of the low ceilings. Stepping through the entry door that was older than the castle itself, Elisiana led Adolph out into the inner bailey.

The moon was indeed full and the sky clear, so it was almost as if they were walking in daylight. Elisiana made sure to stay a good arm's length away from Adolph, who was walking with his hands clasped behind his back. He didn't make any moves in her direction, but even so, she discreetly tried to move further away from him.

"You do not have to see the garden if you do not want to, my lord," she said as she came to a halt. "I could just as easily show you the stables. Or the outer ward. Or the gatehouse. Surely there are other things of more interest to you."

Adolph cocked his head. "I am more interested to know why you are unmarried," he said. "You know they are trying to make a marriage between us."

He was starting out with a heavy volley. Straight to the point. She was taken aback for a moment, but that surprise quickly turned to determination. Determination that he should know the truth so he knew exactly where he stood. If he was going to be honest, then so was she.

"I do," she said. "I am sorry if they are forcing your hand. Surely that was not what you expected when your mother married my uncle."

He shrugged. "Are not all parents trying to marry off their children?" he said. "My mother is trying to break me away from a woman I wish to marry, you should know."

"Oh?" Elisiana said, thinking that maybe there was hope that he'd leave her alone after all. "Why is she trying to separate the two of you?"

"Because the woman has no property," he said. "In fact, she is the daughter of a merchant in the town where we live. I've known her many years and we have always planned to be married, but then my mother heard about you. And here we are."

He didn't seem terribly averse to marrying her, but he also didn't seem completely agreeable. Maybe he was only interested because she came with money and property. Why not marry her and keep the woman he truly wanted to marry as a mistress? That was a horrible thought. Elisiana was trying to determine how to respond, but it didn't matter in the end. All that mattered was what she felt.

She was going to make that plain.

"You should know that I have no intention of marrying anyone I do not approve of," she said. "My parents are in a panic because I have seen over twenty years and have not yet married, but I've not yet met anyone I could imagine spending my life with. No offense, my lord, but I do not intend for my marriage to be a one-sided affair."

"No offense taken, but what do you mean?"

"I mean that I intend that my husband and I should be equals," she said as she began to walk toward the garden she had tried to discourage him from seeing. "I want a husband who will let me do as I please. One that will not tell me what to do. A husband who understands I am a woman of means and does not treat me like a brainless nymph."

"I see," Adolph said, walking next to her. "You want a husband who will share power with you."

"I suppose I do," she said, peering at him. "Do you think that is asking too much?"

He shrugged. "I suppose that depends on what you bring to the marriage."

She came to a halt. "I bring a good deal," she said. "I bring an enormous dowry, of which you have probably already been informed."

Adolph was grinning at her. "I was," he said. "I just wanted to hear it from you."

She was annoyed by that. "What else do you want to know that you have not already been told?"

"I want to know about these indecent drawings you do."

She wasn't shocked that he knew about that, but she was irritated that he'd been told. It wasn't something she ever discussed, and certainly not with a stranger. She began to walk again, the walled garden looming before them in the moonlight.

"I do not know what you mean," she said. "Were you told that I fostered at Pevensey Castle?"

"And were sent home in disgrace? I heard."

"I was *not* sent home in disgrace," she said. "It was simply time for me to return home."

"I was told that a priest deemed you incorrigible."

They were at the gate now, a big iron panel that Elisiana jerked open because it liked to stick.

"Clearly, you have been told untrue versions about me," she said. "I

suspect there is nothing more I can tell you because I refuse to defend myself."

He chuckled softly as he followed her into the garden, cast in silver from the moonlight. "You needn't defend yourself," he said. "I rather like a girl with spirit. But I would like to see some of your drawings."

"Impossible."

"Why?"

"Because it is."

"Then you *do* admit to them."

"I admit to nothing."

He continued to chuckle, but he was coming closer as she stood near the small fishpond that was at the edge of the garden.

"Come, my lady," he said, lowering his voice. "You needn't pretend with me. I find the fact that you sketch lewd drawings completely fascinating. That shows talent and vision. It also shows that beneath that proper exterior beats an impetuous heart."

She didn't like that he was coming closer, so she moved away. "And how would you know that?" she said. "You've only heard what others have told you, things that may or may not be true. You do not know me at all."

"But I would like to," he said, moving closer still even as she stepped away from him. "Here we are, in this lovely garden, and it is very romantic. Your parents sent us out here for a reason. Shall you disappoint them?"

Elisiana frowned. "How can I disappoint them?"

"By not letting me kiss you."

She had a feeling where he was leading, so she took a big step back and extended her arm to put obvious distance between them.

"Stay where you are," she said firmly. "Coming out here was not my idea and it certainly is not an invitation for romantic interludes. You can put that from your mind."

He wasn't deterred. Smiling, he stepped forward so that he was against her outstretched arm. "I kiss very well, I'm told," he said. "If our parents are going to force us together, we may as well make the best of it."

She gave him a shove backward. "Stay away from me," she said. "I do not want you to kiss me. Frankly, I find you repulsive, so you may go back and tell my uncle what I said. There will be no marriage between us."

He laughed softly. "You may find me repulsive now, but you will not when you realize I have a cock the size of a rutting stallion's," he said. "It will bring you pleasure such as you've never known. Many a maiden can attest to that."

Shocked, she scowled. "That is a disgusting thing to say," she said. "I am going to tell my father."

"Go ahead," he said seductively, moving one of his hands down to his breeches to rub himself, trying to bring his manhood to life. "But you should see what you are running from. You may even wish to touch it. I would not mind."

He was moving closer again and she was beginning to feel threatened. He was a big man and stood between her and the garden gate. She could see him rubbing the crotch of his breeches and was genuinely fearful that he might force her into a compromising position. He might even try to hurt her.

But not if she hurt him first.

Her scowl turned into a smile.

"Very well," she said, moving toward him. "Mayhap I *should* see what I am running from."

His smile broadened. "Good," he said. "I like a woman with an adventurous heart."

"A wicked heart is more apt."

"Wicked?"

She was standing in front of him now. Reaching out, she put her hands on his hips, watching him lick his lips lasciviously. But his pleasure was only momentary. Before he could draw another breath, she rammed her right knee, as hard as she could, into his semi-erect manhood. When he howled and doubled over, she stood back and kicked him for good measure. As Adolph folded himself in two, yelping in pain, Elisiana gave him a good shove and pushed him right into the fishpond.

"That is what I think of your vulgar behavior," she shouted. "Next time you will think twice before trying to seduce a woman who finds you repulsive!"

As Adolph struggled in the fishpond, Elisiana ran for the keep. She knew her parents were going to be furious, and her uncle as well, but she didn't care. This was the last straw in a bale that had been full long ago. Little by little, however, the straws had been pulled for various offenses, all of them perpetrated by her parents.

She simply couldn't take it any longer.

No more straws.

The problem was that if she remained, not only would she be forced to apologize to Adolph, but she would more than likely be forced to marry him right away. The price Adolph would have to pay for her large dowry and a castle in Cornwall was a few days of bruised bollocks and a bruised ego. In fact, he could use it against her to force her into doing things she didn't want to do.

She had to get out.

Rushing into the keep, she managed to not catch the notice of anyone in the small hall. They were all still eating and drinking. No one saw her rushing to the stairwell. Once she was up the stairs, she moved very quickly. Grabbing a traveling satchel, she shoved clothing into it, combs and such, and all of her coin. Everything she'd earned drawing pictures. It was money to give her a new life, possibly a new identity, and most definitely a new hope. Let Adolph marry someone else.

It wasn't going to be her.

By the time Adolph made it back to the keep, soaking wet and roaring with anger, Elisiana had managed to slip herself and a sturdy pony from the postern gate, already on the road beneath the full, bright moon.

The road to a destiny that would be more adventurous, and dangerous, than she could have possibly imagined.

PART ONE
THE BLACK COCK

CHAPTER ONE

Six months later
The Black Cock Tavern

T HEY CALLED HIM Sin.

Not that he was a sinner, though he'd been known to indulge and a few things for that people might find questionable, but the very real fact was that it was his name.

Sinclair de Reyne.

He was on his way home.

Having spent the past few years in the Flemish duchy of Toxandria, fighting to regain it for the rightful duke, he'd done what he'd set out to do those years ago. Helping a young man regain that which had been stolen from him.

And, God's Bones, did he have stories to tell.

Most importantly, however, was the fact that he'd returned home to not only his rightful liege, but also friends he'd missed for a long time, friends and colleagues that were more like brothers to him, and he was eager to resume his position alongside them as a Blackchurch trainer.

The truth was that Sinclair served, and was employed by, the Blackchurch Guild.

Located deep in the heart of Devon, in the Exmoor Forest, Blackchurch was as mysterious and feared as the lands around it. It was far from London, far from most of the hustle and bustle of England as a whole, and it tended to have its own legends and ambiguities. There were beasts that roamed the moors and wood sprites waiting to trap unsuspecting men. Fae lingered in the vales and serpents swam in the lakes. Devon wasn't heavily traveled when it came to the Exmoor Forest, an area that sane men would stay away from, and that made it a perfect place for the most elite warrior training ground in England.

Possibly the world.

There were great castles like Kenilworth and Berkeley and Warwick who trained powerful knights that went on to serve great lords and kings. Those were the reputable castles with the reputable training programs, and nearly every nobleman's son in England aspired to train at one of those great training grounds.

And then there was Blackchurch.

It was in a league of its own.

Sinclair was proud to be part of that legacy, proud to be a trainer of the most elite warriors in the world. He'd missed the days of teaching men, and sometimes even women, the finer art of swordplay. He'd missed the days of camaraderie with his fellow trainers. He'd even missed this tavern, smelling of sewage and alcohol and stale bodies. It wasn't much, but it was home. Home to him, home to others. Everyone who knew anything about the Blackchurch Guild knew that the Black Cock tavern belonged to them. At least, that was where they spent their off time, where they were able to relax a little.

And that's why Sinclair had stopped here on his way home.

He was waiting for them.

In fact, he'd sent word ahead two days ago that he would be arriving. He'd only had marginal contact with those from Blackchurch in the time he'd been away, mostly with his close friend, Tay Munro, and the man's wife, Athdara. Sinclair's entire journey to Toxandria was because of Athdara, the daughter of a deposed duke. Her younger brother,

Nicolai, was the rightful heir, and it had been Sinclair who helped the young man regain his property as a favor to both Tay and Athdara. He'd been handsomely paid—*very* handsomely—and even been given the title Lord Brexent and the lands that went with it, so it hadn't been a waste of time. He'd taken pride in watching young Nicolai ascend to his seat. But now he was back and it was time for him to resume his life.

He was ready.

Seated in a private room that was off the common room, he had been enjoying a beef pie, stuffed eggs, and a good deal of ale. The food wasn't elaborate, but it was plentiful. He'd been half-dead when he came into the tavern because he'd traveled for half a night and a full day to reach the place as it was a stone's throw from Blackchurch. Now, with the food and drink, he was starting to feel alive again.

Pushing the used bowls and utensils aside, he lifted one of two big saddlebags at his feet. Digging around in it, he pulled forth a leather-bound book. It was a big book, a journal of his adventures since leaving Blackchurch to go to Toxandria so he wouldn't forget the details. He'd written down every place of interest he visited, every person, and every battle. As he waited for his comrades to show up, which they would now that the sun had set and the evening meal was upon them, he began to read the early pages from his journal.

It seemed like a lifetime ago.

As he read, someone entered the chamber. The remainder of the meal was cleared away and in its place was a bowl of something that smelled sweet and spicy. The scent alone brought Sinclair out of the pages of the book to discover the source. The servant who brought it was still in the room, placing another spoon near the bowl and putting a fresh pitcher of ale on the table.

"That smells good," Sinclair said, pulling the bowl in his direction. "What is it?"

"Pears stewed in wine and cinnamon and honey, my lord," came the reply. "It is favorite around here."

Bowl in front of his face, Sinclair inhaled deeply. "I can understand why," he said, sticking his finger into it and pulling out a pear, which immediately went into his mouth. "It tastes as good as it smells."

"My thoughts also, my lord."

He was about to say something more as he happened to glance up at the servant. After that, speech seemed to leave him for a moment.

But his thoughts didn't.

Behold, perfection!

Standing next to the table was inarguably the loveliest woman he'd ever seen. She had dark and curly hair, very long, that was pulled into a braid that draped over her left shoulder. With pale skin, slightly freckled on the nose, she also possessed full lips, dark brows, and eyes of the brightest blue that Sinclair had ever seen.

She was absolutely astonishing.

"Who are you?" he finally managed to ask. "I've not seen you here before."

She smiled faintly. "And I've not seen you here before either, my lord," she said. "My name is Lisi."

Lee-see.

He looked her over as if struggling to believe what he was actually seeing. "How long have you been here, Lisi?"

"Only a few months, my lord," she said.

"Are you getting along well?"

"I am, my lord."

Sinclair dipped his head in the direction of the common room. "This place can be a little rough at times."

Her smile grew. "Nothing that a good club will not solve, my lord."

He grinned. "Hobbes lets you beat his customers, does he?" he said. "It is about time he took some of these fools to task. He lets them get away with too much. Where is the man, by the way?"

They were speaking of Hobbes, the owner of the Black Cock, and the woman pointed toward the kitchens.

"One of the ovens is not working properly," she said. "Shall I fetch him for you?"

Sinclair shrugged. "When he is finished," he said. "I do not wish to take him away from his ovens. He might take a club to *me*."

The woman laughed softly. "You know him, my lord?"

"I know him well."

"Then I shall tell him that you are looking forward to seeing him."

Sinclair nodded, and she slipped out of the room, but his gaze remained where he'd last seen her. He sat there, staring at the doorway, thinking that she was extremely articulate and well spoken for a serving wench. Coupled with her fine looks, something told him that she was a well-bred woman.

So what was she doing working as a serving wench in the wilds of Devon?

Pondering that very thing, he picked up the spoon and turned his attention to the pears, which he made short work of. He was on the last one when a round man with a halo of white hair appeared.

"Lord Sin!" Hobbes said happily. "Someone said that they saw you come in, but I've been up to my neck in a foul oven. Welcome home, my lord!"

He reached out to shake Sinclair's hand enthusiastically. Sinclair grinned as the man practically shook his arm right out of the socket.

"So you remember me, do you?" he said. "I seriously wondered if people would."

"Why?" Hobbes asked. "It has only been three years. That can change a man, but not enough. Not you."

Sinclair appreciated the complement. "And not you, either," he said. "How have things been around here since I've been away? Quiet?"

Hobbes shrugged. "Quiet enough," he said. "We had a few rough moments, but all taverns do. It is the way of things."

"Rough moments?"

"Fights, stabbings. That kind of thing."

Sinclair nodded in understanding. "The usual."

"Exactly. The usual."

Sinclair pondered that. "I'm glad to see that little has changed," he said. "But I have seen a few new faces around."

Hobbes nodded. "We have a new cook," he said. "And a new serving women."

"I met Lisi."

"Ah," Hobbes said. "She is a very hard worker. And very pretty, though I am certain you did not notice."

Sinclair's brow furrowed as if he were offended by the comment, but he couldn't quite manage it. "And I am certain I am not the only one who has noticed it, either."

Hobbes shook his head, laughing. "You are not," he said. "Your colleague from Blackchurch, Payne, has made a nuisance of himself with her, but she soundly ignores him."

That brought a chuckle from Sinclair. "So the big Scotsman has made his interest in her known, has he?" he said, speaking of the trainer who was known as the Tempest. Every trainer had a moniker at Blackchurch, something that defined them, and Tempest most definitely defined the hotheaded Scot. "I did not know he was capable of such things. He's not had a woman since I've known him."

"And he'll not have this woman," Hobbes said. "She has no interest in him."

"Does she take money for comfort?"

He meant to know if she was a whore, but Hobbes shook his head firmly. "Her?" he said. "Never. She does her work, sleeps, and does it again the next day. She does not speak of herself, of her past, or of anything, truly, but she is friendly and the customers like her. If anyone tries to get too friendly with her, she's not afraid to poke men in the eyes or kick them in the belly. I've seen her."

Sinclair chuckled. "So she fights back," he said. "Good girl. A lass that pretty has had to learn to defend herself."

"She's not afraid to."

"I'll remember that."

From back in the kitchens, someone called Hobbes' name and he scooted away, shouting at them as he went. Something about smoke, Sinclair thought. It was the usual chaos at the Black Cock, and he found that comforting. He was home, and as the minutes ticked away, it was more and more as if he'd never even left. Pouring himself more wine from the pitcher that Lisi had left, he silently toasted his return.

It was good to be back.

As the night deepened, Lisi returned a couple of times, bringing him more of the stewed pears and then a dish sent by Hobbes, beans and onions in a chicken broth that was very good. He ate most of it but was so full from the other food that he'd ordered that he couldn't finish it. It was growing late and he was coming to think his friends wouldn't be coming to the Black Cock to meet him, so he was simply going to have to go to Blackchurch and see them there.

Leaning over in his chair, he was securing his saddlebags when he heard footsteps behind him. Before he could sit up to see who it was, someone hit him from behind and he went over onto the floor. Men began piling on top of him, and he would have been fighting them off fiercely had he not realized one thing.

They were laughing.

He recognized the laughter.

"Ah, my bonny lad!" The Tempest himself, Payne Matheson, was on top of him, kissing him loudly on the cheek as the rest of his face was pressed into the floor. "The Swordsman has returned!"

More laughter as someone yanked Payne off him only to have another body take his place.

"Did you truly think we would not greet you appropriately?" a deep voice asked. "You deserve nothing less than this grand welcome, my friend. Welcome home."

Sinclair recognized the voice of Fox de Merest, the trainer known as the Protector. Fox wasn't usually the rowdy type, but even he was getting in on the friendly beating. Sinclair could feel someone roughing up his legs and torso, not too terribly, but just enough to buffet him around as he tried to push himself up from the floor.

"Release me, you idiots," he said, finally able to push himself onto all fours. "Do you not know that I am a titled lord now? How dare you take to beating me."

More laughter greeted him as he made it to his knees and looked up to see that he was surrounded. Everyone was patting him, pushing him, trying to topple him over onto his bum. But he fought them off, laughing softly as Tay Munro, his dear and close friend, pulled him to his feet and into an embrace.

"We wanted to make your return memorable," Tay said, releasing him long enough to take a good, long look at him. "It really *is* you. Thank God you've made it home."

Sinclair smiled at the big man with the dark hair. Being half Grecian and half Norman gave him a big build and dark coloring. "Aye, I've made it home," Sinclair said. "Finally. It seemed as if it took forever."

"When did you leave Toxandria?"

"Almost eight weeks ago."

"But you're back now." Another man grabbed him by the arm, pulling him away from Tay and directing him toward a chair. Kristian Heldane, a man born in the land of the Northmen, practically shoved him down to sit. "We want to hear about your adventures. You must have great stories to tell."

Sinclair nodded as someone shoved another cup of wine in his direction. "Many stories, for certain," he said. "In fact, I was looking at my journal earlier. I documented everything I could because I did not want to forget anything. And I know that Lady Munro will want an accounting of her brother's new rule."

"She will, indeed," Tay said, sitting down on his right. "She was unable to come because our youngest is not sleeping well at night. New teeth are sprouting. But she will expect to see you in the morning, and you had better be prepared to tell her everything."

"I will," Sinclair said. "I intended to report to her even before Denis."

St. Denis de Bottreaux was the owner of Blackchurch, known as the Lord of Exmoor, the latest in a long line of de Bottreaux men to carry on the Blackchurch tradition. Everyone was sitting at this point and Sinclair found himself looking around the table at men he'd missed a great deal. Men he knew every detail about, the good and the bad.

For example, Kristian was a prince to his people, but he could not return home, so he taught recruits the ways of the Northmen. Next to him was none other than Creston de Royans, a trainer known as the Avenger, from the powerful de Royans family. A more brilliant military strategist had never existed, and there were times in Toxandria that Sinclair had sorely wished he had the man with him.

But there were more.

At the end of the table, next to Creston, sat a dark-haired man who was tall and well built. Cruz Mediana de Aragon was a knight from the Holy Order of Santiago, an expert in negotiation and politics, known the Conquistador. Seated to his right was a man who had a special place at Blackchurch because he had come to England after King Richard's crusade and his father was a great Egyptian warlord. Aamir ibn Rashad was called the North Star because he was strong and constant, and seated next to him was the man that Sinclair had probably missed most of all.

A man who was smiling warmly at him.

Ming Tang was a monk from far to the east and more than likely a better warrior than any of them. Known as the Dragon, he was a man of many trades, many skills, and his wisdom was well respected. He wasn't big like the other men were, men who had been born and bred for battle, but rather smaller in a way that had nothing to do with his strength. He was still one of the strongest men in the group, powerful in a way that wasn't noticeable until one got into a confrontation with him.

By then, it was too late.

Sinclair was very glad to see him.

"Was it a glorious adventure, lad?" Payne shouted from across the table as he grabbed at the nearest pitcher of wine. "Tell us of yer greatness."

Sinclair laughed softly. "If I tell you all of it before I tell Lady Munro, I suspect she might box my ears or worse," he said. "Instead, tell me of everything that has gone on here in my absence. Anything of note."

As Payne waved him off, upset he wasn't going to hear about glorious adventures until Sinclair had delivered his report to Athdara, Tay spoke.

"We've had several classes of recruits move through since you left," he said. "As we discussed before you left, your class was divided up between Creston and Cruz. They combined it with their own teaching segments."

"True," Creston spoke up. Big and blond, he was handsome and congenial, masking the deadly warrior within. "We tried to teach them as you would, but, of course, you are the expert. Quite honestly, I am glad you are back. I feel as if the recruits we've been teaching over the past three years have not received the full Blackchurch experience because of your absence."

"I am certain you did quite well," Sinclair said. "Better than 'well,' actually. I know how you both are with a sword."

"Ah, but we are not you, *amigo*," Cruz said, smiling. "With the Swordsman returned, we are once again whole."

Sinclair smiled at the pair, who were the best of friends. Rarely did one do anything without the other. "Indeed, we are," he said. "Any recruits of note?"

Around the table, the trainers nodded. "A few," Ming Tang said. He had a deep, deliberate way of speaking, something that conveyed comfort and wisdom. "We had a few sons of French *ducs* pass through and the daughter of a Northman king, which was uncomfortable for Kristian."

"Why?" Sinclair asked, looking at Kristian.

"Because I knew her father," Kristian said quietly. "He was an enemy of my father."

It sounded complicated and uncomfortable for Kristian, but given the man's background and how he was an exiled prince, Sinclair didn't delve into it further. Unless Kristian wanted to discuss it, no one pried. In fact, there were a few Blackchurch trainers like that, men with pasts that were better left buried, and everyone respected their privacy. It was an unspoken rule because in the world of Blackchurch, a man's reputation was based on how he performed as a trainer and how he treated his fellow trainers, not the often rocky and mysterious threads of his past.

Sinclair knew that better than most.

"But you survived," he said, glossing over the subject. "We should be just a few weeks into the new group of recruits. Has Tay managed to eliminate the weak with his initiation classes?"

That brought smiles around the table. Tay was the trainer that all new recruits, referred to as dregs, faced when they came to Blackchurch. They'd already had to go through a litany of tests to see if they were even worthy of Blackchurch training, so the ones that faced Tay were usually of the hearty sort. But even Tay was known to wash out more than half of them before they ever faced any other Blackchurch trainer, so Tay's heavy hand with new recruits was well established.

And well feared.

"I have," Tay replied proudly. "You do not think I would let anyone unworthy pass my rigorous tests, do you?"

"Of course not," Sinclair said, grinning. "Is there anyone particularly worthy?"

Creston and Cruz glanced at one another. "In fact, there is," Creston said. "I'm glad you asked. There is a recruit who is a Warwick-trained knight. He descends from the last king of Northumbria, Eric Bloodaxe. His father is the Earl of Bernicia. Honestly, Sin, the man has a pedigree more impressive than anything I've ever seen. He came here right after you left, passed Tay's tests, made it into the recruit group and into the advanced group. He's not only Warwick trained, but Northwood trained as well, so his qualifications are impeccable. So are his sword skills. He has been helping with your class and Exmoor wants him to continue to do so even after your return, but only as support. You are the master, Sin. No one can replace you. But Anteaus de Bourne has been doing an excellent job of educating our recruits while you were away."

Sinclair didn't seem particularly pleased with that. "While I am happy that things have continued in my absence, I am not entirely sure I need help with resuming my duties," he said. "But I look forward to meeting de Bourne."

Tay, sitting closest to him, put his hand on the man's shoulder. "We would never try to replace you," he said. "You know that. Furthermore, I would never allow it. You left to do me and my wife the greatest favor and you did not have to do it. Trust me when I tell you that your position is secure, Sin. We admire you and love you above all else. You are part of us. But de Bourne has talent and was helping Creston and

Cruz when they needed it. In the same manner as Bowen helped me before he became a trainer."

He was speaking of Bowen de Birmingham, a former recruit who had such grit, such stamina, that Tay had recruited him as an assistant years ago. Only to help, never to supersede, but even so, Bowen had worked himself into the position of trainer through Tay's recommendation. Sinclair knew that and, given the example, began to feel a little better about the situation.

"As I said, I look forward to meeting him," he said. "But the moment I see a hint of resentment that I have returned to assume my position, I will throw the man out on his ear and I do not care what his credentials are. Understood?"

He received firm nods from Creston, Cruz, and Tay. Payne, who was drinking up the last of the wine, wiped his mouth with the back of his hand.

"And I'll help ye toss him out," he declared. "But I dunna think it will come tae that. He seems tae have some humility, which is more than I can say for most of us. He knows ye're returning. It'll not be a surprise."

As Sinclair nodded, because Payne would have mentioned if de Bourne had been the ambitious sort, Ming Tang spoke quietly.

"Sin, you have something with us that no one could ever replace," he said. "We are a brotherhood. No one can usurp that, and in this brotherhood, acceptance of outsiders does not come easily. Look at de Bourne as a subordinate and nothing more. But I will say he was very helpful to Creston and Cruz, who worked hard to cover your classes during your absence."

Sinclair looked across the table at Creston and Cruz, lifting his cup. "And I could have no finer brothers," he said sincerely. "You have my deepest gratitude, but I have also intend to split some of the money I received for my efforts with you. I could not have gone had the two of you not volunteered to train in my place."

Creston waved him off. "No need," he said. "I did not do it for money."

"How much?" Cruz said, drawing chuckles from the group. But he grinned and waved Sinclair off, also. "I was only jesting. I did not do it for the money either. I did it for you, so Denis would not replace you."

Sinclair smiled at his friends. "We'll discuss the compensation later," he said. "Rest assured that it is not a dead subject by any means. But tell me about Denis and Sebo. Is everything well with them?"

The man referred to as "Sebo" was St. Denis' son, St. Sebastian. He was the youngest of St. Denis' two sons and the heir after the unexpected death of his older brother, St. Gerard, a few years ago. St. Sebastian was Kenilworth trained, and had gone to the Levant with King Richard's crusade, so he was an excellent and experienced knight, and more of a leader than his father, who was more of an administrator and scholar.

It was a subject that Tay, in particular, knew a good deal about.

"Denis has become the tutor for my children and for Fox's," he said, indicating the only other married trainer in the group. "He has five young boys to teach—my three eldest and Fox's two eldest. Though Denis comes from a long line of Exmoor lords, I do believe his true calling is tutelage. He teaches children while Sebo manages Blackchurch. He would have come tonight but he thought you would like time with us first before he and his father greet you."

Sinclair nodded. "He is an intuitive man," he said, looking around the group. "All I can tell you is that it was difficult and there was hardship. There were plots and schemes and spies, just as you would imagine, but it was good to be in battle again. I had not realized I'd missed it so much until the first battle we had in a village called Bethune. The young duke's uncle heard we were coming and made sure to meet us. After that… Well, I will tell you the rest of it once I've told

Lady Munro, so until then… know that I am glad to be back."

He lifted his cup, and those around the table echoed his sentiment. But there wasn't anything left in his cup, and he was about to send for more when a crash in the common room caught his attention. In fact, it caught everyone's attention. Payne was on his feet first, yanking back the curtain to be faced with an all-out brawl.

It was chaos in the common room of the Black Cock.

And Sinclair, on his feet, noticed someone right in the middle of it.

CHAPTER TWO

TO SAY THE man was handsome was an understatement. Elisiana wasn't in the habit of noticing the patrons that came in and out of the Black Cock, but for some reason, she noticed him.

She had the moment he walked in.

Over the past few months, she'd gotten used to the clientele that the remote tavern attracted. Almost always, they were travelers moving from Tiverton or Yeovil or other points east to the wilds of Cornwall, its coves and port cities. Cornwall may have been remote, but it was quite busy with industry from the sea, including merchant ships and, most importantly, pirates. Because of its many coves and secluded beaches, pirates that roamed the western coasts of England and Wales could always find an empty spot to hide away in. Rumor had it that almost every little cove and cave along the western side of Cornwall had some kind of booty buried in it.

A treasure hunter's paradise.

But there was another side to it. Because of the remote area and the industry that Cornwall was known for, the travelers tended to be a little rough. They could be frightening and even brutal at times, as Elisiana had discovered along the way, so when Hobbes' well-spoken friend entered and was greeted happily, Elisiana found herself taking a second look at the man.

He was most definitely worth a second look.

When he first entered, he had been dressed from head to toe in a weather-worn cloak. Everything was covered up with the exception of his eyes. Hobbes had shown him into a private room, whereupon the man stripped off the cloak and the bags underneath, laying everything down as he made himself comfortable.

That was when his male beauty came to light.

He was quite tall, though she had seen taller. What she hadn't seen were shoulders that size, or arms that size, and when he finally removed his gloves, she caught a glimpse of hands that were as big as trenchers. She was positive one of those fists was the size of her head. And speaking of heads, he had a very nice one. His hair was dark blond, but traveling in the elements had bleached the ends of it. It was wavy and just a little past his shoulders, and when he removed his cloak, he ran his fingers through it to slick it back off his face.

And what a face.

His skin was tan from what she could see, from the time he'd spent in the sun and the wind and the rain, but he had a trimmed beard and mustache that covered more than half his face. He had a long nose and a square jaw, but the thing she noticed the most about him was the color of his eyes. They were intense and bright, and when she came closer, she could see that they were a shade of greenish gold. They were the most intense eyes she'd ever seen set within quite possibly the most perfect male face she had ever seen.

He looked like he belonged with those knights that visited from the training guild to the north. They, too, were young and handsome and had an air about them that suggested breeding and education. They weren't like the rest of the visitors that passed through the old door of the tavern, men who reeked of desperation or depression or greed.

They were much different.

Blackchurch knights.

Oh, she knew about them. Hobbes had told her that they were the most elite trainers of men in the entire world, trainers who had done more and seen more in their lives than most men would do or see in a dozen lifetimes. Though she'd not formally met them, she'd become familiar with the sight of Tay and Fox and the rest of them, including the big Scotsman who was forever trying to impress her. His name was Payne, so he'd told her, and he seemed nice enough, but she genuinely had no interest in him. He was a good enough sport about it, once he realized her disinterest, but that didn't stop him from trying. It had become something of a joke between them. He would come in, give her a big wink, and greet her as his "sweet," and she would impatiently ask him what he wanted to eat. He would always say something extravagant, something the Black Cock had never served, and she would insult him, but he always laughed at her insults, and, quite frankly, she thought he'd looked forward to them.

Truth be told, she looked forward to them, too.

In fact, Payne and his good humor was one of the more pleasant aspects of her life these days, the life she had chosen for herself when she fled her home those months ago. Taking her money and her chances, she had fled east, toward London, because that had been her destination. She reasoned that she could lose herself in the population of the enormous city, someplace where her parents could never find her. She'd had high hopes of making a living off her drawings, a life she very much wanted for herself, but it wasn't going to be easy. Running from home had been the simple part.

Staying away from her father's men had been a little more difficult.

Within twelve hours of her leaving home, the situation had changed dramatically. Every road she needed to take east had been blocked by either her father's men or her uncle's men, which meant she had to take roads that she hadn't intended to. She didn't even know where they went, but that didn't matter. All that mattered was that her father's men weren't there and she had to evade them, so staying to the trees but paralleling the road in order to stay out of sight, Elisiana took a lesser-traveled road that took her north into Devon, into the Exmoor Forest, to be exact, and that was where things went from bad to worse.

It had started out calmly enough. She'd left the pony tied to a tree, with her satchel still on the saddle, and taken soap and a rag down to the nearby creek to wash her hands and face. It was nearing supper and she had only brought what she could steal from the kitchens as she'd fled Fremington, so all she had left was some stale bread and cheese. That was to keep her going until she found a village where she could purchase more supplies.

That had been the plan, anyway.

Unfortunately, there were men who had been tailing her since she'd started on the smaller road, outlaws, to be exact, and they didn't care about her plans. When she'd gone to wash, they'd taken the opportunity to steal everything—the pony, her bags, her money. All of it. They'd almost captured her, too, as she returned from the creek, but quick thinking and hiding in the stump of a rotted tree had saved her. Elisiana had been forced her to hide for an entire night, and when morning finally broke, she was cold and wet and without anything but the soap and the rag she had collected from her saddlebag.

So much for her plans for glory in London.

But she still wasn't going to go home.

Determined to escape Adolph and her parents, Elisiana continued on foot. It was a walk that led her straight to the Black Cock tavern, where she had asked Hobbes if she could work for a meal. He'd let her, though he didn't normally do that sort of thing, but two days of work had turned into five months of a job. The truth was that Elisiana was a hard worker, good with the clientele, and she could carry on an intelligent conversation. That was rare among serving wenches, at least those Hobbes had experience with.

Elisiana had turned out to be an asset.

She enjoyed the work, and it showed. Every day, she met someone new, someone she could talk to and learn from. The merchants that traveled in and out of Cornwall may have been the rough sort, but they weren't unfriendly and had traveled to so many wonderful places. They even brought exotic goods with them from time to time, goods they were either taking to London or bringing out of London, and Elisiana had the opportunity to purchase some lovely things.

As it turned out, the robbery in the woods had been a blessing in disguise.

Between the tips she received and what Hobbs paid her, Elisiana had been able to replenish more than half of the money she'd had stolen. The Black Cock had become a good job. She'd accumulated things like jewelry and clothing from the passing merchants, much more than she'd brought with her in that little satchel, so the position was lucrative. As long as her father's men didn't show up looking for her, she saw no reason not to stay a little longer and earn more money before continuing on to London.

Quite honestly, the Black Cock had been a godsend.

Therefore, the appearance of Hobbes' friend had been a break in the monotony of what normally went on at the tavern, and to say that the man didn't have her interest would have been a lie. But Elisiana hadn't given a hint of that interest, instead remaining polite and professional, providing him with good service. He'd been polite in return, but there had been no conversations between them. He seemed to want to be alone, so she didn't even try. When the entire crew of Blackchurch trainers entered the tavern later that evening and descended on the man as if he were a long-lost brother, she realized her instincts about him had been correct. He *wasn't* the normal traveler that usually visited the Black Cock. She would have liked to have watched the festivities because the men were being fun and boisterous, something they normally weren't, but she had duties to attend to and several tables she was responsible for.

It was one of those tables that started some trouble.

Carrying a tray laden with a pitcher of watered ale and several cups, Elisiana was heading for a table of five men who had come in as the sun began to set. They'd kept to themselves, eating and drinking, and as the night went on and the drinking continued, Hobbes began to water down the ale they were ordering. That was usual with him when he didn't want his patrons to become ragingly drunk and destroy, defecate, or vomit in his common room, so he tried to taper them off a little. Putting the tray on the table in front of the men, she was busy collecting dirty wooden spoons they had been using when one man slammed down his cup, catching Elisiana with some of the spray.

"And ye're a madman for thinking so!" he shouted at one of his friends. "*My* sister? Is that who ye mean?"

Elisiana was trying to get out of the way, but the other man bolted to his feet and plowed into her, sending her sideways.

"I'm going to make her my wife!" he shouted at his companion. "I've offered ye sheep and money for her. What more do ye want for a woman who has already been used?"

Elisiana narrowly avoided being clobbered when the first man launched himself at his comrade. The entire table, and nearby tables, deteriorated into a fight as cups, pitchers, and even spoons and knives began to fly. Chairs flew over the table, hitting people at other tables, and those people retaliated.

Elisiana ended up on her hands and knees, crawling away from the brawl. She scooted under one table, whose occupants were joining the fight, before leaping to her feet. Racing over to the area where trays and cups were kept, she pulled out an enormous club used for moments just like this. The club that Hobbes called the "Lion Tamer" had iron spikes sticking out of it, and Elisiana wielded it with confidence. It wasn't the first time she'd had to. Heading back over to the fight, which was now growing exponentially, she began swinging the Lion Tamer at knee level.

Men began dropping as the club made contact.

But they weren't exactly moving out of her way. One man saw what she was doing and came at her with a pitcher over his head, clearly intent on hitting her with it, but Elisiana swung the club at his groin before he could lower his arm, and he went down in a heap. Another man grabbed her and tried to take the club from her, but she managed to hit him in the face with the back of her hand. When he faltered, she swung the club around and hit him in the neck.

He fell like a stone.

Hobbes was on the outskirts of the brawl, standing on a table and demanding that everyone stop fighting. He had frightened serving wenches bring him buckets of water, which he tossed on the brawling patrons in an effort to stop the fight. The water helped, but it didn't stop it altogether. He was particularly upset when someone tossed a man through one of his windows.

The fight spilled out into the street.

Elisiana was still in the middle of it, swinging the Lion Tamer, knocking men down and yelling at them to stop fighting. Most ignored her, but some cleared away, licking their wounds. She was so focused on what was in front of her that she didn't see what was behind her. A man with a dagger in his hand, one she'd already bashed in the knees, was up and staggering toward her. The closer he came, the more her life was in danger because it was clear that he meant to do her serious bodily harm. He was nearly upon her, dagger lifted, when she raised the club, tipping it backward so that she could get some momentum in her forward blow. But that backward tip hit the man in the forehead and he howled, enough to startle Elisiana when she heard the cry. But the time she turned around, the man was screaming in agony because someone had planted a knife between his ribs. As he fell away, Elisiana saw the Blackchurch trainers breaking up the fight behind her.

And the mysterious traveler was the one who had killed the man stalking her.

His hand shot out and he grabbed her.

"Come with me," he said.

With her club still in hand, Elisiana let the man lead her out of the skirmish. The Blackchurch trainers, all eight of them, excluding the one who had her by the arm, were making short work of the combatants. Even Payne, the big Scotsman, was settling men down with shoves and shouted threats. But Elisiana was removed from all of it by the man she'd been eyeing all evening.

Maybe that was why she'd let him remove her.

It was difficult to refuse that face.

He'd taken her back to the private chamber where he and his comrades had been supping. Coming to a halt, he reached down to take the club from her grip.

"Let me have that," he said, laying it on the table before looking her over. "Are you injured?"

Elisiana shook her head. "Of course not," she said. "You did not need to help me, my lord. I am sorry you felt the need."

His brow furrowed. "The man I killed was about to put a knife in your back," he said. "I should have let him?"

Elisiana shook her head quickly. "That is not what I meant, my lord," she said. "I simply meant that I was sorry to cause you such trouble."

He shook his head. "No trouble," he said, his gaze lingering on her. "But you use that club as if you have done it before."

She grinned. "In a place like this?"

"I made a foolish statement, I know."

Over in the common room, the fight was mostly over and Payne had shoved someone back into a chair, which promptly split. They looked over at the commotion as the man ended up on the floor and Elisiana was preparing to go back into the room to help, but her savior waved her off.

"Nay," he said. "Let the men settle the room before you go back in."

She looked at him in puzzlement. "Truly, my lord, I've faced this kind of thing before," she said. "Hobbes will need help cleaning up."

"Not yet," he said, watching his comrades break up a new fight. "We will wait a moment."

Elisiana wasn't so certain. She wasn't used to staying out of the action, which had caused her bruises every once in a while. This one might have cost her substantially more had her self-appointed protector not intervened with the man who was intent on stabbing her. She supposed that she should honor his effort and not jump back into the fray so quickly.

"I do not even know your name, my lord," she said. "I should like to know the name of the man who rushed to my aid."

He sat back down in the chair he'd been occupying. "Sinclair de Reyne."

De Reyne. That sounded familiar to Elisiana.

"De Reyne," she repeated. "Your family is from the north of England?"

"Aye," he said. Then he eyed her curiously. "What do you know of my family?"

She shook her head. "Nothing, really," she said. "It is simply that I've heard the name."

His gaze lingered on her for several long moments before he spoke. "Where are you from?"

"Cornwall."

"You are not a servant."

"I *am* a servant."

"That is not what I meant," he said. "I mean that you come from nobility."

She averted her gaze. In fact, she noticed the empty cups and pitchers at the table and began to clean them off. "I do not know why you would say such a thing, my lord," she said. "I certainly do not look like I come from nobility."

He didn't say anything for a moment. He watched her gather all of the dirty utensils. When she came near him to collect an empty cup, he reached out and grasped her wrist. Startled, she tried to pull away but he wouldn't let her. He met her gaze for a moment, his pale eyes glittering, before focusing on her open palm.

He studied it.

"These are not the hands of a servant," he said quietly. "It is true that they are rough and chapped, but your callouses are minimal. These hands have not spent a lifetime working back-breaking tasks."

Elisiana didn't try to yank her hand away again, mostly because she was starting to feel something else. Wherever his hand touched her flesh, a wildfire sparked. It was only her hand, but the heat was undeniable. It made her feel… strange.

Heart palpitations.

Quivering in her knees.

Clearly, she was becoming ill.

"That does not mean anything, my lord," she said, managing to slide her hand out of his grip. "It could mean I worked in the kitchens or in the keep. Mayhap I was not subjected to heavy labor so that it wouldn't ruin my hands. Or mayhap my sole purpose was to play with the children. You cannot judge a woman by her hands."

"Mayhap not," he said. "But you do not speak like a servant. You have fine diction."

"Mayhap I was once a servant of a lady who wished that I speak well."

He eyed her, scratching his beard. "So you have a past you are hiding," he said. "I suppose everyone is entitled to their secrets."

"That is an excellent way of looking at it," she said, gathering all of the used things she had collected and piling them into her apron, using it like a basket. "Surely you have secrets of your own that you do not wish to share."

The warmth seemed to leave his eyes. "All men do."

She nodded as she collected the last cup. "Working here, I have come to see that," she said. "But I am grateful to you for saving my life. The next time you come here, you will let me provide your drink free of charge. It is the least I can do."

"How do you know I will be back?"

She nodded her head in the direction of the Blackchurch trainers who were now starting to filter back into the chamber. "Because you clearly know these men," she said. "They serve at Blackchurch, so either you do, also, or you have in the past."

"What do you know about Blackchurch?"

"Nothing, really," she said. "I only know what Hobbes has told me, that it is a training guild for warriors. Are you a trainer, then?"

"I am many things."

He was being evasive, but it didn't offend her. She had been the same way with him. In fact, it amused her because he had a rather impish look as he said it. With more men filtering into the chamber, she began to back away.

"I would believe that, my lord," she said quietly. "Thank you for the conversation, but I must return to my duties. I will bid a good eve to you."

Sinclair simply nodded his head, pretending to be uninterested in her departure until she went through the door, her back to him, and he knew she wouldn't see that he was watching her. His focus returned to her, the way she moved, the way the light glistened off that dark hair.

Servant or not, she was a woman well worth watching.

Perhaps coming home would have some unexpected advantages after all.

CHAPTER THREE

Exford Castle
Heart of the Blackchurch Operations

"AND THAT WAS the last I saw of the new Duke of Toxandria," Sinclair said. "He was standing tall, waving farewell, and fully in command of his army and properties. It is a memory I shall never forget."

Sitting in the large solar of Exford Castle, seat of the Lords of Exmoor, he'd just given his story to several people in the chamber, including Athdara Munro, sister of the new Duke of Toxandria. In fact, he'd spoken directly to her the entire time. Everyone else in the solar was purely incidental. This was her story, one she'd waited a very long time for. Many, many years.

The tears in her eyes were of joy and relief.

"I can never thank you enough," Athdara said. A tall and beautiful woman, she was a good friend to them all. "Truly, Sin… what you did goes beyond friendship. To fight alongside my brother, against my Uncle Atilla, to help Nico gain what is rightfully his is a service we can never repay. But know that we will be eternally grateful to you for what you have done. You have saved my family's legacy."

Sinclair was uncomfortable with the praise, but he was pleased with the gratitude. "It was a good experience," he said, smiling. "Do not misunderstand—I love my position at Blackchurch, but what we lack here is the opportunity for travel and adventure. Now I think I've had enough to last for the rest of my life, so it is good to return home."

And home was where he found himself.

The solar smelled of smoke from the early morning fire, but also of cold leather and old stone. It was a heavy and familiar scent. Over near the hearth, seated on a cushioned chair, was the Lord of Exmoor himself, St. Denis de Bottreaux. It was important for Sinclair to not only give the report of the last three years of his life to Athdara, but to St. Denis as well because he was the man who had made it all possible. Without St. Denis' approval, Sinclair would have never been allowed to return to Blackchurch, to a position that was waiting for him.

But it had been a complicated situation.

Blackchurch wasn't a political establishment. In fact, trainers were forbidden from taking sides in any battle or lending their name or sword to any conflict. It was true that they trained men who went on to side with kings or princes or warlords, men and women who went into the world with extraordinary training, but Blackchurch itself remained neutral in all situations. They were in it for the money they could make training the best warriors in the word, not the politics. They provided a service and nothing more.

Therefore, Sinclair's fight for Toxandria had been in a gray area.

The only reason St. Denis allowed it was because it wasn't an English, Scottish, or even Welsh battle, but one across the sea. Also, Athdara's father had been a friend to St. Denis, so there was a friendship involved. St. Denis' friend had been murdered by his brother, his dukedom stolen, and Athdara had come to Blackchurch to train so she could fight to get it back for her younger brother, Nikolai. During the course of her training, she'd fallen in love with Tay, and he with her, which complicated an already difficult situation. When it finally came to fighting to regain the Toxandrian dukedom, it had been Sinclair who volunteered to do it to save Tay from crossing a line St. Denis didn't want him to cross—choosing sides.

Sinclair had made the sacrifice.

He was in a better position to do it. He wasn't related to Athdara or the duke in any way. He wasn't a friend. He was simply a paid sword, paid by the true heir to the Toxandrian throne, and that was the only reason St. Denis really allowed him to go. Moreover, Tay was the unofficial leader of the trainers at Blackchurch, with a young family in tow, while Sinclair had none of those attachments. It just made more sense for him to go.

And it had been, as he'd said, quite an adventure.

"It sounds as if you have helped form a great and strong dukedom, Sin," St. Denis said in reply to Sinclair's report. "My dear friend, Athdara's father Alexei, would have been so very pleased. I know he would want to thank you for what you did for Nikolai. But who advises the young duke now?"

"A former advisor of Duke Alexei, a knight by the name of Alen, has taken a most admirable role as mentor and chancellor to the young duke," Sinclair said. "Athdara knows Alen. He somehow survived Attila's attack and incendiary rule and now remains for Nikolai. He is in good hands, my lord."

At the mention of her father's former knight, Athdara nodded. "He is a very good man," she said. "Alen held Breda Castle when Attila attacked. He was the one who helped Nico and I cross the river to safety, and I honestly thought he had been killed, so it a great relief to know he was spared."

"Spared for his knowledge of Breda," Sinclair said. "Your uncle knew he needed such a man, so he spared his life, but it was Alen who was feeding information to Duke Alexei's allies. Had it not been for him, we would have never been able to breach Breda Castle and regain control as we did. Alen wanted nothing more than to see your father's legacy returned."

"And so it has," Athdara said, smiling. "It is like a dream, Sin. You are the bringer of dreams."

"Stop," Tay growled. Standing behind his wife, leaning back against the wall, he shook his head at her when she turned to look at him. "You are fawning over the man and I'll not stand for it. I will have to challenge him for your affections."

Those in the room chuckled, including Athdara. She sat back in her chair, rubbing her swollen belly. "You are mad if you think your pregnant wife would openly flirt with a man," she said. "Moreover, it is not fawning you hear, but gratitude. Clean out your ears, Tay."

Tay simply grunted, making a face at Sinclair, who snorted. "I do not want a wife who can best me in fight, Tay, so your marriage is safe," he said. "Besides, I could not manage all of those offspring. Two more since I have been away!"

"And fine children they are, lest you forget," Tay said, still in a threatening tone, but he quickly sobered. "But she is correct—you have brought the dream back to Toxandria, Sin. We can never thank you enough for that."

Sinclair waved him off. "Nico already has," he said. "He had made me a rich man and has given me a title, so I was well compensated. But I must say that I am eager to return to my duties at Blackchurch. Mayhap it is not the travel and adventure of a faraway battle, but I have missed training men."

"A-And you have been greatly missed," St. Sebastian de Bottreaux said with his distinctive, slight stutter. "C-Creston and Cruz have done a remarkable job in your stead, but it has been taxing for them. With their regular duties, and yours, I am certain they are glad you are back also. There is only one Swordsman, after all. But I must say that I'm envious of your adventures in Toxandria. I-I would have liked to have gone with you."

He meant it, too. St. Sebastian, or simply Sebo, was the heir to Blackchurch. He was highly educated and well trained by the Master Knights of Kenilworth Castle, but given that Blackchurch was built on the principle of remaining neutral in any given conflict, accompanying Sinclair had been out of the question.

But he hadn't always been that way.

St. Denis had two sons, once. St. Gerard had been the eldest, a man who was primed to lead Blackchurch into the next generation until he was unexpectedly killed a few years ago. St. Sebastian, the younger and perhaps less aggressive son, had always been second to his ambitious brother. That meant he could say things, and even do things, that St. Gerard couldn't because he didn't have an empire weighing down on him. But with his older brother's death, the world had changed greatly for St. Sebastian.

It had been a difficult transition.

In the first place, he was a thinker. That meant he tended to be a little less neutral than he should have been, something his father was trying to change in him because Blackchurch couldn't afford to have a dog in any fight. If they did, the entire dynamics of what they did would shift. They would immediately became a political training ground, and probably have enemies all over the known world, which wouldn't bode well for the continuation of the guild. St. Sebastian knew that, but he still struggled with it. He had opinions and he felt passionate about them.

But those opinions made his father struggle with the future of Blackchurch.

"Mayhap your father will let you go with Tay and Athdara when they return to visit," Sinclair said after a moment, trying not to encourage the man's natural tendency to voice his thoughts. "Toxandria is a beautiful land and one that is thankfully now at peace."

"Well done, Sin," St. Denis said, picking up the conversation before

St. Sebastian could turn it into a political discussion. "It sounds as if you truly did something noble. That reflects well upon you."

Sinclair smiled weakly. "Thank you, my lord," he said. "And thank you for letting me go. You did not have to provide me with a position to return to, and I am grateful."

St. Denis gestured to the men in the solar. "As if they would have let me replace you?" he said. "Every one of them would have walked out and Blackchurch would be at a standstill, so I was happy to permit you to do what needed to be done, especially since you regained my old friend's kingdom. All jesting aside, of course I would let you lend your skill to a worthy cause. You saved a dukedom, Sin. That is something to be proud of."

"I am," Sinclair said. "But I am also eager to return to my duties today."

"You do not wish to rest after your travels?"

"No need, my lord."

St. Denis could see that Sinclair was eager to get back to work, which was typical of him. He wasn't one to be idle because it simply wasn't in his nature. Therefore, St. Denis looked to Creston and Cruz, standing off to his left.

"Then take him and show him the progress of his recruits," he told them. "Introduce them to our Swordsman so there will be no doubt as to his credentials or our respect for him. You will also want to introduce him to de Bourne, since the man has been helping with his recruits. Sin, do you know about Anteaus de Bourne?"

"I have been told, my lord."

"Good," St. Denis said. "He has an excellent sword arm. Use him if you wish, but if you do not wish to, then tell me. I'll find other work for him."

Sinclair stood up from the chair he'd been seated in, but his focus was on St. Denis. "Then you have made up your mind to make him another trainer, my lord?" he asked.

That was a question the other trainers had been asking, but no one seemed to have an answer. St. Denis had been evasive about it and St. Sebastian, a man who usually spoke openly, had been surprisingly silent on the matter. But St. Denis merely shook his head to the question.

"I am not certain," he said. "All I know is that he is talented and he is capable. He is good with the men. Let him work with you and form your own opinion. I am curious to know what you think."

That was a good way of putting it—letting the trainers evaluate another trainer and make it seem as if the decision was with them rather than simply make a decision that would affect them all, including the tight dynamics of their group. Especially for Sinclair—since de Bourne had already been teaching his recruits, he was essentially giving Sinclair the power to accept the man or send him away.

But there was also something more—both Tay and Fox had assistants, men who helped them with their classes, which was a badge of honor for the more senior trainers. One of Tay's former assistants, Bowen, had even become a trainer himself, and Fox's assistant, Axton Summerlin, was well on his way to becoming one as well. Capable men helping their very capable masters—so Anteaus joining Sinclair was something of an honor.

And Sinclair knew it.

"As you wish, my lord," he said. "I will let you know."

With that, St. Denis waved him on. Sinclair moved for the door first, followed by Creston and Cruz. Payne and Kristian also filtered out after them, along with Athdara, leaving Tay, Fox, Ming Tang, and Amir behind. Once the door was closed, St. Denis turned to Tay.

"Well?" he said. "How do you think he is going to react to de Bourne? Sin tends to teach alone. I am not entirely certain he will work with another."

Tay shrugged. "De Bourne knows that his position here at Blackchurch rests on how he deals with Sin," he said. "The other trainers will side with him in any conflict, but more than that, if there is a conflict, I will remove de Bourne personally. Our recruits cannot see discord between the trainers. It will foster confusion and mayhap even lessen their respect for us. Mayhap, for today, I will have de Bourne work with me so Sinclair can establish himself for his recruits without them looking to de Bourne as someone they are more familiar with."

"Agreed," Ming Tang said quietly from his position near the door. "Let Sin see his recruits alone for today. But if it is of any interest, I have never gotten the sense that Anteaus was overly ambitious. He has been easy enough to get along with and he is quite good with the recruits. Furthermore, he knows that Sin is our sword master. I do not anticipate any problem, but I will keep watch of the situation if you wish."

St. Denis nodded. "That would bring me comfort," he said. "With Sin returned, our full complement of trainers is now complete once again. Sebo tells me our next recruit class is quite large, so this is good news. I feel as if we are full strength once again as Sin has returned to the fold."

"R-Returned from a great adventure," St. Sebastian mumbled. When his father and the others looked at him curiously, he lifted his shoulders. "I-If I had been Sin, I would have never come back. I would have traveled the world in search of money and adventure. I would not have come back to the wilds of Exmoor to train men day after day. It seems like a waste of material."

St. Denis frowned. "Enough with your useless dreams, Sebo," he said, unwilling to change the subject yet again and simply dealing with his son head-on. "God help us when you are in charge of Blackchurch. My ancestors and I did not build this guild into the prestigious establishment it is today only to have someone like you ruin it, so keep your opinions to yourself. No one wants to hear them, least of all me."

It was a sharp rebuke in front of the men, so Tay caught Fox's attention and nodded his head discreetly toward the door. Fox took the hint, motioning to Ming Tang and Amir.

"We have duties to return to, my lord," Tay said as everyone funneled out. "Good day to you."

They moved swiftly, leaving father and son alone, but they weren't two steps away from the door when they heard St. Denis unleash on St. Sebastian. Tay and Fox were several feet ahead, already descending the steps to the entry below, but Amir came to a pause. He had a significant role at Blackchurch because in addition to being a trainer, he was also an advisor and counselor to St. Denis. He'd brought a different view to the man's world from a Muslim perspective of warfare and peace, but better still, even St. Sebastian listened to him. That was the one hope St. Denis had when he passed on, that his son would continue listening to his advisor. Now, hearing the man shouting at St. Sebastian had Amir torn. He felt as if he needed to ease the situation between them because he was naturally a peacemaker. Ming Tang, who had been walking next to him, came to a pause also.

"Do not interfere, Amir," he said quietly. "Denis will resent you for it if you do."

Amir was still uncertain. "This could have been avoided had he allowed Sebo to go to Toxandria with Sin," he said. "You know he wanted to go."

"I know."

"But his father told him he could not," Amir said. "He could not take sides, not in any battle. Even one for a friend."

Ming Tang understood what Amir was trying to convey. "And you suggest he put the needs of Blackchurch over the needs of his old friend, the Duke of Toxandria?" he said. "By preventing Sebo from fighting for him?"

"Possibly," Amir said. "But I also understand that Denis must view Blackchurch from a wider position. Meaning he cannot think of only

Blackchurch and its longstanding policies. He must be able to see into the future and what it would mean to allow Sebo an exception."

Ming Tang sighed. "If he makes one exception, he can never again stand his ground against those who want Blackchurch to fight for them or side with them," he said. "We have an army of over one thousand skilled soldiers. With all of the trainers as commanders, we would be extremely formidable."

"Extremely."

"And Denis must avoid using that power for profit," Ming Tang continued. "If he does, he would be no better than St. Abelard and his pirates. They fight for money and are well-known mercenaries. Blackchurch has always kept clear of that reputation."

They were speaking of St. Denis' cousin, St. Abelard de Bottreaux, who was in command of the other business venture that the de Bottreaux family had founded long ago. St. Abelard was, quite literally, a pirate who ran a profitable fleet of ships known as Triton's Hellions. They used the beaches and coves on the northern coast of Devon to moor their fleet and use it as a launching base for their pirate endeavors. No sane ship entered the Bristol Channel for fear of being confronted by St. Abelard and his pirates, whose activities involved the coastlines of Ireland, the entire west coast of England, Wales, and Scotland, as well as part of the French, Spanish, and Portuguese coastlines. Anywhere there was money to be had, St. Abelard and his skilled men would find a way.

But thinking on those pirates had Amir snorting ironically.

"Sebo should go with Abelard," he said. "He would find enough adventure to last him a lifetime if that is what he chooses."

Ming Tang shook his head. "You know that Denis would throw him in chains for the rest of his life if he expressed his wish to do such a thing," he said. "Blackchurch is Sebo's. His father will not surrender his son's restless heart to Abelard."

"True," Amir said. He paused, listening, and realized that the shouting had died down. "It is quiet now. Hopefully they are discussing things more calmly."

"And Sebo is learning not to test his father so much."

Amir grinned. "That is a son's responsibility in life," he said. "Testing his father until the man shouts at him."

Ming Tang smiled. "Like you tested yours, the great Sheik Rashid Bin Maktoum Al Mana?"

Amir laughed softly and began to move toward the stairs leading down to the entry. "You've never seen a man's eyes bulge as much as my father's do when he is enraged," he said. "It is quite impressive, truthfully."

Ming Tang followed the man to the stairs. "And you did this regularly, I assume."

Amir passed him an impish grin. "He impressed me quite often."

Grinning, Ming Tang followed him down the stairs.

He could well believe it.

CHAPTER FOUR

I T WASN'T A class full of dregs that Sinclair faced, but men, and two women, who had made it through both Tay's and Fox's training. Now they were recruits. They'd proven themselves for the most part.

And they belonged to Sinclair.

He didn't hold back.

God, it felt good to be back in harness again. Back doing what he loved to do, back teaching talented individuals the finer art of sword-play. He'd felt fulfilled and useful as he helped Nikolai regain his rightful dukedom, but he'd missed training men and watching their expressions of pride for a job well done. It was something that gave him great satisfaction, and the class he assumed from Cruz and Creston was properly awed by the introduction from his two friends. They made him sound as if Ares had just come down from Olympus and was now prepared to teach them all how to fight. Of course, Cruz and Creston made him prove it with a surprise attack, and he disarmed both of them, but not without a fight that took about an hour.

After that, he had his class's undivided attention.

The exercises began.

Every recruit in his class had already been through some kind of training except for a farmer who had proven himself extraordinarily hearty, talented, and a quick learner. He was a big man, eager to absorb the knowledge that Blackchurch was imparting, and Sinclair took a liking to him because he genuinely wanted to learn. The man, named Thomas Ram, had an even temperament, too, in contrast to some of the more experienced knights who often didn't think they needed to be taught anything more about fighting with a sword and became frustrated with simplistic exercises.

Sinclair didn't care about their egos.

Even though he'd been properly introduced, even though everyone in the recruit class knew who he was and his qualifications, there were still those who were going to test him. That was normal. Sinclair always took delight in those men because they were a challenge. Admittedly, he had the advantage because if he wanted to fail them, he could, and they would have to leave Blackchurch for good, so that was probably the one thing that really kept the recruits in line. No one was too arrogant or rebellious lest they be booted from the class. But there were still those who thought they didn't need his instruction.

Sinclair proved otherwise.

Truthfully, the entire day was a delight. He'd spent most of it with his new recruit class, taking them back to the basics even though they had been in this particular module of training for about two weeks. Cruz and Creston had explained to him the type of training that those past weeks had entailed, but Sinclair took everybody back to the beginning. He wanted to make sure his class was taught by his methods from the very start of the program that he had devised over years of serving at Blackchurch. It was a schedule that had been proven time and time again to train some of the best swordsmen in the world.

And it all started out with repetition.

As Sinclair explained to the class, learning to be an expert swordsman was purely about repetition. It was repeating the same moves over and over again until you were sick to death of them but knew them intimately. Then he would go to the next move, which they would repeat over and over again as well. He would do this until he had at least ten specific moves with the sword, and then after that, they begin to put the moves together—the first move and the second move would be done at the same time, over and over again, until everyone became very comfortable with it. Then they would add the third and fourth moves so that all four moves would become fluid through repeated practice and continuous repetition.

On and on it went.

When all ten moves were learned and each man or woman had perfected them, they would put those moves to the test against one another. That was another module that Sinclair taught. It was his job to ensure that every Blackchurch recruit could emerge from a sword fight victorious. It was his job to ensure that they could think for themselves in the midst of a battle, that they could anticipate an enemy and still come out with their life intact. His class was purely about the art of swordplay and not the art of strategy in battle, which was more in line with what Fox and Creston taught. They would use what Sinclair had drilled into his recruits and expand on it.

As St. Denis used to say, they were building a warrior from the ground up, and every trainer built on the foundation that other trainers had laid. Like any construction project, the Blackchurch warriors were built from a strong foundation. By the time they emerged from their lessons, they were the most perfect warriors that had ever been produced.

And Sinclair was a big part of that.

Therefore, his afternoon had been truly delightful because he had forgotten how much he loved working with those who were eager to learn and also those who thought they knew everything. There was a great deal of variety in what he did and he enjoyed that immensely. But even as the day begin to wane, it occurred to him that the very man who had been helping with these classes had not shown his face.

Anteaus de Bourne was nowhere to be seen.

Curious, but not particularly caring, Sinclair wound down his class as the sun dipped below the horizon. Classes never went beyond the setting of the sun because men working with swords in the darkness was a very dangerous thing. He'd had his class working on a very basic move all day, the repetition of a simple lift, but by the end of the day everyone was quite weary from lifting heavy swords over and over again. He dismissed the class, watching them trudge off toward the cloister of the old church that gave Blackchurch its name. The cloister was where the recruits slept, big dormitories that housed the dozens of people who were in different stages of training, and the smell of cooking fires from the kitchens was already sitting heavy in the evening air.

Cooking reminded him of food.

Food reminded him of the Black Cock.

Lisi.

He hadn't thought of her since last night, since they'd had their brief conversation after the common room brawl, but the truth was that he wouldn't be sorry if he saw her again tonight. That beautiful, brave, mysterious woman who had been good conversation was someone he'd been attracted to from the start. She was a mystery, and that, more than anything, had his curiosity.

There was something intriguing about her.

As a few servants began to collect the swords used by the recruits, Sinclair headed over to the village where the trainers and those who served at Blackchurch lived. In fact, it used to be a bustling town over one hundred years ago, but Blackchurch had long ago taken over every cottage, every building, and now it was where the trainers and associates critical to the function of Blackchurch lived. They had an entire village to themselves, set within the dark Devon moors, with the burned-out bones of the old, blackened church anchoring the northern end.

This was their sanctuary.

And he'd missed it.

Sinclair truly felt as if he was home as he entered the village, heading for the cottage that belonged to him. He had lived in one next to Tay's cottage, but the crying of Tay's infant children had kept him up at night, so he moved to the edge of the village, away from Tay and his screaming offspring. His cottage was the last one in a row of cottages and now he was only next to Ming Tang, with Amir and Kristian directly across from him. He entered the two-storied cottage, smelling the familiar dusty and smoky smell, although the woman who kept house for him had stoked the fires both upstairs and downstairs, put food on the table in the dining room, and made sure he had clean linens.

It was good to be home.

He'd slept here last night, but nothing had been ready for him since they hadn't known exactly when he would be returning. It had been a little bare-bones, with the exception of a bare mattress and a fire in the hearth. But tonight, everything was prepared for his return and he sat down at the table to inspect the food, talking a few bites of the bread before thinking he might go into town and get his meal at the Black Cock instead.

But first, he thought he'd clean up a bit.

Chewing a hunk of bread, he went over to the hearth because there was an iron pot on an arm over the flames. He peered at it, hoping it was hot water, and was pleased to see that he was right. It was usual in households to keep a pot of water warmed over the coals for bathing or kitchen purposes, so he took the pot off the arm and brought it upstairs where he kept his belongings.

Soap, razor, and rags were pulled out of his saddlebags, which he hadn't unpacked yet, and using the hot water, he proceeded to strip down to his bare skin and wash himself with a rag and soap that smelled of lavender. He couldn't remember when he'd bathed last, so he went ahead and washed his hair and shaved off his beard, getting water all over the floor in the process. But he felt cleaner than he had in a very long time. He dried off with the bed linens and donned clean clothing. Using a comb to slick back his shoulder-length hair, he headed out of the cottage.

The village of Exebridge, where the Black Cock was located, was about a quarter of a mile from the gatehouse of Blackchurch. Huge perimeter walls encircled the guild, manned by soldiers who were paid well for their skills. Sinclair considered stopping by the cottages of some of the other bachelor trainers to see if they wanted to join him, but the truth was that he wanted to engage in conversation with the mysterious Lisi and didn't want an audience for that. It was true that he had missed his follow trainers very much, and this was only his second night back, but there would the hundreds of nights to come to sup with them and speak on his adventures in the east.

For some reason, Lisi had his attention this night.

"Where are ye off to, lad?"

The booming voice came from the cottages off to his right, and he turned to see Payne heading in his direction. Kristian was with the big Scotsman and they moved quicky to catch up with Sinclair, who reluctantly came to a halt.

"The Black Cock," he said. "A quiet supper and I'm off to bed."

Payne slapped him on the back. "Ye've been gone for three years and ye want tae be alone tonight?" he said, tugging on Sinclair's arm as he started to walk. "Tonight is a night we celebrate yer return, lad. Ye'll not be alone this night."

Sinclair let the man pull him along. "I've spent the last several weeks completely alone as I traveled home," he said. "I think I've grown accustomed to the peace and solitude. As much as I love all of you, I think it is going to take time for me to acclimate back into the group. It is an adjustment."

"Then we'll help," Payne insisted. "I'll tell ye about the latest missive I've received from my mother."

"The same mother who beat you regularly as a child and smokes hemp in a pipe?"

"The same."

Payne's Scottish mother was something of a legend in the Blackchurch annals. According to Payne, she was eight feet tall, as strong as an ox, could cook enough to feed half of the Highlands of Scotland, and swung an axe better than any man, among her many attributes. Some of the trainers doubted she was even real, but no one would question Payne about it. They looked forward to stories of his all-powerful mother. Real or not, she was part of her son and he was part of them.

They simply accepted her.

"I look forward to meeting your formidable mother someday," Sinclair said. "Invite her to Blackchurch sometime. Given her litany of skills, I do believe I would like to challenge her to a fight."

Payne flashed his big white teeth. "She's better with a sword than ye are."

"I would believe that."

Sinclair grinned. He didn't feel so much like being alone now. He had Payne on one side, Kristian on the other, and they kept up a running conversation all the way into Exebridge with its muddy, uneven streets and cramped cottages up the main throughfare. The Black Cock was near the village center and the windows were open, emitting light and faint conversation.

As the trio headed toward the tavern, a man went down the street lighting torches affixed to tall iron poles. They gave off light against the darkness, illuminating the street and providing a measure of safety. Exebridge also had the unusual feature of a night watch, something normally only done in the larger cities, but after too many outlaws used the forest as safe havens and, subsequently, harassed the citizens of Exebridge, they formed the night watch for the security of the village. It was no small coincidence that a few of the night watch were soldiers from Blackchurch's compound.

And that presence cut down on robberies and other unsavory activities considerably.

Just as the three of them reached the entry door to the tavern, someone went flying through one of the windows, landing in the street. Clearly there was a fight going on inside, and Sinclair opened the door to see half the common room in another brawl. That wasn't unusual in a place like this, so he and Payne and Kristian entered in time to see Elisiana standing on a chair with the Lion Tamer in her grip, yelling at the men to stop fighting. Anyone who ventured close to her was struck on the head, and as the three of them watched, she hit at least two men who tried to get her off the chair.

That had Payne moving in.

The Scotsman with the temper began bellowing at the combatants, who turned out to be only four men who were making a mess of the place. He put himself between Elisiana and the brawlers, shoving anyone away who came close to her. The fight calmed down unnaturally fast after that, and as Payne played mediator, Sinclair and Kristian headed for the private room that the Blackchurch knights usually occupied. Sinclair, however, went over to Elisiana as she stood on the chair and lifted his hands to her to help her down. When she saw him, she smiled and allowed him to. Payne wasn't even aware—he was still berating the combatants for fighting so violently in the presence of women.

He didn't even realize the lady he'd defended had gone off with another.

"I do not know what is wrong with men today," Elisiana said, following Sinclair away from the confrontation. "That is the third fight we have had. And this one over a dirty knife, of all things."

Sinclair watched Payne as he shoved a man into a chair, which tipped over. "Mayhap the full moon is bringing out the animal in them," he said. Then he gestured to the club. "I see you have the Lion Tamer at your side again."

Elisiana looked down at it, grinning. "You know the name if it, my lord?"

He nodded. "I've seen it used many a time."

She chuckled. "It has been my constant companion today," she said. "To tell you the truth, I do not like to use it. Only when there is no other choice."

"You are a woman of peaceful means, then."

"If I can be."

She was smiling at him, nodding, but he was gazing at her, too, and they both seemed to realize at the same time that they were staring at one another. As her cheeks flamed with embarrassment, Elisiana lowered the club and tucked it against the wall where it would rest until needed again.

"Now," she said, brushing off her hands as she faced him. "What can I bring you on this fine evening, my lord?"

"What does Hobbes have ready?"

"A few things," she said. "I have boiled beef, or a capon pie from the birds that needed to be slaughtered before they grew too old, or pork and beans left over from last week, which I would not recommend because they have all turned to mush. What is your pleasure, my lord?"

"The beef," he told her. "Bring plenty, along with bread and butter and anything else you have in the kitchens. My friends and I are hungry tonight."

"As you wish, my lord."

Suddenly, the fighting flared up again and they both looked over to see Payne caught in the middle of it. Someone knocked over a table with a candle used for light, and the tallow splashed on a nearby chair that started to burn. Kristian hadn't quite made it into the private room, and when the fight, and the fire, flared up, he went to help. Hobbes emerged from the kitchen, wiping his hands on his apron and seeing the burning chair. He also happened to catch sight of Sinclair.

"What happened?" he asked. "Why are Payne and Kristian in the middle of a fight?"

"They are trying to disperse it," Sinclair said, noting that the chair was starting to smoke greatly and no one had moved to take it out. "I'll get the chair."

Reluctantly, he left Elisiana, heading over to the burning chair and grabbing it by a leg that wasn't burning yet. He dragged the thing out of the entry, out into the night. He kicked it into the gutter, watching it burn for a moment, before turning back to the tavern. The moment he did, Elisiana appeared beside him with a bucket of water, which she promptly tossed onto the furniture.

"There," she said as the fire was mostly doused. "That should ensure that no embers travel."

Since they were surrounded by closely packed homes and businesses built out of very flammable materials, Sinclair appreciated her foresight.

"Indeed," he said. "Well done, lady. You've saved Exebridge."

Elisiana grinned at him. "How heroic of me," she said. "You were the one who did the difficult task. I am simply riding on your laurels."

Sinclair laughed softly. "You are welcome to do that anytime," he said. "For a lady who wields the Lion Tamer quite ably, I suspect there is no end to your heroic talents."

"You know much about heroes, then?"

He shrugged. "I've been a knight for many, many years," he said. "I know a little something about men of valor."

"Is that why you've been away?" she said. When he looked at her curiously, she gestured in the general direction of the tavern. "Because the Blackchurch trainers came to greet you last night when you arrived. Hobbes said you were a Blackchurch trainer, too, but that you went away for a few years. He said you were fighting another man's war."

Sinclair nodded. "I was."

"May I ask where? If it is not too bold?"

Sinclair could only sense genuine interest on her part. She wasn't being pushy. Normally, he wouldn't speak about where he'd been or what he'd done, but with the woman he knew as Lisi asking, he was perhaps a bit less resistant about it. He'd come to the Black Cock hoping to see her, and now they were having the very conversation he'd hoped to have until Payne and Kristian joined his solitary party. With his colleagues occupied, he didn't want to waste the opportunity.

"It is not a bold question," he said. "I was in Flanders, fighting to regain a dukedom for the rightful heir."

Elisiana nodded in understanding. "I went to Brussels once with my father," she said. "We went to see an old friend of his, a man whose sole business was buying jewels and then selling them. He owned many mines."

It was Sinclair's turn to nod. "So you are well traveled, then," he said. "I was right."

"About what?"

"You *are* a lady."

She cast him a long look. "Just because I traveled to Brussels does not mean I am well traveled or nobility," she said. "It simply means I went there with my father."

"Who is your father?"

She opened her mouth to reply, but realizing he was trying to extract more information than she was willing to give, she grinned and shook her head.

"You think you are so terribly clever," she said. "It is none of your business who my father is."

Sinclair fought off a smile. "You brought him up, not I."

Her gaze lingered on him a moment. "I will make you a bargain," she said. "I will tell you who my father is if you tell me who your father is."

He pretended to seriously consider it. "Very well," he said. "I will tell you."

She lost all of her humor. She hadn't expected him to call her bluff. "You will?" she said. "Mayhap you should not."

"Why not?"

"Because I cannot tell you mine."

"But you said you would make a bargain. I am accepting your terms."

Unable to form a snappy reply, Elisiana lowered her gaze. "I should return inside, my lord," she said. "Hobbes will need help cleaning up after the fight."

"Wait." Sinclair stopped her before she could turn away. "I was only jesting with you. If you do not wish to tell me, I will respect that."

She paused, unable to look at him. "Thank you, my lord."

"If you do not wish to tell me that your father is the King of the Beggars, I will not force you."

Her head shot up, her eyes wide, but she could see the mirth on his face and realized he was teasing her again. That settled her down a good deal.

"How did you guess?" she said. "Someone must have told you."

Sinclair shook his head. "No one had to tell me," he said. "Or mayhap your father is the King of the Fae. Truly, only a man of such power and magic could have a daughter as beautiful as you."

She cocked her head. "Are you trying to flatter me into telling you who he is?"

"Is it working?"

"It is not."

Sinclair rubbed his hand over his chin so she wouldn't see him grin, but it was a futile effort. "Good," he said. "I am glad I did not spend too much time on it, then."

Her eyes were twinkling at him. "No harm in trying, I suppose," she said. "It was nice to hear the compliment, even if you *were* trying to manipulate me."

"That was not manipulation," he said, oddly serious. "You *are* beautiful. I've traveled the world enough to know such a woman when I see her. Your beauty is rare, Lisi. It seems quite out of place out here in the wilds of Devon."

Her cheeks were turning a delightful shade of pink. "Everyone has to be somewhere," she said. "I happen to be here, no matter how rare... well, how out of place I seem."

"I did not mean to offend you."

"You did not."

"Must you truly go back in and clean up? Hobbes has other women who work for him."

She turned her head toward the door. They could hear people moving around inside, casting shadows on the windows, and her hesitation was obvious.

"That is what I am paid for, my lord," she said. "To clean, to bring food, or anything else that is required, so I should like to keep my position. In fact, you ordered food when you came in. I shall fetch it for you."

"In a minute," he said. "Don't run off. Truly—I am sorry if I offended you by saying you were out of place here. I simply meant that you look as if you belong in a great castle, cherished by those around you."

She was already turned in the direction of the door, but she paused. "You sound like my father."

"The Fae King?"

"Exactly."

"He is not wrong."

"But that is not what I wanted."

Now we're getting somewhere, Sinclair thought. This ethereal, evasive woman who hid behind a shield of secrets was starting to crack a little. He wasn't entirely sure why he was so determined to find out about her, only that he was. For all of her beauty and bravery, there was something about her that seemed strangely sad. Her eyes glimmered with warmth, but deep down there was grief there, and he wasn't sure why. All he knew was that she was an enigma.

An enigma who had his interest.

He proceeded carefully.

"And this is what you wanted?" he said, gesturing to the tavern. "To break up fights and serve ungrateful men?"

She grinned. "They're not all ungrateful," she said. "They're certainly not as probing as you are. They accept me for who I am."

He wasn't surprised that she knew what he was up to. She seemed quite astute. Therefore, he put up his hands in a gesture of surrender or the conversation was going to be over sooner than he hoped.

"Then let us change the subject," he said. "We can speak of me if you wish. Ask me anything and I will answer."

With the empty bucket under her arm, Elisiana thought on that statement. Sinclair could see just by looking at her that she may be inclined to ask questions he didn't want to answer. If nothing else, the lady was sharp. Perhaps she was about to give him a taste of his own medicine.

"Very well," she said. "But only for a moment. Truly, I must go back inside or Hobbes will wonder what has become of me."

Sinclair shrugged. "You are with me," he said. "No harm will come to you. Now, what do you wish to know?"

Elisiana cocked her head thoughtfully. "I cannot think of anything," she said. "You've told me where you came from. I know you serve at Blackchurch. What more is there to know?"

There was an insult in that statement, and a disappointing one at that. Sinclair could see that she wasn't nearly as curious about him as he was about her, and he felt some embarrassment. He also felt some irritation at himself for showing interest in a woman in the first place. In his experience, there wasn't anything redeemable about any of them. Self-centered, callous, and selfish. He should have known better. To save his pride, he simply conceded the point quickly.

"Nothing," he said. Then he gestured toward the tavern. "You should probably return before Hobbes comes looking for you. I should not want to get you into trouble by keeping you away from your tasks."

With that, he turned away from her and back to the chair, which was in the last stages of burning. He kicked at it, breaking it up so the embers would cool. He'd picked up the back of it, the only part still intact, with the intention of smashing it down into kindling, when he heard a soft voice behind him.

"Mayhap you can tell me about Blackchurch. I would like to know more."

Chair still in hand, he turned to see Elisiana standing behind him. There was warmth in her eyes again as she looked at him, perhaps mirth because she knew she'd insulted him. Perhaps she meant to. Or perhaps she hadn't. In either case, he couldn't really tell if she was playing games with him, but then again, he supposed it was no worse than him trying to force secrets out of her.

Perhaps he deserved the insult after all.

"Very well," he said, tossing the chair aside. "What would you like to know?"

"How long have you served there?"

"Nine years."

"Do you like it?"

"Very much."

"May I visit sometime?"

"Any time you wish. But not at dawn or at dusk."

She didn't think Blackchurch was a place for visitors, but he hadn't told her she couldn't come. She felt rather special about that, as if he had granted her some manner of privilege.

"Mayhap I will," she said. "Where did you serve before that?"

Sinclair smiled weakly. "I was a master trainer at Kenilworth Castle," he said. "I grew up at Kenilworth, so they trained me. They knew my worth. I was their master swordsman until the opportunity at Blackchurch presented itself."

Elisiana was impressed. "Kenilworth is where only the greatest families send their children," she said. "And you were a master knight there?"

"For about five years."

"What did you do before that?"

He shrugged, leaning against the wall of the tavern and folding his enormous arms over his chest. "I was still with Kenilworth, but that was during the time of John's reign," he said. "It is a royal castle, you know. It always has been. I served in the royal ranks and fought battles for John that I rather would not have fought, but I was sworn to the king. I had no choice because I was a royal ward."

Elisiana was quite interested. "That makes sense," she said. "The House of de Reyne is quite prestigious."

He shrugged. "It was more that my mother's side of the family descended from the kings of Bernicia," he said. "John liked to keep his eye on anyone with ancient royal blood just in case they decided to challenge him for the throne."

Her eyebrows lifted. "And he kept an eye on you?"

"He did," he said. "When he saw my talent with a sword, I was practically forced into being a trainer to others. He did not want me leaving to serve one of his enemies and using my skill against him."

"But he let you come to Blackchurch?"

"I left Kenilworth right after he died," he said. "William Marshal permitted me to go to Blackchurch because I would be using my skills to train the most elite knights in the world. Not using my sword against young Henry or anyone opposed to his rule."

Her brow furrowed. "What does William Marshal have to do with it?"

Sinclair gave her a wry smile. "You do not know how the man controls the country, do you? Especially after John's death."

Elisiana shrugged, rubbing her arms against the chill that was now descending as the night deepened. "I remember from my days of fostering that…"

She suddenly stopped, looking at him with wide eyes when she realized that she gave him more information than she'd intended, and Sinclair snorted softly.

"I was right," he said. "You *are* nobility. Where did you foster, lass?"

Elisiana lost her humor, her interest in his conversation, and everything else. She stopped rubbing her arms and began to back away from him. "I'll not tell you," she said with a growing sense of alarm. "You'll not force me to go back, do you hear me? I'm happy here. I am living the life I want to live. If my father sent you, I swear I'll fight you to the death!"

He came off the wall, his hands lifted in supplication. "Sweetheart, your father did not send me," he said. "I swear this upon my oath as a knight."

She was shaking with fear, with anger. "Truly?" she demanded. "Do you promise?"

"Of course I promise," he said, somewhat gently. "Moreover, how could your father have sent me? In the first place, I do not know who he is. In the second place, you know I just returned from Flanders. Hobbes, and even my friends from Blackchurch, have confirmed this. Do you understand that?"

Elisiana was quite shaken. She gazed at him for several long moments before he began to see a hint of calm coming to her face. "I understand," she said, taking a deep breath to steady herself. "Of course I understand. Please… forget what I said. I should not have said it. I apologize."

Sinclair was moving in her direction, watching her as she struggled. "There is nothing to apologize for," he said. "I am sorry if I frightened you."

She shook her head. "You did not mean to," she said, forcing a smile that was more like a grimace. "You said last night that I have secrets. I do not wish to reveal them, not to anyone, so please do not ask me again. Not anything."

"I will not," he said, his voice still gentle. "I have a few of my own. But one thing that is not a secret is the fact that I am an elite knight of noble birth. I have served the king. I now serve at Blackchurch. I am considered by everyone who knows me to be most trustworthy."

She eyed him, noticing that he was standing right in front of her now. "I… I would believe that."

"Good," he said. "Because if you are running from something, mayhap you should tell me so I can help you if the need arises. My intentions are only honorable, my lady, I swear it."

He could see in her eyes that his declaration touched her. But it also frightened her. After a moment, she simply shook her head and looked away. "Though I appreciate your offer, I do not wish to put any burden upon you," she said. "My situation is my own. It does not concern anyone but me."

Sinclair didn't push. He'd already pushed enough. He wasn't certain if it was wild curiosity that was making him push for the truth or a genuine desire to help her. The moment she thought he had been sent from her father, she'd taken on the look of a hunted animal. That gave him some indication as to what she was keeping hidden deep.

But she wasn't willing to share it.

"Very well," he said. "If you want to keep it to yourself, that is your privilege. But know I would be willing to help you should you need it."

She kept her gaze averted even as she nodded her head firmly. "I appreciate that," she said. "I do, very much. You are very kind."

"Will you tell me one thing?"

"If I can."

"Lisi is not your real name, is it?"

It was more of a statement than a question. She sighed faintly before shaking her head.

"Nay."

"May I ask what your Christian name is?"

"Elisiana. Lisi was what my family called me as a child."

A smile spread across his lips. "Elisiana," he repeated. "A beautiful name. I will not tell anyone."

She lifted her head then to look at him. "Thank you," she said. "I mean that. You have been very kind to me since we met, Sir Sinclair. I will not forget it."

"Call me Sin," he said. "My friends do. I would like you to be one of them."

She smiled in return. "I am honored," she said. "I never thought I would know a master knight from Kenilworth, much less a Blackchurch trainer, in my lifetime."

Before Sinclair could reply, Payne chose that moment to poke his head from the tavern, immediately spying them.

"What are ye doing out here?" he demanded. "Come inside, Sin. Stop flirting with my lass."

Before Sinclair could answer, Elisiana swung the bucket up into her arms and marched toward the door.

"I told you that I am not your lass, Payne," she said firmly. "You would do well to remember that."

Payne grinned as she walked past him. "'Tis just a matter of time before ye are," he said. "I'll wear ye down one way or the other."

"Never!" she called back to him as she headed toward the kitchens.

Payne watched her until she was out of sight. "What a woman," he said, sighing with appreciation. "Probably the one woman in all of England and Scotland that could take on my mother. She's fearless, that lass."

Sinclair could already see a problem. He hadn't really yesterday, but today, something was telling him there was going to be a problem between him and Payne, because the mere mention of Payne calling Elisiana "his woman" and Sinclair could feel his jealousy rise. Perhaps not jealousy so much as a strong sense of competition. He loved Payne like a brother and he was a good man, but Elisiana wasn't meant for a big, loud-mouthed Scotsman.

She was meant for other things.

Perhaps a former master knight from Kenilworth.

Careful, he thought to himself.

"I wish you luck, lad," he said as he passed by Payne on his way into the tavern. "That's a brave and stubborn lass."

Payne laughed as only he could—booming, joyful. "Ye sensed that, did ye?" he said as he followed him inside. "Truth be told, I think my mother already has a wife picked out for me, so I doubt I could bring Lisi home, but the fun is in the chase, isn't it? Like the hunters who chase down a beautiful stag only tae release it because they dunna have the heart tae kill it."

Sinclair frowned. "You want to *hunt* her?"

Payne laughed again. "Just for the thrill of the chase, lad," he said.

"Nothing more."

Sinclair didn't say anything more. At the moment, he was too confused with what he was feeling about the situation. He let Payne slap him on the shoulder and follow him back to the private room, where Kristian was already sitting down to boiled beef and capon pie. Another serving wench, one that was old enough to be a grandmother, was serving them, and Sinclair sat down to a feast, listening to Payne talk about what had gone on in Sinclair's absence around Blackchurch.

Most interestingly, he mentioned that St. Abelard and some of his pirates had come for a few months, nearly jumping claim on Kristian's water-centric classes to teach some of the recruits how to board enemy vessels in the event of a battle. They were even teaching the recruits pirate ways when Kristian, Tay, and some of the other trainers, including St. Denis, regained control of the class and kicked them out. Sinclair had grinned his way through that conversation, imagining Triton's Hellions against the Blackchurch knights for supremacy of the lake where Kristian taught his classes.

He was sorry he missed it.

The conversation with Payne and Kristian went well into the night, something Sinclair had missed while in Toxandria, but every so often, Elisiana would pass into his line of sight and he would find his attention wandering. To watch her when she didn't know he was looking at her was a sight to behold, indeed.

She was a sight to behold.

It was good to be home.

Now for another reason.

CHAPTER FIVE

Fremington Castle

"I THINK WE found her."

The announcement came from Aristeo as he stood in the doorway of his father's solar, a lavish and vast two-storied chamber that was laden from floor to ceiling with all of the things his father considered precious. Rare books, maps, trinkets—including what was reportedly a sliver of the True Cross—lined the shelves and steps and walls. There were more than a dozen mounted heads from animals Adriano and Aristeo had killed on hunts, and from those heads hung rosaries and silk ties. In all, the chamber was cluttered and full of strange and wonderful things, but those things meant nothing to Adriano at the moment.

His son's announcement did.

"Where?" he gasped. "Where is *mi hija*?"

"Possibly in Devon," Aristeo said as he entered the room, heading for the pitcher of wine on a table near the window. "You know that I have had men all over the roads now for months, traveling in small towns, large towns, looking everywhere for her."

"And?" Adriano said eagerly. "What have they said? And how do they know it is her? Some of those men do not even know her!"

"True," Aristeo said, pouring himself a sloppy cup of wine. He lifted it to his lips and drank deeply before answering. "But I have described her well to them. Pale eyes, very dark hair, freckles on her nose… They know she is a beauty. One man believes he saw her in the village of Exebridge, in a tavern, breaking up a fight."

"A fight?" Adriano exclaimed. Then he put his hand over his heart and sank back into his chair. "Sweet Mary. What is she doing in a tavern? She is an innocent!"

Aristeo cast his father a long look. "Papa, we must face the reality that she may not be innocent any longer," he said. "You know I love my sister and would never disparage her, but what do you think she has done in order to survive?"

Adriano's features rippled with pain. "You will not think such things about her."

Aristeo went to his father, putting his hand on the man's head. "Papa, I do not want to say such things about her," he insisted softly. "But we must face the truth. It is possible she has sold herself to survive."

Adriano put his hand over his face in despair. "Then if she did, it would be better had she died," he said. "It is too much shame for her mother and I to bear. Why could she have not simply married Adolph? He would make a good husband. He will still make a good husband. He has agreed to wait, you know."

Aristeo's expression darkened. "Because he is greedy and without prospects," he muttered. "I do not like the man, Papa. He is not good enough for Lisi."

"After she has run away, she will not be good enough for *him*!"

Aristeo sighed heavily. "He will wait because he knows she will be without prospects after this," he muttered. "This was never a good match, Papa. I wish you had not forced this."

Adriano frowned. "Are you saying I pushed her into running away?"

"I am saying that you should have listened to her," Aristeo said. "She told you that she did not want Uncle Robert's new wife's son. Rather than try to find someone appealing to her, you pushed that pale lump of a man on her."

"He brings money with him, Téo."

"He looks like melted cheese!"

Adriano wasn't prepared to argue with his son. They'd done nothing but argue for six months, ever since Elisiana ran off as Adriano tried to foist a marriage on her. Aristeo wasn't wrong about that—Elisiana had never been obtuse with her wants or desires when it came to Adolph de Rade, but Adriano hadn't listened. He wanted his daughter married and he wanted grandchildren, and Elisiana had reacted by running away and staying away. Perhaps he was willing to admit he had done a few things wrong, but not in front of his son.

He didn't want to give the man the satisfaction.

"Enough," he snapped softly. "Your opinion of de Norbury does not interest me. What *does* interest me is getting my daughter back. Well? What have you planned now that we know where she is? Where is this Exebridge?"

Aristeo drained his cup. "It is a small village near the Exmoor Forest," he said. "It is also near the Blackchurch Guild, which is why no one thought she would make it that far into Devon. At least not near Blackchurch. Everyone knows those lands are full of murderers and pirates."

Adriano grunted. "Your sister is as foolish as she is brave," he said. "She more than likely went that way thinking we would not suspect her to take that path."

"And that is why I am inclined to believe that it is, indeed, my little sister," Aristeo said. "The man who saw her says she spends a good deal of time there. He saw her for three straight days before he left to give me the message."

Adriano pondered the news for a moment before shaking his head. "She has been little more than a day's ride from us all the time," he murmured. "She has been hiding in plain sight."

Aristeo could hear the irony in his father's voice. "She did not go far," he agreed. "Not to worry, Papa. I will bring her home, but I suggest you not tell Adolph. If you have any hope of making her stay, I would not bring him around."

Adriano didn't say anything, but he did nod. That was simply to avoid more arguing with his son. Of course he was going to tell Adolph. He wanted his daughter married, didn't he? A marriage to Adolph would keep her close to him, married to his wife's brother's new wife's son. But he had to make sure the marriage happened. Bringing a runaway bride, who had been living—and surviving—on her own for six months back into the fold was bound to bring up all kinds of questions that Adriano didn't want answered before the marriage could take place.

He had to make sure of it.

As Aristeo went to arrange for the reclamation of his sister, Adriano wrote a missive to his brother-in-law, Robert, telling him the news. Robert only lived about a day's ride south in Hatherleigh. Adriano would make sure that Adolph was at Fremington when Elisiana arrived. In the end, he would have what he wanted.

A marriage to Adolph to pay off the debt he owed Robert.

The man had loaned him a great deal of money a few years ago, something Adriano used to pay some debts he owed to others, but the fact of the matter was that he now owed his wife's brother a good deal of money. But it was something he had never, ever mentioned to Aristeo, knowing how his son felt about his father's scheming dealings and their relationship to one of the most feared Spanish pirates in recent history. Aristeo had tried to distance himself from the feared Santiago Fernandez, leader of the band of pirates known as the *demonios del mar*, or the Demons of the Sea, while Adriano was more apt to accept his family ties.

Distasteful as they were.

But that was the truth.

And now Elisiana was involved in Adriano's underhanded dealings, this one with his own brother-in-law. *A marriage for the money*, Robert had said.

And Elisiana was the one to settle the debt.

CHAPTER SIX

H E'D BEEN WATCHING him for the better part of an hour. Sinclair started his recruit class at dawn, and the elusive Anteaus de Bourne was introduced to him by Tay, who told Sinclair that he'd needed Anteaus' help with his own dreg class for a couple of days and had thus kept the man occupied while Sinclair settled in. In fact, Sinclair had been wondering where de Bourne, a man he'd been told about, had gone to, and now here he was, in the flesh.

A very capable knight who seemed to have a better sword arm than most.

But Sinclair had been polite to him. Anteaus was a tall, well-built man with blond hair and intense, dark eyes. He had abnormally long arms, which was why he was probably so good with a sword, and Sinclair had thanked him for helping Cruz and Creston with the class. Anteaus had been gracious, telling Sinclair how highly the trainers spoke of him and expressing his wish to learn from the man even though Anteaus was as highly trained as most upper-nobility knights were. Moreover, he'd spent a good deal of time with his father's army in the north, fighting Scots and Northmen, and assisting his eldest brother, who was the Sheriff of Westmorland. It seemed to Sinclair that Anteaus had a good deal of opportunity through his father and eldest brother, but still, he wanted more.

He wanted Blackchurch.

That either concerned Sinclair or made him curious. The man was either secretly ambitious or simply wanted to be the best knight he could be. Sinclair wasn't sure which, not yet, but his friends seem to have a high opinion of Anteaus, and the man's strength seemed to be in the swordplay arena, so Sinclair wasn't opposed to an assistant if that's what Anteaus was best suited toward. Sinclair had never worked with one, preferring to operate his classes on his own, but he was older now and presumably wiser. He'd done a great deal already in his life, so if he wanted to stand back and instruct while a capable assistant handled the heavy physical training, then he reasoned that he'd earned that right.

But time would tell just how capable Anteaus truly was.

And if the man secretly wanted to usurp him.

Sinclair's class got underway at dawn, and it was another day of repetition. As Anteaus helped dole out the training weapons that the recruits were using, Sinclair stood on a rise above the field they were using, one that was next to Lake Cocytus, the body of water that all of Blackchurch was built around. Named after a lake in the ninth circle of hell, it was a fitting feature in the midst of the guild's training grounds. Sinclair could see Kristian's class about to embark on their seafaring training using three large cogs that were moored on the northern end of the lake. The same cogs that St. Abelard's hellions had tried to confiscate. They *were* pirates, after all. Sinclair was grinning at the memory of that particular conversation the previous night when Anteaus came up beside him.

"Everyone is armed, my lord," he said. "Is there anything else I may do for you?"

Sinclair looked at him. "You were not here for my first class yesterday."

"Nay, my lord."

Sinclair gestured to the group. "While I realize this class has been in sword training for a couple of weeks already, it has not been *my* training," he said. "I am taking everyone back to the basics right now, so I hope you can tolerate it."

Anteaus grinned. "I am the youngest of three brothers, my lord," he said. "I have been chased back to the basics by those bullies many times in my life. I do not mind it."

Sinclair fought off a smile. "You are Warwick trained, I'm told."

"Aye, my lord."

Warwick, Kenilworth, and Berkeley were some of the finest training grounds in England for knights, so Anteaus had an impeccable education. Truthfully, Sinclair could already see it in the man's manner. There was something strong and precise about him, so he could easily see why the trainers seemed to think that Anteaus was trainer material himself.

But Sinclair wanted the man to know whom he was so eager to learn from. Anteaus' education may have been impeccable, but Sinclair's was elite.

And he wanted to stress that.

"You know that I was a master knight at Kenilworth at one time," he said.

"I was told, my lord."

Sinclair cocked an eyebrow. "The point is that I have my own training system," he said. "Whatever these men have been taught over the past couple of weeks is about to be erased. We will embark on *my* training schedule now."

"I look forward to it, my lord."

"Do you?" Sinclair said. "Good. Because you are going to walk among the ranks and watch every wrist, every forearm. We are doing lifts today and will be doing them for the rest of the week. How a man lifts his sword, and grips the hilt, will prevent him from breaking a finger or injuring his wrist in battle, so we will be working on specific moves for the next several weeks. One move, repetitively made, until it is perfect. Then we move to the next one. Do you understand?"

"Implicitly, my lord."

"You may find it rudimentary."

"Anyone who feels that a basic move is a wasted effort will not long survive in battle, my lord," Anteaus said. "That is not how the world works."

Sinclair's gaze lingered on him a moment. "Well said," he said. "Now, let's get on with it."

Anteaus nodded, standing aside as Sinclair lifted his voice and gave the recruits the day's instruction. A simple lift, but an important one, moving the weapon into a defensive position.

Over and over again.

The class commenced.

Sinclair, too, walked among the ranks, watching the recruits as they lifted repeatedly. As he walked, he clapped his hands, forcing the men to move to the beat. He went to stand next to Thomas Ram, who was trying very hard to be graceful with his lift. Being a farmer, he'd never really held a weapon with skill before, only strength, but because Sinclair liked him, he was willing to be less harsh with him. In fact, he had Anteaus pull Thomas aside, personally instructing him on how to lift the weapon because most in the class were already trained knights and were able to do the move with ease.

He didn't want Thomas to fall behind.

Into the morning it went. When the men were showing signs of exhaustion lifting the weapon with their dominant hand, Sinclair had them switch to their non-dominant hand. That was more of a challenge. The recruits seemed to slow down a little because of it, and Sinclair was forced to clap his hands again in rhythm, compelling them to keep pace. He went over to see how Thomas was doing with Anteaus and had to admit that he was impressed by the man's patience and skill.

But he also had to admit he was still suspicious of a Warwick-trained knight infiltrating his class. As he turned away from the pair, he caught sight of someone approaching from the village.

It took him all of two seconds to realize it was Athdara and another woman.

Elisiana.

Pleased to see her but trying desperately not to look like it, he made his way in her direction, coming up from the sloping training field. When Athdara saw him coming, she lifted her hand and waved.

"Sin!" she called. "I've brought you a visitor!"

Sinclair couldn't help the smile then. Both Athdara and Elisiana were grinning at him, so he returned the gesture.

"So I see," he said, his focus shifting mostly to Elisiana. "I told you to visit any time that wasn't dawn or dusk or mealtime. And here you are."

Elisiana nodded. "You did not say that I could not come today, but this is the day that Hobbes has given me to rest," she said. "I have already completed my chores, so I thought I would visit. I hope my visit is not inconvenient."

Sinclair glanced at Athdara, who was looking at him as if she knew something he didn't. Perhaps she knew that the serving wench might have a romantic inclination toward him. Or he toward her. Perhaps she wanted to tease him about it. In any case, she was smiling so annoyingly that Sinclair wanted to give her a shove or a sneer, anything to chase her off just like he would an irritating sister. It was difficult to keep his composure when Athdara was a hairsbreadth away from taunting him about it.

"Nay, it is not inconvenient," he said, but then he turned to Athdara. "How did you come to be the escort?"

Athdara gestured toward the gatehouse. "Today is market day in Exebridge and I went there early this morning," she said. "I saw Lisi at the gatehouse upon my return and she told me why she had come, so I invited her in. If you are in the middle of your instructions, I can bring her to my cottage until you are done. I've not seen her in a while."

"You know each other?"

Athdara nodded. "Tay takes me to the Black Cock from time to time, and Lisi and I have met," she said. "But I've never had much opportunity for a conversation because she is always working."

"I have been honored by your attention, Lady Munro," Elisiana said. "Although I realize we are not of the same social station, I've enjoyed the brief conversations we've had."

Athdara rolled her eyes. "Brief conversations as men yell, or fight, and minstrels play, and you are in great demand to bring food and drink to the masses," she said. "And I do not care about social station. I do not have many female friends here, so it would be nice to talk to someone new."

Sinclair shook his head and reached out to grasp Elisiana by the wrist. "She has come to see *me*," he said. "Go away, Valkyrie. You can talk to her another time."

"Valkyrie?" Elisiana repeated as Sinclair gently pulled her away from Athdara. "Is that your name, my lady?"

Athdara shook her head, displeased that Sinclair was taking charge. "Nay," she said. "It is a nickname. I'll explain it to you another time."

Long ago, Athdara had actually been a recruit at Blackchurch and her moniker had been "Valkyrie." Sinclair didn't want her to explain all of that to Elisiana now, not when his time was limited, so he waved his hand at her in a dismissive gesture.

"Thank you for your escort, Lady Munro," he said. "You are no longer needed. *Go*."

Athdara frowned. "I understand," she said. "But you do not have to be rude."

"If I was being rude, I would have said, 'Begone, witch,'" he said, casting her a threatening glance. "I still might if you do not leave promptly."

Athdara fought off a grin. "I am going to tell my husband what you said."

"Tell him. I'm not afraid of that big bull."

Athdara was giggling as she walked away, which told Elisiana that they were teasing one another. She thought it was rather sweet the way they got along. In fact, after a long night of lying awake and thinking about the mysterious Sinclair de Reyne, she had come to the conclusion that *he* was rather sweet.

And that's why she was here.

"Truly, if this is inconvenient, you only need tell me," she said. "I've never been to Blackchurch before, so this might be a misplaced impulse on my part."

Sinclair's smile broadened. "Not at all," he said. "I am happy to have you visit, though I am in the middle of a class. We can talk while the recruits run through an exercise."

"Are you sure you do not need to pay close attention?"

"I have an… assistant who is helping," he said, eyeing Anteaus in the distance. "At the moment, I'm simply observing and making sure everyone is completing their exercise correctly."

The subject seemed settled. Elisiana smiled timidly, nearly forgetting the basket she had tucked under her arm. It was partially covered by her cloak, and she produced it, holding it up for him to see.

"Because I have never been one to be idle, sometimes during my rest days, I make food for the tavern," she said, uncovering the basket. "I've brought you some. Surely you must eat midday, so if you like, you can have this."

Sinclair peered into the basket, poking around at what seemed to be a veritable feast. "It smells delicious," he said. "What did you bring?"

Elisiana watched him inspect the offerings. In fact, she hadn't been able to take her eyes off the man since she saw him only a few moments ago. He was glorious by candlelight in the darkness, but in the daylight, he was positively magnificent.

Her heart was pounding simply from looking at him.

She had planned this day well. This wasn't simply a random decision to take him up on his invitation of a visit to Blackchurch. This was something she had been calculating since last night because the conversation had been both curious and enlightening. Normally, Elisiana didn't spend a lot of time speaking with patrons of the Black Cock. Not that they weren't able to carry on a conversation, but most of them weren't there to talk. They were there to eat and drink and be left alone. Therefore, she had become accustomed to simply delivering food or clearing away dirty dishes. Sometimes, she helped Hobbes manage the kitchens because of her training as a chatelaine. The truth was that not only was she an extremely proficient chatelaine, but she knew a little something about everything that had to do with running a house and hold, and that included cooking.

Drawing wasn't her only talent.

While it was unseemly for a noblewoman to cook or do anything that was considered the duties of the servants, Elisiana liked to cook a great deal. When she had fostered at Alnwick, the cook had been from Bavaria and the woman made all sorts of incredible dishes. Elisiana had spent a good deal of her time in the kitchen, managing the stores as well as the schedule of meals, so inevitably she spent time with the tall, round woman with the great belly laugh. She and the cook had become friends, as much as a noblewoman and a servant could be, and the woman had imparted her knowledge of dishes upon her. Elisiana learned to make a good deal of traditional Bavarian dishes along with some Parisian and English dishes as well.

She brought these talents to the Black Cock, and one of the very first things she ever did for Hobbes was cook. He saw fairly quickly the talent he had in her. Taverns normally weren't terribly elaborate with their dishes, but with the addition of Elisiana, they had become quite upscale as far as taverns went. Therefore, on her day of rest, she loved working in the kitchens, making breads with different flavors and textures as well as pies and other delights. After Sinclair invited her to visit Blackchurch, she had begun planning last night what she would bring to him today. Perhaps it was foolish of her, thinking this man wanted anything she should bring him, but watching him eagerly pull forth a ginger cake with honey and pepper, she was hoping that it wasn't so foolish after all.

Someone once said the way to a man's heart was through his stomach.

Maybe his heart was her ultimate goal.

Maybe.

"Those are ginger and honey wafers," she said, watching him pop one in his mouth. "They're made from breadcrumbs and honey and pepper and then baked."

Sinclair chewed twice before pausing and closing his eyes in delight. "God's Bones," he muttered. "This is delicious. Did you actually prepare them yourself?"

Elisiana nodded. "I've learned how to make dishes over the years," she said. "I do believe that is why Hobbes allowed me to stay those months ago. He wanted to exploit my skill with food."

Sinclair put another one in his mouth. "I do not blame him," he said. "But how did you come to the Black Cock in the first place? Exebridge is not exactly well traveled. Were you simply journeying through?"

Her smile faded. "I think we should establish something right away," she said. "I will not ask about your past and you will not ask about mine. Agreed?"

He swallowed what was in his mouth. "Agreed," he said. "But it makes it a little difficult to have a conversation if all you will speak of are the past six months of your life."

She shrugged. "What about my future?" she said. "Will you ask me about that?"

He nodded and took the basket from her. "I will," he said, reaching out to take her hand. "Come over here and watch my class train, and you can tell me about your future."

Elisiana's heart threatened to pound right out of her chest as he held her hand. It didn't seem to be in a romantic gesture, or affectionate, but simply companionable. At least for him, but for her, it meant more than that. He pulled her over to the top of a rise, and down below was an entire gang of men raising a sword and lowering it in rhythm. Up, down. Up, down. Beyond them was a stone wall and another field where men seemed to be doing something else, and then at the very base of the hill was a beautiful lake spread out before them. It was a large lake, in fact, and off to the north, she could see three cogs moving in unison. She pointed.

"There are ships out there," she said. "Is that part of Blackchurch, too?"

Sinclair looked off to the north, seeing the fine cogs. "Aye," he said. "That is Kristian's class. He is a Northman and his expertise is fighting on water, so that is what he is teaching."

She looked at him curiously. "Kristian?"

Sinclair let go of her hand and dug into the basket again. "Big lad," he said, pulling out another ginger wafer. "Hair to his shoulders, the color of honey. Dark blue eyes. Young. He and Payne are close friends."

Her eyes widened in recognition. "Ah," she said. "*Him.* Aye, I know who he is, but Payne always calls him 'Princeling.'"

"He is," Sinclair said, chewing. "He's the son of a king."

That surprised her. "And he teaches at Blackchurch? He is not ruling his people?"

Sinclair looked at her, winking. "You are not the only one with a past that is not spoken of," he said. "Most of us have things we do not wish to discuss."

"Even you?"

"Especially me."

Since Elisiana understood that kind of thing, and she'd already established their conversation rules, she didn't push him. Instead, she looked to the group of men training below. There had to be forty or fifty of them, all of them lifting a sword and lowering it. Raising her hand to shield her eyes from the sun, she watched a couple of men working together as one tried to show the other one how to hold the hilt. The second man, the one being taught, seemed rather clumsy, but eager. The rest of the recruits, however, seemed quite proficient.

"How do men come to be trained at Blackchurch?" she asked, changing the subject away from their obvious secrets. "Are they special men? Do you select them?"

Sinclair swallowed the last of the ginger wafer. "In a way, we do," he said. "Anyone can come to Blackchurch for training, but they must pass a variety of tests to prove their worthiness."

"What kind of test?"

"Strength, endurance, skills to a certain extent," he said. "A man, or woman, must prove they have the foundation of what is necessary to become a Blackchurch-trained warrior. And there is no failure—if they fail at any of the tests, then they must wait a full year to try again. If they happen to make it through the initiation tests and then fail in any one of the courses we teach during the course of their training, they are out."

"Forever?"

"For a full year. That is the rule."

Elisiana turned her attention back to the field of men lifting the sword, over and over again. "Are the classes at Blackchurch given in any order?" she asked.

He nodded. "They are," he said. "Tay is the first course that any dreg faces."

"Dreg?"

"New recruits until they pass Tay's course of endurance and strength."

"What's next?"

"Fox comes next," he said. "Recruits learn how to fight with small weapons, how to protect themselves and others. Things like that. I follow with swordsmanship classes. I teach them how to fight with a sword. After that, the classes usually split into two. Some will train with Payne, some with Kristian. As this is going on, other classes are with Creston teaching interrogation and torture, with Cruz teaching diplomacy and politics, or with Ming Tang teaching how to fight without a weapon. Then there is Bowen to teach about knightly honor and warrior etiquette, and after that to Amir, who teaches them military tactics and history. If a recruit fails to excel in any one of these classes, they are dismissed."

Elisiana pushed some stray hair out of her eyes. "That seems very sad," she said. "To go through all of that only to be dismissed if you make a mistake. Everyone makes mistakes. They should be given another chance."

"They are when they are permitted to try again," Sinclair said. "We are not a school of failure. We do not believe in learning from one's mistakes. We believe in doing it right the first time."

"That seems harsh."

"Not if we are training the most elite warriors in the world."

She conceded the point. "I suppose," she said. "I am assuming recruits pay to attend Blackchurch?"

Sinclair nodded. "They either pay outright or they pledge a percentage of the money they receive from a new position when they finish their training," he said. "It usually takes a recruit about five years to get through all of our training. The men you see in my class have been here at least nine months, if not more."

"Do they pay again if they fail?"

"Certainly."

It seemed like a unforgiving way to run a business, but then again, they *were* training the most elite warriors in the world.

Perfection *was* the standard.

"And you?" she said. "Did you have to go through the training, too?"

"Of course I did," he said. "Initially, I went through it to return to Kenilworth to use methods to teach our own knights, but Lord Exmoor offered me a position as the master swordsman and I accepted."

"And it has been lucrative for you?"

"Verily."

Elisiana pondered that. As she watched, the recruits switched hands and began lifting with the left one while Sinclair took a few steps toward them, clapping out a beat of repetition. But her gaze moved around the guild, for it was a good deal of property as far as the eye could see, all of it nestled around the large lake. There were stone walls creating pens where the recruits were working, and she could see several groups of them dotted throughout the landscape. Everyone working toward one goal—to survive Blackchurch and to become an elite warrior, ready to face the world. It was on such a grand scale that the entire guild was most impressive. She was watching the cogs in the distance again when Sinclair caught her attention.

"The class is going to break for a rest period and some food," he said. "Would you like me to show you around?"

She lifted the basket still in her hands. "Don't you want to eat?"

He grinned and took it from her. "I did not want to be rude, since you came for a visit," he said. "I was willing to show you the grounds, but if you insist, I shall eat first."

Down the slope, men were sitting, some of them lying down, recovering from hours of lifting a sword. They were waiting for servants to come down from the kitchens near the cloister to provide them with cheese and bread and fruit. Sinclair sat down on the cool green grass, as did Elisiana, the basket between him as he began to pull out more delights.

"I feel like a king," he said, food in both hands. "And quite pampered. Thank you for bringing this."

Elisiana smiled. "You are welcome," she said. "I... I suppose I also wanted to apologize for last night."

"Why?"

"Because you tried to help me with the fight and I made it difficult," she said. "I did not mean to seem ungrateful."

"Ah," he said. "So your true motive is revealed. You did not come simply to visit me. You came to ply me with food as an apology."

She laughed softly. "That is *not* true," she said. "Well, not entirely. I enjoy speaking to you and I cannot say that about many people. The food is merely so you wouldn't turn me away so quickly."

He shoved part of a meat pie into his mouth. "Clever," he said as he chewed. "But I would not send you away in any case. I do not have the chance to speak to many women like you."

"Serving wenches?"

He shook his head. "You are most definitely *no*t a wench," he said. "I meant well spoken. I suppose if I knew more about you, we might know some of the same people and the same places. But I am afraid to venture into questions of a personal nature lest you run away and take your food with you."

She hung her head a little, unable to really look him in the eye. "Do you know why else I came today?"

"Why?"

"To make sure you really *were* a Blackchurch trainer."

His gaze lingered on her a moment as he understood her meaning. "You mean that you wanted to make sure I hadn't lied to you by telling you I was a Blackchurch trainer when I was really one of your father's men?"

"Exactly."

He put another bite in his mouth. "Look around you," he said. "This is my domain. This is where I belong. I am part of Blackchurch and it is part of me."

"Were you born in Devon?"

He shook his head. "Nay," he said, swallowing the bite in his mouth before continuing. "I do not speak of my past, Lisi. But I will tell you what you want to know. I suppose it is no great secret. I simply do not wish to talk about myself."

He handed her half of the pie he'd been eating. "You do not have to," she said. "I understand well the need for privacy."

"It is not privacy," he said quietly. "The truth is that my birth, and upbringing, is inglorious."

"Shameful?"

"Not really," he said. He dug around in the basket a little more, and Elisiana wasn't sure he was going to finish that thought until he began to speak quietly. "My father was the second of four brothers. Our family line can be traced back to the days of the Duke of Normandy. I had an ancestor who was part of his squad of knights, highly trained men who led the battle for him. They called themselves the *anges de guerre*."

"Angels of war," Elisiana translated softly. "Sounds fearsome."

"Aye, they were," Sinclair said, shifting so he was lying on his left side, propped up by an elbow. "Very fearsome. My father had that sense of warfare in his blood—he was a brutal, aggressive knight. All he knew was war and death. There was very little humanity about him."

"What was his name?"

"Rhodes de Reyne."

"Where did he serve?"

"Thropton Castle," he said. "That is the seat of the House of de Reyne, at least our branch of the family. He served his eldest brother and hated it with a passion. He was always at odds with him, especially when his brother gifted the younger brothers with property and gave Rhodes nothing. So Rhodes became something of an outlaw. Traveled around with a band of unscrupulous bachelor knights, stealing and looting to gain his fortune. He caused a good deal of trouble, including his meeting with my mother."

Elisiana was listening with interest. "What happened?"

"As the story goes, she was traveling north to Coldingham Abbey with her father because she was destined to take the veil," he said. "My father and his outlaw friends attacked their escort, killed the soldiers, and robbed them. My father, who was drunk, saw my beautiful mother and abducted her. Took her straight to the nearest church, forced the priest to marry them, bedded her, and didn't remember any of it the next morning. When he woke up and found her in his bed, he accused her of lying about how she got there."

Elisiana's mouth was open in outrage. "How terrible for her," she said. "What happened?"

He shrugged. "The priest confirmed they were married, so my father accepted what he had done," he said. "He went back to the site of the ambush and found my mother's father tied to a tree. He'd been there all night. My father told him what he had done. Oddly enough, my grandfather accepted his fealty, and my father tried to settle down after that. He returned with my mother and her father back to their home and attempted to resume a normal life."

Elisiana shook her head. "After all that, how could he?" she said. "He stole your mother's life away."

"He did," Sinclair agreed. "But this is where it becomes fortuitous, as least for my father. As it turned out, my mother was a descendant of the kings of Bernicia. Her father was Lord Ebchester, descended from St. Ebba, a Bernician princess, so when my grandfather died, my father inherited the title through my mother and all of the property, which was substantial. What his brother wouldn't give him, he ended up acquiring by marriage. Ironic, is it not?"

Sitting on the other side of the basket, fiddling with a blade of grass, Elisiana smiled. "Did it finally make him happy?"

Sinclair sat up, his gaze moving over the recruits in the field, the lake, the sky. "I do not know," he said. "I had two sisters, born right after me, and my father was killed in an ambush after the second child was born. My mother, in a state of apparent grief, decided to finish what she'd started those years ago when planning to take the veil. She went to Coldingham Abbey, my sisters were given to relatives, and I was sent to Kenilworth Castle because my uncle, the eldest de Reyne brother, made arrangements to send me there after my father's death. I was not quite five years of age."

Elisiana's smile was gone. "You were so young," she said. "I'm so very sorry, my lord."

He glanced at her. "What did I tell you last night?"

"You told me many things last night," she said. "To what do you refer?"

"I told you to call me Sin."

A smile tugged at her mouth. "My apologies," she said. "I'd forgotten."

"No harm done."

"Are you named for someone?" she said. "Is Sinclair a family name?"

He snorted. "Not that I am aware of," he said. "The rumor is that my grandfather named me. You see, my mother's name was Claire. I was born from sin. Hence, Sinclair."

Her mouth popped open. "That is a terrible thing if that is true," she said. "It is a terrible person who would saddle a child with a name like that. It's not true. And the circumstances around your birth were not your fault."

"Your defense is flattering, but unnecessary. It is my name. I am not ashamed of it."

She simply shrugged. The basket was in front of her, and because everyone in the field was eating now that the servants had come to dispense some food, she peered into it to see that there were a few ginger wafers left as well as some cheese. She pulled out the cheese with one hand and a ginger wafer with the other.

"Regardless of your name, or how you came to be, you have done very well for yourself," she said, taking a bite of the white cheese. "Losing your parents at such a young age could have been quite damaging. But you did not let it stop you, and that is an admirable quality."

He saw that she had a ginger wafer in her hand and reached into the basket to confiscate the other two. "I had no choice, really," he said, popping one in his mouth. "I was fortunate that the castellan of Kenilworth's wife took me under her wing because I was so young. Lady Bethania was her name, and she was very kind to me. Raised me as one of her own children until I was eight and her husband insisted I become a page. But I will always be grateful for the stability she brought to my life. I was fortunate."

"And you hold no hard feelings toward your mother for abandoning you?"

He shook his head. "My father changed her life so drastically," he said. "She had always intended to take the veil, not become the mother of three small children. When he died... I remember that she cried for days. She spent that time in the chapel of Ebchester, praying and weeping, and when she was done, that was when she decided to send her children away and take the veil as she had always intended. I honestly do not know if she is alive or dead. I've never cared enough to find out."

"You resent her, then?"

He shrugged. "Not resent," he said. "She did what she had to do. But I do not intend to open up the wounds of a five-year-old child who did not understand at the time. I still remember the fear, the abandonment. I remember the men that came to take me to Kenilworth. I cried for my mother but she did not come to me. But that is all the past now and I've no desire to dredge anything up. Sometimes it is better to simply let things lie."

"And your sisters?"

"Ophelia and Eloise," he said. "They, too, came to Kenilworth, but not until they were older. I did not even know who they were until Ophelia told me. They did not seem to want much to do with me, so I returned the favor. I do not know what became of them after they spent a couple of years fostering at Kenilworth."

"Do you ever wonder?"

"Nay."

Elisiana let the conversation fade, thinking of her own life and how different it was from his. She had her parents, her brother, and had been raised in luxury and comfort all of her life. Even when she was fostering. Running away from home had been the most exciting, or terrifying, thing she'd ever done, and she was acting as if she was the only person who had ever done anything so questionable. As if she had suffered more turmoil than anyone alive.

But Sinclair had suffered far more than she could have ever imagined.

It made her feel foolish that she thought she'd had the worst of it.

"Pevensey," she said quietly.

He looked at her. "What did you say?"

She took a deep breath and met his gaze. "You asked me where I fostered," she said. "Pevensey Castle."

It was clear from his expression that he was surprised she had answered him, belated though it was.

"I've never been there," he said after a moment. "I've heard it is quite large."

She nodded. "Large and busy," she said. "I learned everything a lady could learn but have a particular talent for drawing. I like to draw very much."

"Oh?" he said with interest. "Do you still?"

"When I have the time and the materials."

"May I see your drawings sometime?"

With an embarrassed smile, she lowered her gaze. "Probably not," she said. "You see, I was sent home from Pevensey because of my drawings. They were not what a proper lady would draw. Lady de Valcourt was scandalized by them, so she sent me home."

He frowned. "God's Bones," he said, somewhat incredulous. "What on earth did you draw?"

Elisiana was quickly backed into a corner. She hadn't intended to talk about this aspect of her life, but she'd brought the subject up. There was no use avoiding it now that he was asking about it.

"I draw pictures of women," she admitted. "Men and women, actually. Romantic drawings that I was able to sell for a great deal of money. But the women, most of the time… are without apparel."

His eyebrows shot up. "You draw nude women?"

He said it with a bit of volume, and she hissed at him, quieting him. "Please," she begged. "I should not have told you, but you had told me so much about yourself that I… Oh, God's Bones. Please do not tell anyone, because if Hobbes hears, he will dismiss me. And I need this position."

Sinclair could see how upset she was and hastened to reassure her.

"I'll not tell anyone, I promise," he said, reaching out to grasp her hand because she was clearly nervous. "I'm very glad you told me. It means you are a brave woman, much braver than I imagined. It takes great courage to do something that you are passionate about."

She eyed him warily. "Passionate, aye," she said. "I am very passionate about my drawings, and I am very good at it. But what I draw is considered unseemly by some."

He chuckled. "Aye, it is, but it is wonderful," he said. "Proper women bore me to tears. I like women with fire and brilliance and the courage to do something different."

She was starting to calm down a little. "Do you?"

He nodded. "Very much," he said, smiling. "Is that why you've run off? Because of these drawings? Don't tell me your father wants to punish you because of them."

She shook her head. "I ran off because he wants me to marry a fool of his choosing," she said stubbornly. "I will not do it. I will not marry that pasty-faced imbecile who leers at me and smells like cheese."

In those few short sentences, Sinclair knew everything he needed to know about the mysterious Elisiana.

It had been an eye-opening morning, indeed.

In truth, he wasn't sure why he'd told her so much about himself, only that she was easy to talk to. It all came pouring out. In turn, she had felt comfortable with him, and the conversation, and some dark little secrets of her own came tumbling out. Running from an arranged marriage, drawing naked women… He'd been honest when he told her that proper women bored him to tears. He liked women with a sense of adventure.

Elisiana had that and more, evidently.

"So you ran," he said. "Is there a chance he will find you?"

She shrugged. "Possibly," she said. "We live in Cornwall."

"You did not run very far."

"I did not have the means to do so," she said. "What I managed to bring with me was stolen, so my only choice was to find work to earn money and I have—with Hobbes."

"Who is your father?"

She hesitated. "If you think to send him a missive to tell him where I am and collect a reward, you will be disappointed," she said. "I am certain he would not pay for such information. My father is quite tight with his purse strings."

Sinclair grinned and shook his head. "You are quite mistrustful."

"I've learned to protect myself."

"Understandable," he said. "But I have better things to do than write fathers about their errant daughters. Besides, if he found you, I would feel bad."

"Why?"

"Because I would have no fiery lass to talk to and tell me about her sinful drawings."

Elisiana fought off a grin. It wasn't that she didn't trust him, but merely the fact that she'd grown accustomed to keeping her secrets buried deep. But he already knew a good deal about her thanks to a lovely morning and good food. Yet he didn't seem the greedy type. He was a well-paid trainer for Blackchurch, a former master knight from Kenilworth, and she doubted there were many men in England with more honor than he.

She relented.

"Do you promise not to tell anyone or send word to my father?" she said after a moment.

He nodded. "You have my vow."

She sighed. "Then I suppose I will tell you in case you happen to see his standards in town," she said. "You can warn me. My father is Adriano Celestino Fernandez y de Verra, head of the House of de Verra and the hereditary holder of the title *Conde de Pontevedra*. Our home, in Cornwall, is Fremington Castle and my father's colors are red and blue with a sea serpent in the center. I've been at the Black Cock for six months and he has yet to make his way to Exebridge, but I am certain my luck will not hold out forever. At some point, I will be moving on."

Sinclair was listening seriously, becoming increasingly impressed with what he was hearing. "Your father is an Aragon earl?" he asked.

"Castilian," she said. "Pontevedra is a port city and the title has been in my father's family for centuries. But do not think he is a noble earl, because he is not. My father bears some secrets as well. His cousin is Santiago de Fernandez, the fearsome pirate. His home port is Pontevedra, my father's town, but my father also lets him hide his ships at Fremington, which sits on the River Taw. Santiago pays my father a tribute from his raids on the English coast for the privilege."

The information was becoming more impressive by the moment, and Sinclair chuckled. "Incredible," he said. "Have you ever met Santiago?"

She waved him off. "Too many times to count," she said. "He is big and loud and drinks too much, but he always brings me expensive gifts that I'm sure he has stolen from a queen or a princess somewhere. He tells me that I am his very favorite niece and that he loves me more than my father."

Sinclair smiled. "I do not blame him," he said. "But when you ran, why did you not run to him? Mayhap he would have protected you."

She nodded. "He would have," she said. "But he was out to sea at the time, so I had no choice but to find my own safe haven. But I suppose I could find him and become a pirate."

Sinclair struggled not to laugh at the thought of a lady pirate. "Do you think he would accept your fealty?"

She looked at him to see that his eyes were twinkling with mirth. "You do not think he would?" she said. "You would be wrong. If he knew how much I hated this man my father wishes for me to marry, he would allow me to serve him. He would not force me to return. Mayhap he would even make me a captain of one of his ships, and then I would be the most fearsome pirate of all."

Sinclair did chuckle, then. "That I *can* see," he said. Then he threw a thumb back in the direction of Exmoor Castle. "You *do* know that the Lords of Exmoor are related to St. Abelard de Bottreaux and the pirates known as Triton's Hellions, don't you?"

Elisiana shook her head. "Nay," she said. "I've not heard that. But I think I have heard of Triton's Hellions. I think my father has mentioned them."

Sinclair waggled his eyebrows. "If your cousin is Santiago de Fernandez, then I am sure he and St. Abelard have gone up against one another from time to time," he said. "Abelard controls the Bristol Channel to the north, and if your cousin is docking his ships in Fremington, that is fairly close to the channel. They have surely had run-ins with one another."

"Santiago has cannons," Elisiana said. "Big, loud things. He is very proud of them."

Sinclair chuckled, shaking his head at the thought of a well-armed pirate as his attention moved to the lake and the cogs that were moving southward on the water. He thought about Abelard and his men trying to take the Blackchurch cogs, which did not have cannons. Probably for the better, or he would have returned to a much different Blackchurch.

One with holes in it.

"Well," he said after a moment, "it would seem that you have more in common with Blackchurch than you realized. You both have pirate relatives."

"I am not certain that is something to be proud of."

He looked at her, laughing softly. "Probably not," he said. "But thank you for telling me about your father. If I see his standards, I will be able to warn you."

"I would appreciate it," she said. "I must earn a little more money before I set off to London."

"Why are you going there?"

"To sell my drawings," she said. "That is where I intend to live. I think I could make good money selling them to women who would appreciate them."

He fell silent for a moment, mulling over her plans. "And that is the future you wanted me to ask about?" he said. "It is very ambitious."

"I know," she said. "But I know I can do it. I have the talent. I can go door to door, to every house in London, and sell my drawings or even accept commissions. I can draw people very well."

He looked at her. "Can you draw me?"

She looked at him, smiling. "Of course I can."

He fought off a grin, moving to face her. "Do you need me to sit still for you while you do it?"

She shook her head. "I can do it from memory."

He thought that was rather impressive. "Can you?" he said. "Then get a good look at me. My class is resuming in a few minutes and you'll not see me again until tonight. Can you draw it this afternoon?"

"I can," she said. "But I need to inspect you. May I?"

He had no idea what she meant until she crawled over to him, on her knees, and lifted her hands to his face. He sat stock-still while her fingers drifted over his cheeks, his chin, his nose, and his forehead. In fact, the mood of their conversation was quickly changing.

Now he was the one with a thumping heart.

There was something profoundly intimate about her touch to his face. He closed his eyes when she reached his forehead, feeling every flit of her fingers as if it were a lightning bolt. They were making him quiver, something magical flowing from her touch and into him, though his skin and into his veins like the headiest wine. His head was beginning to swim, but in a delightful way. When he finally opened his eyes again, Elisiana was right in front of him, just a few inches away, looking at his chin. When she saw that he was looking at her, her cheeks turned pink.

"You have a dimple in your chin," she said. "I must make sure to include that in the drawing."

She sounded breathless. As breathless as he felt. Quite honestly, he'd never felt this way before, but the more he looked into her pale blue eyes, the more he couldn't seem to breathe. But a shout off to his right captured his attention and he turned to see Anteaus ordering the men onto their feet. The rest period was over.

For Sinclair, too.

He took one of her hands, still on his face, and kissed it.

"I will expect to see that drawing tonight," he said, standing up and pulling her to her feet. "And if you make me look like a toad, I shall be very upset with you."

Wide-eyed at his kiss, Elisiana started to giggle. "Please?" she said. "Just a little like a toad?"

He turned his nose up at her. "Nay," he said. "I'll swat you like a naughty child, I swear it."

She was still gigging as he released her hand and was able to bend down and pick up her basket, which was now empty. His men were gathering, ready to resume their training, and Sinclair smiled at her as she brushed the grass off her cloak.

"Thank you," he said softly. "This was such a memorable visit. I am very glad we have become friends, Lady Elisiana."

She couldn't help but smile in return. "I am glad also," she said. "But I will not keep you any longer. I know you have these men to train."

"I do," he said. "But I will see you tonight."

"I look forward to it, Sin."

He snorted softly. "Good lass," he said. "You are learning to use my name."

She chuckled, moving away from him with some reluctance. She really didn't want to go, but she knew she had to. He was busy, and she evidently had a drawing to complete with the rest of her day.

"Best of luck with your class today," she said. "I have things to attend to as well."

"Like my drawing?"

"Of course."

"No toad. Remember that."

She laughed, casting him a rather flirtatious look, and headed off the way she'd come. Sinclair watched her go, his gaze lingering on her until she disappeared from view. He was still smiling when he turned back to his class, only to realize that they were all watching him. Every single one of them was watching and waiting for the next command. Feeling like an idiot at being caught watching a woman, Sinclair came at them with a vengeance.

For the recruits of Sinclair de Reyne, the second part of the day was much more difficult than the first. But for Sinclair himself, he realized he couldn't wait for class to be over.

He had a drawing to see.

CHAPTER SEVEN

I T WAS A wild night at the Black Cock.

Because it was market day, more people were in the village than normal, and as the sun began to set, that crowd filtered into the tavern, filling it to the rafters with men and women and laughter and song.

A band of traveling minstrels from Bohemia had also come to rest at the tavern that night, and for their supper they agreed to play all evening. They had a woman with them, dressed in an elaborate costume with silver tassels on the end of her skirt, and she danced and sang while the music filled the stale air. One of the two hearths in the common room was malfunctioning, sending streams of blue smoke into the air and adding to the chaotic ambiance.

The kitchens at the Black Cock were working at full capacity on this night. Hobbes usually had two cooks and at least three kitchen servants in addition to the four serving wenches he employed, and also an old woman who cleaned up every morning after the mess, but tonight he had engaged two more serving wenches because of the unusually large crowd. Because they were filled to capacity, the kitchen had prepared food that was easier to serve crowds rather than the roasts or pies that they normally served. There were enormous pots of beans and pork and carrots, plus other pots full of beef and gravy and dumplings made from flour and water and butter. Numerous loaves of bread were baking every hour, and the lad who took care of the livery, including the cows and chickens, was churning butter as fast as he could.

When it became particularly busy after sunset, Hobbes put Elisiana in charge because she was very organized. She served food, dealt with unhappy customers, and took payment for their food and drink with a smile. If customers got too friendly and tried to pinch her, she was quick with a slap. That usually settled them down. If it didn't, the Lion Tamer was always within reach.

Everyone knew she wasn't afraid to use it.

But tonight, the mood seemed to be good. Everyone w happy, enjoying the beans or the beef or both. Everyone was allowed two servings of a dish, and if they wanted more, they had to pay for it. Tonight, there happened to be piles of those sweet ginger wafers that Elisiana had brought to Sinclair, so when the Blackchurch trainers arrived—all of them—that was one of the first things Sinclair demanded as they walked in and headed for their usual private room.

Elisiana and another wench named Aster gathered cups and pitchers of wine from the kitchens, heading into the private chamber as the trainers found their seats. They were chatting between themselves, but once Payne saw Elisiana, her hands full of cups, he called out to her.

"My bonny lass," he said loudly. "When are ye going tae marry me?"

Elisiana fought off a grin as she began to set the cups down in front of the trainers nearest her. "Only in your dreams," she said. "My mother would roll over in her grave if she knew I'd married a Scotsman, so it is best not to tempt fate."

"Yer mother is dead?"

"She is not, but if I marry you, it will kill her."

The group laughed at Payne's expense as Kristian spoke up. "And she is far too pretty for you," he said. "Why would she want to marry the likes of you?"

Payne tried to grab him by the neck, but Kristian just laughed. As those nearest Payne found amusement at his misfortune, Elisiana came to Amir and Ming Tang, seated next to one another.

"I'll have ginger beer for you," she told them, as neither drank wine or ale. "We received a new shipment of it yesterday and I've set some aside for you."

Amir was pleased because he liked ginger beer a great deal. "How kind of you," he said. "Did you get it from the supplier who makes it with lemon?"

She nodded. "The man in Bilbao who makes it with lemon and orange," she said. "I tasted it myself. It is delicious, but it is quite bubbly."

"Thank you, Lisi," Ming Tang said. "You are an excellent hostess. How Hobbes survived before you came, I do not know."

Elisiana smiled at the man who was from a country far to the east. He was always very polite with her, and she wanted to talk to him more about his country. Unfortunately, in her position as a serving wench, there simply wasn't the opportunity, but she was fascinated by him.

"Hobbes survived before and he'll survive after," she said, putting the last cup down in front of him. "But it is kind of you to say so."

"You are not leaving, are you?" Ming Tang asked.

She shook her head. "Not anytime soon," she said, her gaze moving to Sinclair, who was sitting next to Ming Tang. "But someday."

Sinclair was smiling up at her as she spoke, and he didn't miss the coy expression she threw him before heading out to collect the ginger beer. He watched her leave the room, trying not to be obvious about it, but beside him, Ming Tang spoke up.

"She is quite lovely," he said quietly. "I am certain that has not escaped your notice. It has not escaped Payne's, either."

Sinclair coolly eyed Payne across the table. "So I have been told."

Ming Tang looked at Payne, too, as he said something to Kristian that must have been very funny. That side of the table erupted in laughter.

"If it means anything, I do not believe he is serious about her," Ming Tang said. "She is another pretty face. He likes to tease her."

Sinclair sighed faintly and looked away. "I adore Payne," he said. "The last thing I would want to do is steal something he very much wanted."

Ming Tang looked at him. "You have only been back a couple of days," he said. "Has she caught your eye so much?"

"She brought me food today," Sinclair said, avoiding the question mostly. "We had a long conversation. She is bright and kind and humorous. But she is also a lady with many secrets."

"I know," Ming Tang said. "She does not belong here, Sin. I am certain you could see that from the start. She is elegant and lovely, and if I could guess, I would say she is a woman of high birth, either hiding from someone or has mayhap fallen on hard times."

"The first one."

Ming Tang looked at him curiously before he realized what the man meant. *She's hiding from someone.* He nodded his head in understanding.

"She told you?" he asked.

Sinclair nodded. "She did."

"Payne has trying to get that information for six months."

"She keeps it very guarded."

"But she told you," Ming Tang said, looking at him seriously. "Sin, I think you have returned to us a changed man."

There was something in his tone that made Sinclair look at him. Other than Tay and probably Fox, he had missed Ming Tang the most. Sinewy and powerful, he was not only an anomaly in England, but he was an anomaly anywhere in the Western world. There were few like him, this man who had made his way from the Far East by way of land

and sea, finding his way to Blackchurch, where he taught skills that put them head and shoulders above any warrior on any field of battle. A Shaolin monk by training and education, he brought mysterious arts with him that he imparted to the worthy. Recruits in his class used to fight with hands and feet, using technique over sheer strength to subdue an opponent.

Ming Tang was a legend.

But he was also a great friend and unafraid to make his opinions known. Something else he'd brought with him from the Far East was wisdom that exceeded anything the Western world was capable of, because those in Ming Tang's land thought differently. They viewed life differently. It was that difference that made him so incredibly valuable as a friend, an advisor, and as a colleague. As Sinclair looked at him, he knew Ming Tang could read him like a book.

"Is it that obvious?" he finally asked.

Ming Tang nodded. "To me, it is," he said. "You look like the same Sinclair, but something has happened to you. There is more depth to you. More generosity of soul. Confucius teaches us that generosity of the soul is key to a man's happiness."

Sinclair smiled faintly. "I do not even know what that means," he said. "I will have to take your word for it."

Elisiana came back into the room bearing two pitchers. The other serving wench was with her, bringing a big tray with food upon it. Ming Tang and Sinclair watched Elisiana as she came in their direction.

"It means you are concerned for Payne's feelings for the woman," Ming Tang said softly. "If you feel strongly enough about her, you must speak with him. And you must be prepared for him to tell you that he loves her. I do not believe he does, but he might tell you that simply to stake his claim. If he does, what will you do?"

Sinclair sighed faintly with disappointment. "I will no longer speak to her without his permission," he said. "And I will not pursue her. I will defer to him, of course."

"That is what I mean by generosity of the soul. You think of Payne's happiness over your own."

Elisiana was upon them, putting the pitcher of ginger beer in between Amir and Ming Tang. "There," she said. "It is strong this time, but good. I hope you enjoy it."

Amir, who had been speaking with Creston on his other side, picked up the pitcher and poured himself a cup. "Thank you," he said. "I am going to have to learn how to make this myself. All we have at Blackchurch is boiled apple juice or boiled pear and quince. Sometimes strawberries or raspberries."

"Ginger beer is much better for you," Elisiana said. "It has great health benefits."

"Like what?"

"It keeps you well and helps with digestion," she said, putting the second pitcher of wine in front of Sinclair. "When you have an illness of the chest, ginger will help cure you. It is very good for you."

Amir lifted his cup to her and took a swallow, realizing that it was very strong this time. Strong but delicious. He smacked his lips, nodding his approval, as Ming Tang poured his own ginger beer. Seeing that those two were satisfied, Elisiana turned to Sinclair.

"I have some ginger wafers saved for you," she said for his ears only. "There are so many people in the tavern tonight that our supply has run low, but I managed to set some aside for you."

He smiled at her. "Thank you."

"My pleasure, my lord."

Gazing up at her, Sinclair realized he would be damn disappointed if Payne was serious about her. But Ming Tang was right—he valued his relationship with his fellow trainers too much to step into another man's territory. That wasn't something he'd truly thought about until this afternoon after she left and he'd had time to think.

That was when the thoughts truly came.

It was a repetitious afternoon with the class, so he stood over them and watched them perform the exercise over and over as his mind wandered to the woman with the nearly black hair and pale blue eyes. It wasn't merely her physical beauty that had his interest, but there was a fire in her that couldn't be dimmed. He could see it in her eyes, in everything about her. She was strong and resilient, and she believed in what she was doing. She believed that she was going to go to London and sell her drawings and make a life for herself. That kind of confidence was rare. Some men would call it stubbornness, or arrogance, but not Sinclair.

It was like a light in the darkness.

And like a moth to the flame, he was drawn to it.

Abruptly, he stood up.

"Payne," he said, quickly moving around the side of the table, "come with me."

Payne, who had a mouth full of the beans that the other serving wench had brought, looked at him in surprise. "Me?" he said. "What's it about, Sin?"

Sinclair reached him, grasping him by the arm and pulling him out of his chair. "Come," he said. "With me. Now."

Payne was chewing as Sinclair pulled him out of the chamber, through the crowded, smoky common room and out into the night air beyond. Once they were outside and away from the door, Sinclair turned to him.

"I have a need to speak with you," he said, lowering his voice. "But I want to start this by saying I love you like a brother. You have always been dependable and honest, and those are qualities I admire greatly."

Payne, his jovial manner subdued, was looking at Sinclair with great curiosity. "I admire ye as well," he said, unsure where Sinclair was going with this. "There's no finer swordsman in the world than ye, Sin. I'm honored tae call you my friend."

Sinclair waved a hand at him. "I wasn't looking for compliments," he said. "The truth is that I have just returned from a three-year absence at Blackchurch. Things change, the world changes, but I hope our relationship will never change."

"God himself couldna change it, lad."

"Could a woman?"

Payne's brow furrowed. "What woman?"

"Lisi."

That cleared up all of Payne's confusion, and his expression shifted from puzzled to almost wary in nature. "Ah," he said. "I understand now. The lass."

Sinclair shook his head. "It sounds absolutely mad for me to say this, but she has my attention," he said. "I do not know how, or why, but I feel comfortable when speaking to her. She makes me smile. I've known the woman for two whole days and you've known her for much longer, so I must ask… are you serious with your intention toward her?"

Payne's eyes glittered at him in the torchlight. "And if I was?"

Sinclair sighed heavily. "Then I would not go any further in my interest with her," he said. "I would not wish to offend you because your friendship means more to me than… that whatever I feel for Lisi. I want you to know that."

Payne, who was usually jovial and happy and joking the vast majority of the time, was oddly serious on the subject matter. That wasn't his usual expression, but then again, nothing about him was usual when it came to being a Scotsman. In the first place, he didn't look like a typical Scots—hairy and red-headed—but instead had dark blond hair, mussed on the crown but short on the sides, and a faint growth of beard that was lighter than his hair. He was fair-skinned, but big and muscular like the rest of the trainers. He wasn't unhandsome in the least, and had an oddly refined look to him until he opened his mouth, but he was at least six or seven years younger than Sinclair.

Maybe that was what threatened him.

He was younger and less civilized than the mature and responsible Sinclair.

Truth be told, if he shut his mouth and stopped being so loud and obnoxious, he might make a fine prospect to a lady like Elisiana, but Payne knew that he was too young and too immature to consider such a thing. At Blackchurch, he taught men how to size up an enemy and exploit their weaknesses, and he was damn good at it, but when it came to women, he had no idea how to handle them.

And he knew it.

But Sinclair did.

Damn...

"I appreciate yer honesty, lad," Payne said after a moment. "I thought ye might feel an attraction for her when I saw ye out here with her last night. I saw how ye looked at her. It's probably the same way I look at her."

Sinclair put up his hands in a gesture of surrender. "If you are truly intent on wooing her, I will not pursue her," he said sincerely. "As I said, I've not been here for three years and there may be much more to your attraction to her than I am aware of, so if that is the case, all you need do is tell me. I will relinquish any interest I may have. That is a promise."

"And I believe ye," Payne said. "But the truth is that she looks ye in a way that she doesn't look at me. I saw it yesterday and I saw it tonight when she came with our drink. I also heard she brought ye food today."

"She did."

"She's never brought *me* food."

Sinclair wasn't sure what to say to that. Payne didn't seem angry, but he did seem concerned. Or maybe even disappointed. Sinclair really wasn't sure.

"I was not aware of your interest in her until after I'd already invited her to visit Blackchurch," he said. "At least, I was not aware of your serious interest, so if I overstepped, I apologize. *Are* you seriously interested in her, Payne?"

"And if I am?"

Sinclair shook his head. "Then you only need tell me and that will be the end of it."

Payne thought about that and, after a moment, simply nodded his head. Sinclair took that to mean that his friend was, indeed, serious, and the disappointment he felt was overwhelming. He wanted to remind Payne that Elisiana had brought *him* food, not Payne. He wanted to remind Payne that she had come to visit *him* after only having been home for two days, while she'd never come to visit Payne in the entire six months that he had tried to woo her.

But he didn't.

He forced himself to be gracious in defeat.

"Then I wish you well," he said quietly. "I truly do."

With that, he headed back to the tavern door, but thought better of it and turned the other way.

"Tell the others I went home to bed," he told Payne as he walked past him. "I'm still exhausted from my travels."

Payne watched him go. He truly loved Sinclair like a brother—a man who was rather quiet and stoic, but once in battle, he turned into an archangel of vengeance. No one could move with the skill Sinclair had, and Payne had always admired that greatly. In truth, he was jealous that Sinclair had been able to charm Elisiana to the point where the woman actually came to visit him at Blackchurch. Payne hadn't managed to do that in six whole months. Therefore, if anyone should surrender their suit, it should be Payne.

He knew that.

But he was sure he could woo her given more time.

… couldn't he?

"What happened? Where is Sinclair going?"

Payne turned to see Elisiana standing just outside the tavern door, a pitcher in her hand as she watched Sinclair head down the street, illuminated by the night watch torches.

"He is going tae bed," Payne said. "He's still weary from his travels."

Elisiana's gaze never left Sinclair as he moved away from her. "Oh," she said, sounding disappointed. "Was he feeling ill, then?"

Payne shook his head. "Nay," he said. "Just weary."

Elisiana's gaze lingered on Sinclair for a moment before she turned away. She was heading back inside, but Payne stopped her.

"Tell me something, Lisi," he said. "Will ye answer a question for me?"

She paused and looked at him. "If I can," she said. "What is it?"

Payne, a man with a considerable ego, found it difficult to form his thoughts when it came to personal feelings he knew weren't returned. He struggled for a moment before finally speaking.

"I know I annoy ye," he said. "I know I tell ye that I'm going tae marry ye, but do ye think… do ye think ye might ever be agreeable?"

Her eyebrows lifted. "To marrying you?"

"Aye."

She smiled, but it wasn't one of joy or adoration. It was one of regret. A twisted little gesture of regret. "Are you serious, Payne?" she asked. "Because if you are, I must tell you that there is no chance that I would ever be agreeable. I am sorry if that is disappointing, but it is true. I think you are a kind man and I have enjoyed knowing you, but there could never be more between us. I am truly sorry."

That was a bit of a blow for Payne. Not a surprising one, but a blow nonetheless. "What about Sinclair?" he asked.

"What about him?"

"Could ye see yerself marrying him?"

"I do not see where that is any of your business."

Payne shrugged. "Ye brought him food today," he said. "Ye've never done that for me. Why did ye do it for him?"

She sighed and hung her head. "Payne, there has simply never been anything special between us," she said. "I do not know what more to say. I do not want to hurt your feelings, but it is the truth."

"Are ye telling me that there is something special between ye and Sinclair?"

Elisiana's cheeks flushed as she kept her gaze lowered. She didn't want to answer him because she didn't want it to get back to Sinclair. Having no idea how the man felt about her, she didn't want to shame herself by declaring her interest in a man who was just being nice to her. Secretly, of course, she hoped it was more than that, but one could never be sure. And she certainly wasn't going to declare it to Payne.

"I'm telling you that it is none of your affair," she said quietly. "My business is my own. You are a nice man, Payne, and your annoying ways make me laugh, but that is where it ends. I cannot be much clearer than that."

He sighed heavily. Loudly and heavily. Payne never did anything quietly. "Well," he said after a moment, "ye've been honest with me. I canna fault ye for it. But is there something ye dislike about me? Something I can change?"

Elisiana shook her head. "Nay, it's nothing like that."

"Do I smell bad?"

"Nothing like that, I promise."

"Am I too ugly for ye?"

Elisiana put up her hand to stop him. "Payne, it is nothing like that, I swear it," she insisted. "Who is to say why we are attracted to others? I'm sure you've met lovely girls in your life, but you did not want to marry them, did you? And you do not know why. Sometimes there is no way to explain such things. They simply… happen."

He shrugged. "I suppose," he said. Then his gaze moved to the road where Sinclair had disappeared. "Do ye want me tae fetch him for ye?"

Elisiana shook her head. "Nay," she said quickly. "Why would I?"

"Because he's sweet on ye and I told him that I saw ye first."

Elisiana's eyes widened. "You… you said *what*?"

Payne could sense that she wasn't pleased. Fearful that he'd upset her, he took a step back, afraid she might try to smack him.

"He asked me if I was serious in my pursuit of ye," he said. "He told me that he wouldna try tae woo ye if I was serious."

A hand flew to Elisiana's mouth. "He said that?"

"He did."

Elisiana was astonished. "And you told him you were serious?"

Payne shrugged weakly. "I did," he said. "I thought if I had more time, I could… but I suppose it doesna matter now. If ye are fond of the man, I'll fetch him for ye."

She almost told him that it wasn't his business again, but she couldn't bring herself to do it. If Sinclair wanted to woo her, then she was more than willing to let him. She couldn't even think of the plan she'd had, of how she wanted to sell her drawings in London and live well, experiencing life as it was meant to be experienced. All she could think of was the handsome man with the pale eyes and winning smile, someone who made her feel alive in a way she'd never experienced before.

She was nodding her head before she could stop herself.

"Aye," she said after a moment. "Fetch him."

"I'll not fetch him if ye mean tae toy with him," Payne said warningly. "Only if ye mean it."

"I mean it."

Payne nodded, perhaps with some regret, and headed off into the darkness, following Sinclair's path back to Blackchurch. As he disappeared down the street, Elisiana went back into the tavern.

Feeling just the least bit giddy.

It was warm and stale and smoky in the common room, and the minstrels were still playing as the woman with silver tassels continued to dance for the coins the patrons would throw to her. But Elisiana wasn't paying any attention. Her mind was elsewhere.

He wants to woo me!

She'd never been wooed in her life, at least not by someone she was actually receptive to. Adolph's foolish attempt seemed like a bad dream. *Was this God's plan all along?* she wondered. *Running away only to find a man like Sinclair?*

As if in a daze, she headed to the rear of the tavern where there was a small staircase that led to rooms above. She had a small room to herself because of the extra work she did for Hobbes, and she went into her chamber, tiny as it was, and shut the door. Over the past six months, she'd accumulated quite a collection of finery from passing merchants and she pawed through the careful piles, coming across a lovely lavender gown. It wasn't terribly fancy, made from a durable cloth that had been dyed pale purple, so she supposed she could get away with working in it. It had long sleeves, nicely showing off her round breasts and narrow torso, and she quickly put it on, running a comb through her hair and braiding it so it draped over her right shoulder, which was her usual style. She took the apron off the clothes she had been wearing, putting it on over the lavender gown to protect it from the fools who would spill, vomit, or do any number of things that would stain it.

Perhaps Sinclair might like to see her in something other than brown broadcloth and a leather girdle. Knowing how he felt, she wanted to look presentable to him. She'd never wanted anything more in her life. This was a moment she never thought she'd face in her life, but here it was. A most unexpected moment.

But a moment that would change her life forever.

And she was ready.

CB

"SIN!"

Sinclair was nearly to the main gatehouse of Blackchurch when he heard someone calling him. He wasn't in any mood to stop, so he simply kept walking, drawing closer to the gatehouse until someone grabbed him by the shoulder and forced him to stop. He whirled around, right fist balled, only to see Payne standing behind him.

He had to take a step back or risk throwing that fist into the man's nose.

"Leave me alone, Payne," he said, backing away. "I'm exhausted and I need to rest. Just… leave me alone."

Payne followed him, but at a safe distance. He hadn't missed the balled fist. "I dinna come for me, Sin," he said. "I came for her. She told me tae fetch ye."

Sinclair frowned. "Who told you?"

"The lass. Lisi."

Sinclair came to a stop then, eyeing the man suspiciously. "What do you mean she sent you to fetch me?" he said. "Why would Elisiana do that?"

Payne's features twisted in confusion. "Elisiana?"

"That is her true name. And you will never repeat it, not unless she tells you herself."

Payne had to think about that revelation. It seemed that Sinclair knew more about Lisi than he did, which perhaps only served to reinforce the reason why he'd come. He gestured back in the direction of the tavern.

"Did ye not see her come out as ye were leaving?" he said. "She wanted tae know why ye were leaving, and I told her."

Sinclair's eyes widened. "What did you tell her?"

"That ye were sweet on her but I told ye that she belonged tae me."

Sinclair grunted unhappily and hung his head. "I see," he said. "Payne, I do not wish to talk to her or to you. I've done quite enough talking for one day."

"But—"

Sinclair cut him off. "I do not need her to tell me that although she is flattered, she has no interest in me," he said. Then he jabbed a finger at Payne. "You should not have told her anything. You have a big mouth, Payne. You should have kept it shut."

With that, he turned for the gatehouse, but Payne stopped him again. "*Sinclair*, listen," he said. "Listen tae me or I swear I'll not tell ye that she told me I'm ugly and she wants nothing tae do with me. No amount of wooing will win her. I'll not tell ye that she's as sweet on ye as ye are on her. Walk away from me and ye'll know none of it!"

He was practically shouting by the time he was finished and Sinclair had come to a halt. He simply stared at Payne as if he had no idea what to say, but at least he wasn't trying to walk away anymore. For several long and painful moments, he simply stared at him.

The mood of the conversation shifted.

"Did she tell you that?" he finally asked.

Payne nodded. "After she told me that there was no chance between us, I asked her if she was fond of ye," he said. "She told me it was none of my affair, but I knew she was disappointed because ye were heading back tae Blackchurch, so I told her I would only fetch ye if she was keen on ye. If she was serious. She said that she was."

Sinclair drew in a long, slow breath. He retraced his steps back to Payne, looking the man in the eye.

"You know it was never my intention to come between you and a woman you wanted," he said. "I hope you believe that."

Payne smiled weakly. "She's simply not the right lass for me," he said. "But she may be the right one for ye."

"Are you certain this will not come between us?"

Payne nodded, clapping him on the shoulder. "Go to her, lad," he said. "If ye have feelings for her, tell her. Whatever has happened between the two of ye has happened quickly, so it must've meant tae happen. How do I know? Because I put six bloody months in on the lass and she never looked at me twice. But ye… She looked twice at ye the day she met ye."

That seemed to settle it. Truthfully, Payne didn't seem all that upset by it, and Ming Tang's words came flooding back to Sinclair. *I do not believe he is serious.* Perhaps the man had been right after all.

The only one serious about Elisiana was Sinclair.

After a moment, he forced a smile and patted Payne on the cheek before heading back toward Exebridge and the Black Cock. He was trying not to run, but by the time he hit Exebridge's perimeter, he was very nearly skipping. He slowed down once he came into the glare of the torches, with the Black Cock directly ahead and full of people. He could hear the music and conversation as he approached. Reaching the door, he ducked inside, his gaze immediately searching for Elisiana. A perusal of the common room showed that she wasn't there, so he headed to the private room where the trainers were.

She wasn't in the private room, either. He wondered if he should go looking for her, but Cruz reached out and tugged on his arm, pulling him down into the nearest chair.

"Sit," Cruz commanded. "We've been waiting for tales of your grand adventures. Will you indulge us?"

Sinclair didn't want to. He had a woman to see. But there were several eager faces looking back at him so he relented, picking up the cup nearest him and drinking the sweet red wine.

"Of course," he said, smiling weakly at the men around him. "As you can imagine, I'm quite weary from the travel and today has taken more out of me than I had anticipated, but I shall try to remember a few of the greater moments. Mayhap I should simply start from the beginning."

"How *was* Niko, Sin?" Tay asked from across the table. "Athdara is not here now, so you can say what you will about him. I know he is rather headstrong."

They were speaking of the young duke of Toxandria, who had barely been on the cusp of manhood when he sailed with Sinclair back for his home and the battle that awaited him. Thinking back to that time, Sinclair pushed thoughts of Elisiana aside and focused on those early days of uncertainty and excitement.

"He was actually quite obedient," he said. "Niko was eager, of course, but he wasn't foolish. And he listened when I told him to behave himself. When we took the cog out of London, heading for Dunkirk, I do not think he sat down or slept once. All he could think of was the fact that we were returning to the scene of his uncle's crime. He paced, he chewed his nails, and he watched for the shoreline. I thought I was going to have to tie him to the ship when we finally reached our destination. He was so eager to jump onto dry land that I was afraid he was going to break his neck."

"And the uncle?" Fox asked. "What happened to the man who stole his dukedom?"

Sinclair sat back in his chair, puffing out his cheeks as he thought on a subject with a long and complex answer. "Niko wanted to challenge him," he said as concisely as he could. "He was eager to fight him, to punish the man for what he did to his father and older brother. Both of them were killed when Atilla brought a mercenary army in to overthrow Athdara's father, you know. Niko felt strongly about avenging them."

"Did he?" Fox said.

Sinclair shrugged. "It took two years before we had the opportunity to deal with Atilla, and that was only because he had been captured trying to escape Breda Castle," he said. "Niko was determined to challenge his uncle and kill him, but I wasn't convinced he could actually do it. Men cannot fight effectively if they are overwrought with emotion, so…"

He suddenly stopped as Elisiana entered the room, carrying more wine. Aster was with her and they began to move around the table, filling cups and trying to stay unobtrusive. Elisiana was nearly finished filling Tay's cup when she happened to look up and see Sinclair. Clearly unaware he'd returned, she fumbled the pitcher and it hit the table, splashing a little, but Sinclair was already on his feet, moving in her direction.

"Come with me," he said to her, grasping her by the wrist. "I must speak with you."

His abrupt departure had his fellow trainers looking at each other with puzzlement, but Sinclair couldn't worry about that. Not now. He pulled Elisiana out the back of the tavern, into the rather large livery yard that was quiet and dark at this hour. A few torches burned just for some light to see by, but there was very little near the livery for obvious reasons. Sinclair led Elisiana over to the corral that was stuffed with sleeping horses before he finally came to a stop, turning to her in the faint torchlight.

For a moment, he simply looked at her, realizing she'd changed out of the clothing he'd seen her in earlier. She was wearing a pretty lavender dress, something that looked magnificent on her. As the smell of dung and horses rose up around them, he struggled for something to say, something profound, but settled on something simple instead.

"Payne told me what happened," he said quietly.

She smoothed at the errant strands of curly hair in her face. "He told me, too," she said. "He said that you asked him if he intended to court me."

"I did."

"Why did you ask him that?"

Sinclair had never had an embarrassed moment in his life. No chagrin, no mortification, nothing. He was a man of supreme confidence in everything he did. Therefore, the heat coming to his cheeks at her question was something unfamiliar. He actually thought he might blush.

"Because if he wasn't going to ask to court you, I was," he said.

A smile spread across her lips. "*Was?*" she said. "You do not intend to any longer?"

He started to chuckle nervously. "I *do* intend to," he said. "I've simply never been in this position before. I am not certain where to go from here."

She started to giggle. "You must simply speak the words," she said. "It is not difficult. Shall I help you?"

He frowned, or at least tried to. "Nay," he said. "I will do this myself."

"My apologies."

He could see she wasn't serious and was trying not to smile at her. "I suppose I should tell you what you will be facing with me before I ask," he said. "As you know, I am a Blackchurch trainer. It is my vocation, my passion. I do not intend to leave, so your life would be spend with me as the wife of a Blackchurch trainer. It is a good life, however. I have some wealth and we could purchase anything you wish. We would have our own home. You would have servants and good food. And you could spend your days drawing to your heart's content."

He was trying to sell her on the life she would lead, but the truth was that he didn't have to. She'd already decided when Payne had told her about Sinclair's intentions that she would be perfectly happy as long as she was with him. London and her plan to sell her drawings didn't seem to matter anymore because the prospect of a future as Sinclair's wife had her as giddy as drunken nun.

"What else would I have?" she asked.

He wasn't quite following her. "What else do you want?"

She shrugged. "Would I have you?" she said. "Would I have your affection? Or would you expect us to live separate lives?"

He did frown then. "Of course not," he said. "I would expect you to be by my side, always. You would manage my house and manage me if the mood strikes you. You would most definitely have my affection and I would be loyal to you, and only you, until I die. I am not an eloquent man, Elisiana, but I know how to speak from the heart. I do not ask to court you lightly. I do it because over the past two days, I've realized that you are someone I want to know. And I want you to know me. I want to have you bring me food and I want to have conversations about your drawings, your dreams, and I want you to trust me with your secrets. For I will most assuredly trust you with mine. If this is the kind of marriage that appeals to you, I will do my very best to provide it."

By the time he was finished, the smile was gone from her face and she was looking at him in astonishment. Perhaps not astonishment so much as overwhelming delight. After a moment, she smiled brightly, reaching out to put a hand on his arm.

"That was the most eloquent speech I've ever heard," she said softly. "And most convincing."

He smiled timidly. "Was it?"

"It was."

"Your life will not be in London, you know," he said. "It will be here, with me, in the wilds of Devon."

"I think I would rather be in the wilds of Devon with you than in London without you."

That, by far, was the most eloquent part of the conversation. Unable to reply to that, because it touched him deeply in his vulnerable state, he simply pulled her against him and slanted his lips over hers. He kissed her sweetly at first, acquainting her with his touch, but her scent filled his nostrils and he was overwhelmed with her. His big arms went around her, holding her tightly as his lips suckled hers, tasting what was surely the sweetest mouth in all the world. He was pulling her closer, feasting on her, squeezing the breath from her, when he suddenly stopped as if only just aware of what he was doing.

"Forgive me," he said hoarsely, releasing her so she could breathe. "Did I hurt you?"

Elisiana grinned, her mouth red from where his stubble had rubbed her tender skin. "Nay," she said. "Not at all."

Seeing her reaction made him smile, and he pulled her into his arms again, this time far more gently, and kissed her sweetly.

"There," he murmured. "Better?"

"Better than what?" she said, her hands on his shoulders as she gazed into his eyes. "Better than the moment before? Aye, it was better than the moment before. And your next kiss will be better than the one before it. Every moment from this day forward will be better than the one before it. With you, it could be nothing less."

He gave her a lopsided grin. "You flatter me, lady."

"It is the truth."

He was still holding her close, his gaze moving over her thick fringe of dark lashes, the dusting of freckles on her nose that he could see in the weak light. He was studying her, memorizing her face, a face that belonged to him as he was coming to belong to her.

"I hope it is always the truth," he whispered. "I will endeavor to make it so."

"I believe you."

He gazed at her a moment longer before loosening his grip. "But there is something we must discuss, I think," he said. "Before this goes any further, we must discuss your father. The truth is that I should ask his permission to court you. That is the proper way to go about these things."

Her smile faded. "Mayhap it is, but he wants me to marry a man of his choosing," she said. "If you ask him for permission, he will deny you. It would be better to marry and tell him after the fact. That way, he could not separate us."

He lifted an eyebrow. "You think he would?"

"I know he would."

Sinclair didn't like that thought in the least. "Who is this man he has selected for your husband?"

She sighed heavily with displeasure and pulled out of his embrace. "His name is Adolph de Rade," she said. "My mother's brother married a woman recently and Adolph is her son. He serves the Earl of Lincoln."

"Have you met him?"

She rolled her eyes. "Why do you think I ran away?" she said. "My uncle has told him everything about me, including the drawings and why I was sent away from Pevensey, and he seemed to think that was reason enough to be vulgar with me. My parents forced me to show him the garden, and he was quite forward. He wanted me to touch him… where men find pleasure… but I refused. Instead, I kicked him in his privates and pushed him into a pond."

Sinclair was listening seriously until she told him what she had done. Then it was all he could do not to smile at her brutal, but brave, act. Instead, he pulled her into an embrace again and gave her a tender hug.

"Good lass," he whispered into the side of her head. "You did the right thing."

Elisiana clung to him, enjoying their embrace, holding him tightly as he held her. "Do you think so?"

"Of course I do," he said. "But I doubt Adolph does. Sounds as if he deserved what he received."

Elisiana hugged him a moment longer before loosening her grip enough to look at him. "But that is why my father will deny you," she said. "He is convinced that Adolph is the husband I need and I do not think you could change his mind. As wonderful as you are, my father is very stubborn when it comes to his wants."

"So am I," Sinclair said. Then he cocked his head thoughtfully. "So, it seems we have a quandary on our hands. But the fact is that you did run away six months ago."

"True."

"And your father has not seen you since and he does not know where you are."

"Quite true."

"That being the case, we could marry and send him word," Sinclair said. "How big is his army?"

She shrugged. "I am not sure," she said. "I heard my brother say once that my father has an army of eight hundred fools and men, but that was a while ago."

"Good," Sinclair said. "Even if he discovered we were at Black-church, he could not get to you. The Lords of Exmoor have a highly trained army of over a thousand men. They could easily withstand any assault."

"I would feel terrible if that happened."

He leaned down and kissed her forehead. "It would not be your fault, but your father's," he said. "In any case, we will address the issue if, and when, it comes. Meanwhile…"

"Meanwhile *what*?"

"I should probably let you resume your task so Hobbes does not come looking for you," he said. "I do not want him to become angry."

She smiled, watching him take her hand and kiss it gently. "But you will return on the morrow?"

"I will return every single day until such time as we decide to mar-ry," he said. "Let us take the time to know one another, Lisi. We are already moving quite swiftly in this relationship. I should like to take the time to come to know you very well, so we can both be very sure that this is what we want."

She nodded. "That is wise," she said. "I will win your heart with ginger wafers until you're too fat to walk through the door. Then you will not be able to run away from me."

He laughed. "And I will be a willing victim," he said. "But you have the situation wrong. You will not win my heart. I will win yours."

"I do not think it will take much effort, to be truthful. You have a good start."

He grinned and kissed her hand again before walking with her over to the rear door. With one last kiss to her fingers, he let her hand go and watched her enter in front of him. For a few moments, he simply watched her, this graceful and beautiful woman he was quickly growing obsessed with. When he'd returned home yesterday, he could have never imagined the turn his life would take. It seemed like a dream.

A dream he was more than willing not to wake up from.

CHAPTER EIGHT

ELISIANA WAS FAIRLY certain she hadn't slept all night.

Not that sleeping was at all important. She couldn't surrender to something as mundane as sleep when her life was on the precipice of something wonderful. Sleep meant nothing in the grand scheme of things. It only meant that she wasn't thinking about Sinclair, and all she wanted to do was think about the man.

She'd jumped out of bed well before dawn and dressed in the lavender garment. It reminded her of Sinclair and she wanted to wear it again. Bundling an apron over it, she entered the kitchens just as the kitchen servants were stoking the big ovens for the day, and she proceeded to make several loaves of bread with currants in them, basted with butter and honey.

Feeling industrious, she left the kitchens while the bread was baking and headed into the common room, which was strewn with people sleeping. They were on the floor, on the tables, on chairs—anywhere they could find space. She noticed that the room was particularly filthy, so as people slept, she went out to the well and drew several buckets of water. After mixing the water with vinegar, she brought the buckets back into the common room and began kicking people off the tables so she could wash them.

And also so they could purchase a morning meal.

Ignoring the complainers who were upset that they'd been roused, Elisiana proceeded to splash the vinegar water across the tables and mop it up with a rag. This was one of her chores in the morning, so she was simply going about her duties. But she was also wondering when she would see Sinclair again. It was daylight, after all. Shouldn't he be here to bid her a good morning?

The thought made her smile.

Already, she was making plans to visit Blackchurch around the nooning hour and bring him some food. He would love the currant loaf, she was certain, but there was also leftover stew from the previous night. She would bring him some of that.

Perhaps he really *would* be too fat to run away from her.

It was a delightful thought. Aster and a couple of the other serving women joined her in her duties in the common room, kicking people off the floor and forcing them to rise as they swept and cleaned. Outside, in the village of Exebridge, merchants were opening their shops and farmers were bringing their goods in from the countryside. There was a large market every sixth day of the week, but there were also a couple of merchants in town with smaller stalls who sold things like vegetables and other consumable items. Not everyone in or around Exebridge had gardens big enough to supply their families, so the vegetable merchants did a good business.

Elisiana had just finished scrubbing off a layer of spilled, dried wine from a table when the entry door opened. Glancing up, she saw Athdara and another woman she recognized. Gisele, Lady de Merest and the wife of Fox, lifted a hand in greeting as Elisiana smiled and left the table she'd been working on.

She made her way over to the women.

"Good morn to you, my ladies," she said. "To what do we owe the honor of your visit?"

"It seems that my husband may or may have not lost some coin he had in his purse," Athdara replied. "When he came home last night, he found that his purse had a slight hole in it and he thought some money was missing. I thought I would see if you've found any on the floor."

Elisiana gestured toward the private room that the trainers always used. "If he did, it might be in there," she said, leading the way as they headed over to it. "We have yet to clean in there, so it may be on the floor."

Entering the chamber, she went straight to the side of the room Tay had been sitting on as Athdara and Gisele lingered by the door.

"He did not lose any money," Gisele said. "He purchased too much wine and simply does not remember."

Athdara chuckled. "I know," she said. "But the excuse has served a purpose. We now have Elisiana to ourselves."

Elisiana, who had been crouched under the table looking for Tay's lost coinage, heard her name. Everyone except Sinclair knew her as Lisi, and she stood up, immediately suspicious that they'd called her by her given name. She'd known these ladies for six months, not too terribly well, but she assumed them to be women of honor, since they were married to Blackchurch trainers.

But now...

She wondered why they'd come.

"Who told you to call me by that name?" she asked.

Athdara could immediately see that she was uncomfortable. "Please do not be angry," she said. "We will not tell anyone, I swear. But Payne... He talks too much sometimes, and he returned from the tavern last night, drunken and depressed, and spent most of the night in my cottage, telling my husband that he'd lost the only woman he wanted. He meant you."

Elisiana puffed out her cheeks, letting out a heavy sigh. "I see," she said, no longer suspicious as it was explained to her. "I am sorry if he is upset, but it could not be helped. I never gave him any encouragement if that is what you are here to discuss. And if you are here to convince me to accept his affections, I will tell you that I cannot. I will not. I simply do not feel that way about him."

Both Athdara and Gisele were nodding. "We know," Gisele said. A petite, beautiful woman, she had a soft and comforting way of speaking. "We know everything. Tay sent for Sinclair when Payne came to him and Sinclair roused my husband, so all four of them were up most of the night, discussing the… situation."

Elisiana wasn't sure what to say. Suddenly feeling weary, and perhaps a little irritated, she plopped down in a chair and lingered over what they'd said.

She didn't like that she'd been the topic of discussion.

"And what was the resolution that I am to be part of?" she finally said. "Did they decide, collectively, that Sinclair should surrender his intentions because Payne is so upset about it? Have men I barely know decided my future for me?"

Gisele and Athdara came closer and Gisele sat down next to her, turning the chair toward her. "No one has decided anything," she said quietly. "Sinclair would not surrender his interest in you, and he was adamant. At least, according to Fox he was adamant, but the point is that no one is making decisions for you. Only you and Sin make the decisions that are the best for you both. But he did send us over here this morning. He has recruits to teach and could not come himself."

Now they had her curiosity. Elisiana looked between Gisele and Athdara. "Why did he send you to me?"

Gisele smiled. "Because he wants to know if you will come to Blackchurch and manage the kitchens," he said. "It would be a far better-paying position than what you have here with Hobbes. And you would be safe. No one can breach the walls of Blackchurch."

That told Elisiana that Sinclair must have told them about her father. A secret she'd never intended to tell, and when she did, it seemed to spread. She wasn't happy about that. When she sighed heavily and lowered her gaze, Gisele hastened to reassure her.

"Truly, Sin only told us out of concern," she said quietly. "At Blackchurch, we are like a family. We all care for one another deeply and what affects one affects us all. Athdara knows Sinclair better than I do, but I know that he is a great and honorable man. He deserves to be happy in life, and from what my husband says, the mere mention of you sparks a light in his eyes. Will you at least think about coming to manage our kitchens? Sin says that you are very talented in your management and cooking skills."

Elisiana was still looking at the floor. It took her a moment to answer. "It is a very generous offer," she said, finally looking up at the pair. "What else do you know about me?"

This time, Athdara took a seat on the other side of Gisele. "That you are a noblewoman hiding from your father," she said. "What more do we need to know? Sinclair believes you are a remarkable woman, as does Payne. These are two men that are well loved and trusted by those at Blackchurch. I would say that speaks very well for you, my lady. We only wish to help."

Elisiana believed that. She truly did. She didn't get any sense of judgment from the pair—judgment in her actions, that she'd run from her father, that she was hiding out. They seemed to genuinely want to help her and, truth be told, she was touched. She'd spent six months taking care of herself, working a labor-intensive job, so she was used to being solitary as of late. She was accustomed to not having anyone by her side, friend or family. It was just her. But looking at the women in front of her, she could see that she wasn't solitary anymore.

There were those who wished to help her.

But she wasn't so sure she wanted the help.

"I do believe you," she finally said. "And I am very grateful. The fact that you would take the time to come to me like this speaks of your good intentions."

Athdara's eyebrows lifted. "*But…?*"

The woman was intuitive. She could sense that there was something more on Elisiana's mind, and she was right.

"But I must think on it," Elisiana said. "You must understand that Sinclair and I have only just met. We have only just begun this journey between us and nothing is certain yet. Nothing is definite. We are only just coming to learn about one another and I fear that if I go to Blackchurch too soon, and it does not work out well between us, then I will have nowhere else to go. I will be dependent on Blackchurch and will be forced to see Sinclair every day. It would be torture if… well, if our future is not meant to be together."

Both Athdara and Gisele nodded. "That speaks well for your independence," Gisele said. "You do not wish to be dependent upon anyone but yourself, and provide for yourself, and I think that is very honorable. I think if you would have been too agreeable to this I might have been suspicious of you, but instead, you are suspicious of us."

The three of them broke down in snorts of laughter. "I would not say that I am suspicious of you," Elisiana said. "But I only just met Sinclair. I cannot be dependent on him so soon. I must still have a space, and a position, that is separate from him. I will explain it to him when I see him. But you may tell him… Please tell him how much I love that he wants to make sure I am safe. That is such a wonderful thing."

Athdara and Gisele were smiling. "He is a good man," Athdara reassured her quietly. "He is loyal to the bone. He will kill, or die, for his friends, and he will make you a fine husband, my lady. I swear it."

Elisiana lifted an eyebrow. "You address me as 'my lady'?"

Athdara looked at Gisele, and they passed nervous glances between them until Gisele finally broke down and confessed. "You are the daughter of a Castilian count," she said. Then she shrugged. "Athdara is the daughter and sister of a duke, and I… I am the bastard of a king. We *all* have secrets, Lady Elisiana. But yours is safe with us, I promise."

Elisiana looked shocked for a moment before closing her eyes and shaking her head. Then she started to laugh.

"God's Bones," she muttered. "Remind me never to tell Sinclair anything. The man cannot keep his mouth shut."

Athdara grinned. "In fairness to Sin, it was Payne who mostly spoke," she said. "Sin told him about you as they were discussing who had the better chance of wooing you, and then when Payne ended up in my cottage, drunk and distressed, more of your background was discussed and my husband told me. Please do not be upset. I swear to you that it will not go beyond the trainers. They may talk to one another, but they do not gossip to others. I am sorry if you are angered by it."

Elisiana shook her head. "I am not angered," she said. "But I do wish he hadn't told anyone. Still, I suppose there is nothing to do about it now."

"But you *will* think about coming to Blackchurch to manage the kitchens?"

"Aye, I will."

"Good," Athdara said, reaching across Gisele to clasp Elisiana's hand. "You would be most welcome, Lisi. Those big bulls need us to keep them in line, and I think you would be a fine addition."

Elisiana really wasn't peeved. Not too much, anyway. She was flattered and honored by Athdara and Gisele's attention toward her. She'd spend so much of her life without the comfort of good friends that the prospect of becoming close with these ladies was an exciting thing, indeed. Perhaps part of a better life than she could have ever imagined for herself.

Becoming part of something important.

"When you put it like that, I can hardly refuse," she said. "You will have to let me speak with Hobbes first. He has been good to me and I must tell him that I am leaving. I am not entirely sure he will be happy about it, but I do not want to sour our relationship. I will need a few days before I can consider going to Blackchurch."

Athdara and Gisele beamed. "Take as much time as you need," Athdara said, standing as Gisele stood up beside her. "We shall return and tell Sin that you are, at least, receptive to joining us."

Elisiana stood up also. "Please don't," she said. "I was planning on taking some food to him at the nooning hour, so I will tell him myself. But… will you take something to him for me in the meantime?"

"Anything," Athdara said.

Elisiana held her hands up, silently instructing them to stay where they were, as she scooted out of the room. She was barely gone a minute before she returned with a piece of vellum in her hand. It was rolled, tied off with a small strip of leather.

"Please give this to him," she said.

She handed it to Athdara, who took it curiously. "What is it?"

Elisiana grinned. "He will show you when he opens it, I am certain," she said. "He is expecting it."

That didn't help their sense of curiosity, but Athdara and Gisele nodded. Gisele even took the vellum from Athdara and tried to peer inside of it as Elisiana laughed. She made no move to actually open it, but she was definitely curious, which amused Elisiana. The three of them were coming out of the room when the entry door to the tavern opened and a few men spilled inside.

The sight of them had Elisiana stopping in her tracks.

Hell, for her, had arrived.

CHAPTER NINE

H E'D BEEN WATCHING her since last night.
He saw her in the darkness and saw her this morning, and he genuinely saw no need to wait.

Aristeo was on the move.

He and his men had rolled in just after sunset the previous evening, coming in on the outskirts of town as the village was settling in for the night. He brought with him about fifty soldiers and the man who had seen his sister at a seedy tavern called the Black Cock. The man had been able to give him precise directions, straight to Exebridge, and Aristeo found it rather odd that the very tavern where his sister had been hiding was less than a day's ride from his parents' house.

She hadn't run far.

It was, however, in a village tucked against the Exmoor Forest, with the famed Blackchurch Guild to the north, and the woods in this area were said to be full of outlaws and cutthroats. His father and his uncle had patrolled all the major roads in and out of Devon in Cornwall karma, and they believed that was sufficient because the smaller roads were dangerous and they didn't think Elisiana would have attempted traveling on those alone.

But they hadn't given her enough credit.

Evidently, not only had she traveled the dangerous roads, but she had found a haven in a tavern that didn't look terribly appealing. It was a single story in the front, but the back had at least three stories to it. It also looked as if over the years they had added to it, so there were sections that didn't look as if they quite fit. Appearance notwithstanding, it seemed to be very popular, because last night it was full to the rafters with patrons.

When Aristeo and his men first arrived, he had planned to go inside and locate his sister, but he was afraid she might cause a scene, and with all of the people in the tavern, there was a possibility that he might lose her in the crowd if she tried to run. He had seen her, one time, when she briefly stepped outside to talk to a big man who had evidently chased away another man. He couldn't hear what they were saying, but it was some kind of a confrontation between two very big men. One of them had taken off toward the north and his sister had emerged about that time. It was only a brief glimpse, but Aristeo would know that dark, curly hair anywhere.

His little sister had been found.

Therefore, Aristeo and his men sank back into the shadows and remained out of sight for the rest of the night. Because he didn't need a big crowd to fight against when he was trying to collect his sister, he figured the best time to take her would be in the morning when the crowds were either asleep or gone. No one had seen her leave, which meant she was still inside.

All he had to do was wait.

Sunrise came after a sleepless night in the woods surrounding Exebridge, and Aristeo and his men made it back into the village as soon as the eastern sky turned shades pink and blue. It was a cold, crisp morning as they spread out around the tavern in case Elisiana decided to run again. It was most likely that once Aristeo went in after her, she was going to flee and someone had to be ready to catch her. Already, at this early hour of the morning, people were heading in and out of the tavern, and Aristeo mostly saw people leaving after a night of too much drink and too little sleep. He saw two women go in as well, assuming they were either workers of the tavern or perhaps even whores who found clientele among the unwashed and the dangerous. Once Aristeo's men were spread out and he received the signal from a soldier at the corner of the tavern that all positions were set, it was time for him to make his move.

Into the tavern he went.

What happened next seemed arranged by fate. It was quite surprising because Aristeo had no sooner walked into the tavern than he saw his sister with the two women he'd seen entering earlier. They were all talking and smiling until his sister looked up and saw him standing there.

He saw her jolt with shock.

"Elisiana?" he said. "God's Bones, woman, we've been looking everywhere for you. And here you are? So close to home?"

Elisiana seemed to jolt again at the sound of his voice, as if bolts of lightning were striking her. She dashed away from her friends, collecting an enormous club that was leaning up against the wall. The club had metal spikes on the head, and she wielded it like a sword.

"Get out of here, Aristeo," she demanded. "Get out of here or I will beat you with this club, I swear it."

Beside her, the two women seemed very concerned, one of them going so far as to approach Aristeo with caution.

"Who are you?" she asked. "What do you want here?"

"Athdara, get out of here," Elisiana commanded. "*Go!*"

Athdara stopped approaching him. "Why?" she asked. "Who is he?"

Elisiana came forward, putting herself between Athdara and Aristeo. "This is my brother," she said evenly. "Please, Athdara. You and Gisele… go. Run back to Blackchurch!"

There was a message there that Gisele caught on to. She was standing by the corridor that led to the kitchens and the livery out back, and when Elisiana mentioned who the man was, she slipped into the corridor and began to run back to the livery, where the stable boy was watering a pair of small white horses. She ran up to the lad, shoved him out of the way, and grabbed the reins of one of the ponies. Leaping onto the bare back, because it was a small horse, she kicked it and slapped the rump, sending the pony into a dead run right away. As she headed for Blackchurch at breakneck speed, Elisiana was still trying to convince Athdara to leave.

The tall woman wouldn't budge.

"I'm not leaving you," Athdara said, knowing Gisele had fled because she'd seen it in her periphery. She knew help would soon be coming, so she had to stall until it arrived. "What does he want here?"

"That is a very good question," Elisiana said, her eyes riveted to her brother. "What do you want here, Téo? If you've come to bring me home, I'll not go with you. You have wasted your time looking for me."

So far, Aristeo hadn't moved. He remained by the door, his gaze steady at his sister. "That is a foolish question," he said. "You know what I want. You know what Papa wants. You must come home."

"I will not," Elisiana said before he'd finished his sentence. "This is my home now. My family. I will not go back with you. I thought I'd made that clear."

Aristeo sighed patiently. "Lisi, I know that Papa wants you to marry Adolph," he said. "Will it truly be so bad? He is rich, I hear. He inherited money from his father. You do not even have to like him."

"I do *not* like him," she said, her temper rising. "He was vulgar and forward toward me, Téo. Did you know that?"

"What did he do?"

"He wanted me to touch him in his privates."

Aristeo's jaw flexed. "He said that to you?"

"He did!" she said. "That is why I kicked him between his legs and ran! I will not marry that disgusting excuse for a man. Let him find another wife!"

Aristeo wasn't entirely unsympathetic. "I understand," he said. "I can't say that I have any regard for the man either, but that wasn't the way to go about it. You must talk to Papa. He's hardly slept or ate since you ran off, and Mama is inconsolable. She will not get out of bed. You must come back, Lisi. Please."

Elisiana shook her head. "Nay," she said. "I cannot and I *will* not, because no matter what I tell Papa, he will still force me to marry that vile creature. I would rather die."

Aristeo shook his head in frustration, in sorrow. "Then what do you want to do?" he said. "Work as a tavern wench for the rest of your life? Papa will have fits about this, you know. You are the daughter of an earl, Lisi. This is no place for you."

"It is a wonderful place," she said seriously. "I have met wonderful people who are my friends. I've never had many friends, Téo. It feels wonderful to be respected and needed. Something neither you nor Papa or Mama have ever made me feel. I'm staying."

Aristeo knew exactly where she was coming from because her entire life had been one of disregard until she started creating those lewd drawings. Then her parents paid attention to her, but only to condemn her. Not to try to understand her. Aristeo loved his sister, but he had been busy with his own life, too busy to pay attention to her. She was sinking in the quagmire of propriety and disapproving parents, and he couldn't even thrown her a lifeline. He'd seen it most the night she'd run off, when Adolph was practically salivating over her and Aristeo was too drunk to care.

He should have paid closer attention.

"What if I bring Papa to you, just to talk?" he asked. "You wouldn't have to leave—he'll come to you."

"Nay," Elisiana said flatly. "He'll force me to come home."

"Not even if I tell him not to?"

Elisiana grunted as if that were a ridiculous statement. "Téo, he will not listen to you," she said. "You know he will not."

"Won't you even try?"

"If you bring him here, I'll only run somewhere else."

Aristeo sighed heavily. "Then you simply have to come home with me," he said. "I know you are unhappy and you do not want to marry Adolph, but you ran out on your family and that is simply not the way to behave. Abuelo and Abuela have been praying six hours a day, every day, since you left because they are terrified for safety. Would you truly cause your grandparents such worry?"

That caused her a bit of doubt, but only momentarily. "I am sorry they are upset, but I am not going back," she said. "You'll simply have to tell Papa you did not find me."

"I will not," he said, crooking his finger at her. "Put the club down and come with me, Lisi."

"I will not."

"If I have to take you by force, then I will."

"If you want me, you will have to fight for me."

Aristeo could see that she meant it. Seeing that he had no other choice, he opened up the entry door and motioned to someone outside. Very quickly, men began filtering in—men with swords—and Athdara, who was unarmed, backed away. She came close enough to Elisiana to grab her and pull her back, back toward the corridor that led to the kitchens and the livery.

"Get out of here," Elisiana whispered at her. "But not through the door because there are probably soldiers back there. Climb through a window and get out. Hurry!"

Athdara had been a recruit at Blackchurch several years ago. That was how she'd met her husband, so she was no stranger to a sword or a fight. But she did turn for the corridor, without another word to

Elisiana, and headed back to the kitchens to tell them to hide because there was about to be an armed incursion. When Hobbes tried to get a look at who was in his common room, Athdara scolded him and shoved him under a table. But she went for the long iron rod that was used to tend the fire in the ovens, before heading to the common room just as Aristeo was advancing on his sister.

That was when the fight began in earnest.

ↂ

"Sin!"

Sinclair was teaching his class yet another repetitive move, an over-head swing, and so far, three of his recruits had managed to cut themselves. One man nearly cut his ear off, and surprisingly, it wasn't Thomas Ram. Anteaus was in the middle of the group, helping those less adept at the move, as Sinclair heard his name being shouted. Glancing over his left shoulder, he saw Fox running in his direction.

"Sin!" Fox bellowed. "Trouble at the tavern! You must come!"

For a moment, Sinclair thought he hadn't heard right. Puzzled, he frowned. "What trouble?" he asked. "What is happening?"

Fox was upon him. "Gigi came racing back here from town," he said, breathless from the run. "Lisi's brother has come for her."

Sinclair's eyes widened. "Her *brother*?" he repeated. "Christ, my sword. I need my sword."

Fox shook his head. "No time," he said. "Grab one of the practice swords. They're sharp enough. Anteaus! With us!"

Everyone began to run. There was no time to get the horses because the stable was at least a half-mile away in the wrong direction, so Sinclair grabbed the sword out of the hand of the nearest recruit and began to sprint toward the gatehouse. What he didn't know was that Tay and Ming Tang were already rushing into town because Fox had seen them first and informed them of the situation. Tay had grabbed the soldiers at the gatehouse, at least twenty of them, and the entire group was running into the village.

Sinclair, Fox, and Anteaus were bringing up the rear.

Gisele, however, had gone to Creston after she'd told her husband, and Creston had collected Cruz and Payne. Kristian was out on the water with his class and beyond their reach. Amir was with St. Denis, and no one wanted to tip St. Denis off. Bowen, the junior trainer in charge of etiquette and other things, was in a barn near the stable and too far to reach, and Axton, Fox's assistant, had charge of Fox's class and couldn't leave. Therefore, the available trainers dropped what they were doing, left their classes, and headed into Exebridge at a dead run because one of their own was in trouble. At least, that was what Gisele had said.

By the time Sinclair arrived, it was already a hell of a fight.

De Verra soldiers were all around the Black Cock, and the clash between them and the Blackchurch soldiers rocked the entire village. Residents were running and screaming, steering clear of the battle, as Sinclair tried to fight his way in. The man they called the Swordsman was working with a sword that wasn't his own, and a practice sword at that, but his precision and grace was unmatched. He managed to dispatch three de Verra men and bust in through the front door, along with Tay, only to see more chaos spread out in front of him.

As they stood in the doorway, looking for their women, someone swung a chair at Tay's head. He was a tall man, so the chair only managed to smash on his shoulder, but it was enough to throw him off balance. As he crashed back into the wall behind him, more Blackchurch soldiers filtered in, fighting the de Verra men who were already in the common room, but they were mixing with the patrons who hadn't yet left the Black Cock. That created a situation of bedlam because everyone was fighting everyone—patron against de Verra, de Verra against Blackchurch, and Blackchurch against patron. No one seemed to know who they were fighting, only that they had to fight. Across the room, Sinclair could see Athdara using an iron rod with considerable skill.

"Athdara!" he bellowed. "Where's Lisi?"

She saw him over the madness. "The private room!" she shouted. "Her brother has her! He won't let her go!"

Sinclair started to push through the crowd, kicking men out of the way, slashing those who didn't move fast enough. There were bodies and broken furniture on the floor, and he struggled across it as he tried to get to the private room.

"Lisi!" he yelled. "*Elisiana!*"

Screaming filled the air from the private room because Elisiana heard Sinclair's voice. Her brother had managed to disarm her of the Lion Tamer, and now he was simply chasing her around the table, trying to get a grip on her. Knowing Sinclair had arrived had her faltering.

"Sin!" she cried. "Sin, *help!*"

That was all he needed to hear to fuel his sense of terror. That strong, brave woman he'd come to know was actually calling for help. It was something he never thought he'd hear from her. Sinclair continued to fight his way across the common room, but it was nearly impossible. Two de Verra soldiers came at him, and he found himself engaged until Athdara appeared behind one of them and cracked the man over the head with her rod. As Sinclair was dispatching the other soldier, the screaming from the private room abruptly stopped.

Unbeknownst to them, Aristeo had captured his prize.

Hand over his sister's mouth, he knew he had to subdue her if he had any chance of carrying her away without a fight, so using the butt of his sword, Aristeo cracked her on the side of the head and she fell like a stone. Meanwhile, Sinclair shoved a de Verra soldier aside only to be hit from behind by another. Blades began to fly. But not before he saw a dark-haired man with Elisiana over his shoulder disappear into the corridor that went to the livery yard. He tried to follow but had a fight of his own to attend to.

It wasn't getting any easier.

In a fit of rage, Sinclair dispatched the de Verra soldier and rushed back out the way he'd come in because the way was clearer. Unfortunately, that took longer than he had hoped, so when he made his way outside and around the side of the tavern to the livery yard, it was just in time to see several horses rushing down the road, heading west, and he caught sight of someone draped over the saddle of one of the horses.

It was Elisiana's lavender dress.

Seized with panic, he rushed into the livery yard only to find the stable boy weeping because the de Verra soldiers had either stolen or scattered all of the horses in the corral. There were horses running wild in the yard and escaping out into the village. Realizing he had no mount, Sinclair turned back for the tavern only to see Ming Tang emerging from the building. Sinclair started to run out of the yard but Ming Tang stopped him.

"Sin!" he called. "*Wait!*"

"I cannot," Sinclair said, though he slowed his pace. "Her brother took her. I must get her back!"

Ming Tang caught up and grabbed him, forcing him to stop. It was a strong-arm move, not at all like the man from the east who was usually much more composed. But he had something to say and wasn't going to let Sinclair get away from him.

"Stop," he said firmly but quietly. "Sinclair, stop. Listen to me. *Listen!*"

Sinclair was trying to pull away from him. "Listen to what?" he said. "We are wasting time!"

But Ming Tang shook his head. "Nay, my friend," he said. "Stop and listen to me. You cannot go after her."

Sinclair looked at him as if he'd gone mad. "Of course I am going after her!"

"You cannot," Ming Tang said. "That was her brother, was it not?"

Sinclair nodded. "If was."

"And he is taking her home to her family?"

"Who told you that?"

Ming Tang shrugged. "From the conversations last night and from what Tay and Fox have told me," he said. "She told you that she had run from her father and an arranged marriage, did she not?"

Sinclair had a suspicion as to where this was leading. "She did."

"Then her brother has come to retrieve her and take her home."

"Over my dead body!"

Ming Tang had his hands on Sinclair, now patting the man on the chest. "You cannot go after her," he said again, patiently. "Think, Sin, *think*. Helping her in the midst of a fight in a tavern is one thing. If you were to reclaim her and take her to safety, her brother would not know where. She would be safe from him and he would continue his search for her because you could have kept her out of sight. But this way... if you follow, the trainers will want to go with you. If they go, Black-church soldiers will go. Do you understand what I am saying to you?"

Deep down, Sinclair did, but he didn't want to acknowledge it. "But I *must* go after her," he said. "If I—"

Ming Tang cut him off. "If you and the trainers follow her back to her father's home, what then?" he said. "You have no army to retrieve her. Do you plan to steal her away? And your friends would help you? Sin, that simply is not wise. If she has an arranged marriage, her father could have you executed for interfering with that. And he probably would. Then what happens to those who went with you?"

Sinclair was losing ground fast with the logic. "I cannot stand by and do nothing."

Ming Tang knew that. He wasn't trying to be heartless. But the truth was brutal. "Denis allowed you to fight in Tay's stead when you went to Toxandria, but this is something completely different," he said steadily. "If you follow her and try to reclaim her, you will violate everything Blackchurch stands for. You will create chaos. Already you've created chaos, and you will be fortunate if Denis does not relieve you of your post because of it."

The truth was sinking in as much as Sinclair railed against it. "I did *not* violate Blackchurch's rules," he said. "I came to the aid of the woman I... I'm going to marry her, Ming Tang. I will *not* see her married to another. Do you understand me?"

Ming Tang, ever wise, nodded patiently. "I understand," he said. "But you cannot chase after her to wrest her away from her brother. What happens if the man is killed? That will bring her father and his allies down around Blackchurch if, in fact, they know who you are and where you are from, and given this fight, they have probably figured it out. Denis will be furious. You are not thinking clearly. Whatever you do, it cannot involve the Blackchurch trainers or the soldiers. You cannot involve Blackchurch at all. We will have to think of something else."

Sinclair was almost agreeing with him. *Almost.* But more de Verra soldiers thundered down the road, passing them, and it brought about his panic again. By this time, Tay, Fox, Creston, Payne, and Anteaus had come into the livery yard, seeing Ming Tang with Sinclair.

They converged on the pair.

"What happened?" Tay demanded. "Where's the lady?"

Sinclair was looking at Ming Tang and, suddenly, everything the man said to him made sense. Perfect sense. He couldn't jeopardize his friends, who would want to go with him. As much as he loved them, this simply wasn't their fight, and if he let it become their fight, he *would* be violating everything Blackchurch stood for.

And he would ruin their careers.

Closing his eyes tightly, he turned away and hung his head.

"Sin?" Tay said when he saw Sinclair's reaction. Then he looked at Ming Tang. "What happened? *Where* is the lady?"

"Gone," Ming Tang said simply. "We must return to Blackchurch and tell Lord Exmoor what has happened. And we must come up with some solutions for Sin so he will not charge after the lady and get himself killed. How is Athdara?"

Tay was looking at Sinclair as Ming Tang spoke, distracted by the question about his wife. "She is inside helping clean up the mess," he said. "She's perfectly fine, the bold wench. Holding off a room full of soldiers with an fire poker."

That was good news. Tay wasn't really as casual about it as he pretended to be. He lived and breathed by his wife, so he was relieved more than any of them. But the situation, for now, was over, and Ming Tang nodded to Tay and Fox, who turned around and began moving the Blackchurch trainers and soldiers back for the guild. Everyone seemed oddly happy, energized by a good fight with no significant injuries.

It was all in a day's work.

Ming Tang hung back, however, waiting for Sinclair to compose himself, and it was fortunately a short wait. Sinclair was a professional and understand better than anyone else how emotions could cloud judgment. He'd just never had it happen to him.

In silence, he headed back to Blackchurch with Ming Tang by his side.

And St. Denis was waiting for him.

CHAPTER TEN

"I DID NOT mean to cause him such trouble," Gisele said sadly. "I only meant to help Lisi."

Gathered in Athdara's cottage because it had a view of Exmoor Castle where the trainers, including Sinclair, had been since morning, Gisele and Athdara stood in the front bedroom on the second floor because it afforded a better view. Marina, a woman who minded Athdara's children and sometimes Gisele's as well, had all of the children down on the ground floor, feeding them soup and bread and cheese for supper as their mothers worried overhead.

It was a day of great worry.

Not only had Elisiana been kidnapped by her brother, but Sinclair was in a good deal of trouble. Gisele knew that because when she'd gone to rouse the rest of the trainers so they could go into Exebridge and help Sinclair, St. Denis and St. Sebastian saw the commotion and came to find out what it was. That had forced Gisele to tell him, and when everyone returned, including the twenty Blackchurch soldiers, St. Denis had been waiting at the gatehouse for them.

Now, all of the men who had gone to Sinclair and Elisiana's aid were at Exmoor Castle, where they were undoubtedly being reprimanded. Gisele and Athdara paced the floor and watched the distant castle, wondering if they were going to have to clear the children out and move when their husbands lost their position.

A day of worry turned into a night of worry.

☙

"SIN, I HAVE listened to every man who went with you to the Black Cock defend you and your actions," St. Denis said. "What I have yet to hear is you defend your own actions. You have been at Blackchurch for nine years and you know our code. You know our rules. What can you tell me about this situation that the others have not?"

The solar of Exmoor was rife with tension. It was true that every trainer who had gone to Sinclair and Elisiana's aid had spoken on Sinclair's behalf, and that included Anteaus, who hadn't even known the man a full two days yet. But everyone had made it clear that Elisiana, a Castilian count's daughter, had been in danger from her brother and the soldiers he'd brought with him. The woman didn't want to go with him and was fighting back, so Sinclair and the others went to help her. Even Payne had made a rather passionate argument about it. St. Denis understood all of it, but what he didn't understand was anything from Sinclair's perspective because he wouldn't speak. He wouldn't even defend himself.

No one quite knew what to do.

When sunset descended, St. Denis had had enough of the stalemate. Everyone in the chamber was sympathetic to Sinclair and he knew that, so how he handled the situation would tell whether or not he even had any trainers in the morning except for Amir and Kristian, who hadn't been involved. Seated behind the table of his forefathers, the elaborate piece with lions for legs and inlaid gold on the surface, he finally stood up.

"Sinclair, I do not think a trainer has been dismissed from Black-church in over fifty years, but you are giving me little choice," he said. "If you do not speak on a matter that you were directly involved in, then there is nothing more I can do."

"Father, wait," St. Sebastian said, quickly holding out a hand. "Do not say it. Don't even think it. You cannot dismiss him."

"And why not?" St. Denis said angrily. "He is giving me no choice. He will not even answer my questions."

Tay, who was standing near Sinclair, turned to the man as he sat in a chair, his gaze muddled, his mind a thousand miles away.

"Sin," he hissed. "You must speak. *Please.*"

"Sin," Fox whispered, seated behind him. "Please say something. I know you are distraught, but for God's sake, save yourself, man. We cannot do it for you."

Sinclair had been seated in the chair for hours without moving. He was like a statue. As his friends passed concerned glances, fearful that he was going to continue the act of silence and end up being shamefully dismissed from Blackchurch, Sinclair finally shifted in his chair. He'd been sitting with his chin in his hand, staring off into space, but his head came up and his hand came away from his chin.

When he spoke, it was barely above a whisper.

"I have broken no rules," he said. "I went to the aid of the woman I am to marry because she was being attacked by her brother. I was defending her, the very ethics and morals we teach at Blackchurch. Because the trainers are loyal to one another, they came to my aid. We fought to defend a woman who could hardly defend herself against dozens of armed men. We would have been poor excuses for knights, indeed, had we not gone to her aid, because before we ever took the Blackchurch oath, we took an oath much older and much more powerful. We took the oath before God to fight enemies, to be loyal, to be just, and to protect the weak. And you are telling me that I broke the rules because I protected a weaker woman?"

He lifted his eyes to St. Denis as he finished speaking. Their gazes locked and St. Denis faltered somewhat upon hearing Sinclair's reasoning. He wasn't wrong and St. Denis knew it. In fact, everyone in the room knew it. That brief sentence had just destroyed St. Denis' righteous position. Frustrated, he shook his head.

"You took sides in a fight," St. Denis pointed out. "That is against our rules."

"I sided with *me*," Sinclair said. "I did not side with another warlord, or a king, or the church. There was no 'side' to take. It was my own side and nothing more."

St. Denis looked at St. Sebastian for support, but St. Sebastian lifted his eyebrows at his father, silently telling the man that he agreed with Sinclair. That was literally the case. But St. Denis wasn't ready to surrender.

"Mayhap you did only side with yourself, but you sided against a Castilian earl," he said. "It is a fine line you are walking, Sin. You chose a side in a battle and we simply are not allowed to do that."

Sinclair eyed the man, his jaw twitching with displeasure. "Then you are telling me that when I volunteered to go fight for Toxandria, that wasn't taking a side?" he said, his voice stronger now. "I went to fight for the son of *your* old friend. *You* let me go. *You* let me take sides in the battle against an enemy. And now you are telling me that it was wrong of me to take a side in a fight to save a lady because she was not the daughter of your old friend and, therefore, it means nothing? If you truly have such double standards, my lord, then you do not need to relieve me of my post. I will resign this very moment. Tell me if fighting for your old friend in Toxandria was different than trying to protect the woman I intend to marry. Well?"

He'd backed St. Denis into a corner. All eyes turned to the leader of Blackchurch and St. Denis knew, as he lived and breathed, that there would be no more Blackchurch if he answered this question incorrectly. It was a question of ethics and, indeed, standards and rules. The problem was that St. Denis knew he couldn't give a good enough explanation as to why the two were different. He *had* let Sinclair go to fight for the son of an old friend. He *had* changed the rules for his benefit. Sinclair knew it and every man in the chamber knew it. Therefore, he couldn't justify what he'd done versus what Sinclair had done.

There *was* no justification.

With a heavy sigh, St. Denis reclaimed his seat.

"Mayhap there is no difference," he said after a moment. "Mayhap defending her was not a slight against our rules. I am willing to concede the point. But her brother came to return her home, to an arranged marriage, and you tried to interfere. The implications could be severe—from the church, from the law. We are above trouble with the church and the law and I want to keep it that way. Do you not understand that?"

Sinclair nodded, relieved more than he would admit that St. Denis had backed down. In fact, everyone was. Sinclair's argument had been sound. But that didn't mean the situation was resolved.

Not in the least.

"I do understand that," Sinclair said. "Truly, I do, and I have been sitting here all day trying to figure out how to go about reclaiming her."

St. Denis shrugged. "I do not think you can," he said. "A marital contract is binding, Sin."

"I know," Sinclair said. "But I think I know a way to reclaim her without involving anyone at Blackchurch."

St. Denis frowned. "How?"

"Pirates."

"What pirates?"

Now that he was talking, someone handed Sinclair a cup of wine, and he took it, draining the entire thing, before speaking.

"Lady Elisiana's cousin is Santiago de Fernandez," he said, wiping his mouth with the back of his hand. "I'm sure you know the name, my lord. He is the commander of the Demons of the Sea."

St. Denis nodded. "I know who they are," he said. "But how can they help?"

Sinclair sat forward in his seat, elbows on his knees, hands hanging. "Because Lisi told me that Santiago is very fond of her," he said. "He knows about the arranged marriage and he did not approve of it. I wonder if Santiago would be willing to intervene and stop the marriage if he knew how much she did not want to marry the man her father chose for her? I cannot think of any army that could accomplish more than Santiago de Fernandez could if he was properly persuaded."

St. Denis sat back in his chair, torn between the outrage of the suggestion and the possibility that it might actually work. "Do you not think that is a bit far-fetched?" he said. "You actually think this man would help you?"

Sinclair shrugged. "What other choice do I have?" he said. "I have no army. I do not serve a lord who can summon an army and I cannot, nor would I, use Blackchurch's soldiers or trainers. To do that *would* be to violate Blackchurch's rules. Therefore, what alternatives do I have? Do you think Abelard would help me?"

St. Denis waved him off. "He might, but it would be at a high price," he said. "You do not want to be in his debt, Sin. That is a very bad idea."

"Then mayhap he could simply help me find Santiago," Sinclair said. "Lisi said that Santiago docks his vessels at Fremington. That is where she lives, where her family lives. If I can make it to Fremington, then I can arrange a meeting with Santiago and ask for his help."

"And if he won't?" St. Denis said. "What then?"

"Then I will have to think of something else."

"I-Is she worth so much to you, Sin?" St. Sebastian asked quietly. "Y-You have only known the woman a couple of days and already you are willing to risk everything for her?"

Sinclair looked at the man. "I am not sure what to tell you," he said.

"All I know is that I am not a man of whims. I do not act rashly. But I can tell you, with God as my witness, that Elisiana is worth risking everything for. It does not matter if I know her for two days or two months or two years. She will always be worth risking everything for, and I hope that I am always able to stand up for her and risk everything to keep her safe. Because I will—time and time again."

St. Sebastian wasn't going to dispute him. He looked at his father, his expression suggesting that he was completely on Sinclair's side. But St. Denis was unhappy with the turn the conversation was taking.

Pirates, he thought. *Ridiculous!*

"Nothing will be settled tonight," he said after a moment. "I think we have all had a long day, so I suggest we find our beds. Tomorrow, we may find a new perspective on this, but until we do, I expect that training will continue as usual. That means you, too, Sinclair."

Sinclair stood up from the chair. "As much as I would like to think we have time on this matter, the fact is that we do not," he said. "I am serious about locating Santiago, my lord. I would like to speak with Abelard first, to find out what he knows about the man, but if I cannot speak to him, I will go alone and seek him myself."

St. Dennis shook his head. "Sin…"

"Need I remind you again that I went to fight in Toxandria for your old friend?" Sinclair said, unwilling to be put off. "More than that, Fox once went to Canonsleigh Abbey to protect his future wife from danger against William Marshal, of all people, and, still, you permitted it, so why is my request so different? I will not be put off, so you may as well tell me what I want to know now. Help me or I will resign my post this very moment and find help on my own."

He'd said it as an ultimatum. Tay caught Fox's attention, and the two of them knew they had to support Sinclair in this. St. Denis had indeed made exceptions for them and the man had to know that if Sinclair left, so would they. It was true that they had wives and children, but there wasn't one warlord in England, including the king, that wouldn't readily accept their fealty. Therefore, there was no hesitation when they went to stand by Sinclair, but not before Tay cleared out the room. Silently, he waved to Payne and Amir, and the two of them herded everyone out quickly. The conversation about to happen didn't need an audience.

This was the moment.

St. Denis had seen the others leaving the chamber even as Tay and Fox remained. He knew that a confrontation was coming whether or not he wanted it. Standing before him in Tay, Fox, and Sinclair were his most powerful and longest-standing trainers. He didn't want to lose any of them, least of all his Swordsman.

"I did not say that I would not help you, Sin," he said quietly. "I appreciate that you have something personal to attend to and, believe it or not, I do support your right to do it. I appreciate that you are careful about not involving the other trainers, who are also your friends and would do anything for you. But do you truly wish to work with the pirates? That is like traveling to hell and demanding assistance from the devil."

Sinclair nodded. "I know," he said. "But something tells me that if Santiago knows a worthy man wants to marry Elisiana rather than the fool she is betrothed to, he will intervene. It is worth a chance because it is the only chance I have. There is nothing else."

St. Denis could see how sincere he was. Sinclair was usually a man who kept his emotions hidden, but in this case, he couldn't. That told St. Denis of the strong feelings he must have for Elisiana.

Strong enough to risk the life he knew.

That being the case, St. Denis knew what he had to do.

"Very well," he said reluctantly. "I will send word to Abelard. At least let the man tell us what he knows of Santiago. And then you can make a more solid plan."

Tay put his hand on Sinclair's arm. "That is reasonable," he said quietly. "You must know what you are facing, and if Abelard can tell you something about Santiago, you are forearmed."

Sinclair nodded, though he hadn't much choice. "You will send word right away?" he asked.

St. Denis nodded. "I will send a messenger up to the coast first thing tomorrow," he said. "If Abelard is there, he will receive the message tomorrow. But if he is out roving, it may be a few days. Or even weeks."

Sinclair knew he wasn't going to wait weeks. They all knew he wasn't going to wait weeks. "Then please send it on the morrow," he said. "I would be grateful. If we do not hear from him in a day or two, then I will have to make other plans."

St. Denis didn't argue with him, but something did come to mind that he needed to be clear about. "Pirates do not work for free, Sin," he said. "I can talk Abelard out of extracting anything from you, but Santiago may want something for helping you. Are you prepared for that?"

Sinclair shrugged. "I will give him what he wants."

"What if he wants money?"

"I have money."

"But what if he wants you?" St. Denis persisted. "Your skills are very valuable, and conscription with the pirates is a very real thing."

Sinclair didn't have a ready answer for that. "I suppose I shall have to be prepared for anything," he said. "I do not know if I would make a good pirate, but if it frees Lisi from marrying her father's choice, then I will do it."

"That means you cannot continue here at Blackchurch."

"I would not expect you to hold my position for me, my lord."

St. Denis thought the idea of serving with pirates might cause Sinclair to reconsider, but he could see that it didn't. His bluff hadn't worked. After a moment, he shook his head.

"Do not fear," he muttered. "It will be here when you return. Even if you are one hundred years old and St. Sebastian's grandson is in command. You are our one and only Swordsman, Sinclair. Blackchurch would not be Blackchurch without you."

Smiling weakly, Sinclair thanked the man. It had indeed been a long and exhausting day and, truthfully, he respected St. Denis. He'd always gotten on with him.

He hoped this situation hadn't changed things.

With a nod to St. Sebastian, Sinclair quit the chamber with Tay and Fox on his heels. They made it down to the entry level, emerging into the cold night outside. A million stars blanketed the heavens above, but Sinclair didn't notice. He was focused on the village ahead.

"May I speak with Athdara, Tay?" he asked. "She may know more about Elisiana's conversation with her brother. Mayhap she can enlighten me on a few things."

Tay nodded. "Of course you can," he said. "Gisele, too. They both spoke with Lisi this morning before the fight. Mayhap they can give you some guidance."

"Thank you," Sinclair said sincerely. Then he looked between Tay and Fox. "And for the trouble I have caused you both with Denis... I am truly sorry. I never meant for my fight to become yours."

Tay smiled weakly in the darkness. "My fight became yours the moment you went to Toxandria," he said. "Your fight became mine the moment Lisi's brother appeared, and if I can support you in your fight to claim Lisi, I will humbly do so. And if the pirates want you serve on their ships in exchange for their help, I will do that, too. Mind you, I will have to negotiate being able to see my wife and children, and I have been known to get sick from the rolling of the vessel, but I would do it anyway. Long have I owed you a debt, my friend. I'll pay it however I can."

Sinclair looked at him. "I did not fight in Toxandria so you would owe me a debt," he said. "I did it because I was best suited for it. And if you had done it, you really *would* have been taking sides because the duke is your brother-in-law. What I did, I did because it was the right thing to do. It spared you from having to make the choice."

Tay put a hand on his shoulder, a gesture of thanks and of brotherhood, as they headed toward the arch on the edge of the village. As they reached the arch, a figure stepped out of the shadows.

"Sin?" Payne came into the weak light. "I must speak with ye. Alone."

He was looking at Tay and Fox, who took the hint and continued on. When they were out of earshot, Payne spoke quietly.

"This is an awkward conversation," he said, scratching his ear. "I suppose what I want tae say is that if I'd lain claim tae Lisi, and her brother had come, I know ye would have come tae my aid tae protect her. No matter how ye felt about her, or how ye felt about me, I know ye would have done it."

Sinclair nodded. "I would have," he said. "And you did the same. Thank you for your assistance. I will not forget it."

Payne smiled weakly. "It was a good time," he said. "We dunna have the chance tae fight like that too often. I miss it!"

Sinclair broke down into soft laughter. "I spent the past three years fighting like that," he said. "But I will admit that I do enjoy it."

"Of course ye do," Payne said. "It's in yer blood."

"That is true."

Payne scratched the other ear, and Sinclair was starting to think it was a nervous gesture from a man who had probably never had a genuine nervous moment in his life.

Until now.

Something was afoot.

"I wanted tae tell ye something else," Payne said. "Lisi has a special place with me and I'm sorry if that offends ye, but 'tis true. I only wish the best for her and her brother taking her back tae an arranged marriage is not what she deserves. If ye go to the pirates for help, I want tae go with ye."

Sinclair regarded him carefully. "Why?"

"Tae help ye get her back, of course."

Sinclair's eyebrows lifted. "You do realize we are speaking of some of the most dangerous pirates of all, don't you?" he said. "Santiago de Fernandez is notorious for cutting the feet off his prisoners so they cannot run away and chaining them below decks to row his ships. I didn't mention that to Elisiana when she told me who her cousin was because I'm not entirely sure she knows, but I do. And so do you."

Payne scowled. "And Abelard cuts the noses off men who lie tae him," he said. "He's not exactly a choirboy, Sin."

"Quite true."

"But I still want tae go with ye."

Sinclair looked at the man whom he genuinely liked. He knew Payne had a good heart because he'd seen it, many times. But he also needed the man to be sure.

"What will your mother say?" he said. "I do not think she will be happy with a son who wants to join with pirates to fight a fight that is not his own."

Payne waved him off. "She would understand."

"Would she?"

"My mother was a pirate for years," he said. "I was in her belly when she was fighting the French and the Irish, so dunna bring her up. She would praise me."

Sinclair was trying not to laugh. "She probably would," he said. "But I want to be clear—you want to go for Elisiana, not me. I will not be upset if you admit it. But you are going to save *her*. You are not going to support *me*."

Payne thrust his chin up. "A man can have two reasons for doing something he feels strongly about."

Sinclair fought off a grin. "Have it your way," he said. "I do not mind if you come along. But I do the talking and you do what I tell you to do."

"I will."

"And you must clear this with Denis. He will not be happy about it."

Payne shrugged. "Mayhap not," he said. "But ye did nothing wrong today, Sin. Denis was wrong for berating you the way he did. We all feel that way. And he'll keep Tay and Fox here, so someone should go with ye. It should be me."

Sinclair gave in without any further discussion. He simply nodded and patted Payne on the side of the head, leaving the man to take his offer up with St. Denis. As Payne headed toward the castle, Sinclair continued across the village toward Tay's cottage. His thoughts shifted from the big Scotsman to Athdara because she was the last one who had spoken to Elisiana. He wanted to know anything that had been said that could help him in recovering her. Or perhaps he simply wanted to know if Elisiana had said anything about him. Now that the rush of the day was over, Sinclair realized that grief was beginning to settle. He could feel distress filling his veins and didn't want to feel any of those things at the moment.

He needed to focus.

He *would* get her back.

As he approached Tay's cottage, the door flew open and Tay was standing there, waiting for him. Behind him, children were running around, screaming and playing, and Sinclair could hear Fox trying to settle the boys down. Tay had four little boys and an infant daughter while Fox had three boys, the middle child of which was called the Beast by the Blackchurch trainers. Canon de Merest, at almost six years of age, was almost as big as Tay's older boys, who were several years older. When Canon spoke, everyone listened, and as Sinclair came to the door, he could see Canon shoving some of the other boys around and Fox intervening.

The Beast started howling when his father dragged him away.

"That is not a happy beastie," Sinclair commented with a grin.

Athdara, who had been on a chair with her small daughter, was already walking over to the door.

"Canon is a terror," she said. "The only one he'll listen to is Milo because he's bigger than Canon is, but even Milo has to fight to hold his own against him. He says Canon has taken to biting these days."

"Christ," Sinclair grunted, shaking his head. "He'll bite off fingers with that mouth."

Athdara chuckled. "Hopefully not," she said, but quickly sobered. "Tay told me what happened with Denis, Sin. I'm so very sorry he was cross with you. You truly had no other choice than to do what you did."

Sinclair waved him off. "It is not the end of the world," he said. "But I did want to speak with you about Elisiana. You were the last one to speak with her and… Well, I was hoping you would tell me what was said… what she was feeling…"

He trailed off as if unable to even mention that it could have been a last conversation with her, ever, and Athdara nodded, motioning him inside. Tay's cottage had two big chambers on the ground floor, one with a big hearth and a table that seated about ten people, and then a second, smaller chamber where food was prepared. There was a smaller table there, and Athdara led them into the room to get them away from the playing boys as Tay joined them. Gisele, who had been with Fox as he disciplined Canon, emerged from the small yard behind the cottage and returned to the larger room to tame the frolicking boys.

But Sinclair didn't notice her. He was currently having to take Tay's youngest child from her mother's arms because she was trying to climb over her mother to get to him. Sinclair set little Lisabette on his knee and pinched her nose, and the little girl laughed as Tay and Athdara watched. They knew he was upset, and weary, an unusual state for Sinclair. But they also felt a strong affinity toward him because of what he'd done for them and for Toxandria, so they both wanted to help him as much as they could. No detail was too small or too great.

"Lisi was receptive to coming to Blackchurch to manage our kitchens," Athdara said, watching her daughter stick her hand into Sinclair's mouth. "We told her that we'd come on your behalf with the offer because you were busy with your class and she seemed receptive, but not at first."

Sinclair had little fingers between his teeth. "Why not?"

"Because she felt that she did not want to be dependent on you and on Blackchurch so soon, I suppose," Athdara said. "I admire that, Sin. She did not want to be a burden on anyone, or take advantage of anyone. That speaks well of her."

Sinclair let the little girl slide off his knee and down to the floor before he replied. "Behind the broadcloth and ale stains, I think we had a truly remarkable woman in our midst," he said, trying not to grow despondent. "Did you know that she is an artist?"

Athdara suddenly jumped up and ran off as Tay reached over and picked up his daughter. Sinclair looked at him curiously about his wife's behavior, but Tay couldn't explain it. He simply shrugged as he cradled the baby. Sinclair continued to sit there, pondering the day and what the future would bring, when Athdara abruptly reappeared with something in her hand.

"Here," she said, handing it over to Sinclair. "Lisi gave this to us before she was taken because she wanted us to give it to you. She said you were expecting it."

Quite interested, Sinclair untied the leather strap that was around the scroll of vellum, and when that fell away, he unrolled it.

For a moment, he simply stared at it.

Over his shoulder, Tay took a closer look even as his daughter fussed in his arms. He handed the child back to her mother before reaching over to take the vellum out of Sinclair's hands.

"Remarkable," Tay said. "Did Lisi do this?"

Sinclair nodded, his eyes never leaving the vellum. "She told me she was an artist so I challenged her to draw an image of me," he said. "It *looks* like me."

Tay smiled and handed it back to him so he could show Athdara. "It truly does," Tay said. "She has drawn you true to life, not the stylized nonsense we see in Bibles or in royal portraits. No one really looks like that."

"That is beautiful, Sin," Athdara said, admiring the drawing but now faced with a fussy daughter who was beginning to cry. "What a great talent she has."

That was as much as she could say before she was forced to leave and take her child to bed. That left Tay and Sinclair sitting there, alone, because now Gisele and Fox were separating their brood from the playing mass of boys. It was time for everyone to go to bed. Tay bade them a farewell as they took their children and departed, but Sinclair was still looking at the drawing. He couldn't seem to take his eyes off it. When Gisele and Fox left and Tay instructed his boys to go upstairs and prepare for bed, Sinclair spoke softly.

"Tell me that I am going to get her back, Tay," he muttered. "Tell me that this is not at an end."

Tay looked at him. "It is not at an end," he said. "And you will get her back. Sin… if I have to kill her husband and make it look like an accident, I will. She will be yours, one way or the other, so please do not do anything foolish. A well-thought-out plan with a reasonable chance for success is the best way to see both you and the lady come out of this unharmed. Agreed?"

Sinclair rolled up the vellum and held it against his heart as he lowered his head and closed his eyes.

"Me, Payne, and a gang of damnable pirates are the answer to this problem," he mumbled. "I never thought I'd see the day when I needed the help of pirates."

"Payne?"

"He asked to go."

Tay shrugged. "Stranger things have happened, I suppose," he said, clapping the man on the shoulder as he stood up. "But there's nothing you can do tonight, so go to bed. Try to sleep. I will see you on the morrow and I will personally make sure Denis sends the missive to Abelard. I do not want you to worry about this, Sin. We shall be victorious in the end."

Sinclair could only nod. He didn't have the energy to do anything else. Rising to his feet, he thanked Tay quietly and headed out of the cottage, back to his empty home, where the lady who tended it had stoked the fires, warmed the bed, and left food on the table. But it was quiet, dark, and as solemn as a tomb.

So empty...

Just like his soul at the moment. Sinclair wasn't sure how a woman could get under his skin in just a matter of days, but one had. Elisiana's weapons had been her warmth and charm and beauty, and any walls that Sinclair might have had around his heart had crumbled beneath her tender onslaught. Truth be told, she hadn't done much of anything. He'd been the one who had shown interest and she had simply responded in kind. What a glorious thing that had been. He'd never had a real courtship, so this was something quite special to him.

She was special to him.

But now... now, he was without her.

Was it madness to feel such a connection to a woman he'd known just two days? He'd known plenty of women, but he'd never felt this way for any of them. Sure, there had been a lady or two that had caught his fancy, but those had faded quickly. In this case, his attraction toward Elisiana was growing. But what if her abduction had simply muddled his feelings and he was only experiencing a natural surge of protection, the same as he would for any woman in peril? But in this case, he was confusing those natural surges with affection. Adoration.

... love?

God's Bones. Was it possible he actually loved the woman? Two days and he'd fallen in love with her like a silly squire? Anything was possible and anything was probable. He wasn't going to guess at it. For the first time in his life, he was simply going to give in to feelings so strong that he couldn't control them.

He was going to get her back.

And then he was going to marry her.

When Sinclair finally drifted off to sleep that night, it was with Elisiana's drawing clutched against his heart.

PART TWO

THE ARGOS, THE NAVIA, AND THE FRENCH SWORDSMAN

CHAPTER ELEVEN

S OMEONE WAS SINGING softly.

Elisiana was gradually aware of singing, of a horribly aching head, and when she opened her eyes, it was dark but for a taper next to the bed.

The bed.

She recognized it.

Emitting something between a grunt and a roar, Elisiana propelled herself off the bed and onto the floor. Whoever had been singing screamed at the action, and as Elisiana tried to crawl away from her childhood bed, her mother was suddenly in her path.

"Lisi, *nay*," her mother begged, putting her hands on her daughter and trying to soothe her. "You have been injured! You must not exert yourself!"

Elisiana yanked herself away from her mother, kicking at the woman as she scrambled away. But the room was rocking and there wasn't another way out because she could see that she was in her childhood bedroom. There was one way in and one way out.

She was trapped.

She was home.

Cowering against the wall, Elisiana kicked at her mother again when the woman tried to come to her aid.

"Leave me alone," she spat, kicking again. "*Leave me alone!*"

Sybil de Norbury de Verra did exactly that. She stopped. Wide-eyed, she looked at her daughter with something between fear and sorrow in her expression. In fact, her daughter favored her a great deal in her beauty, except that Elisiana had inherited an ancestor's pale blue eyes and Sybil possessed brown eyes.

Brown eyes that were full of turmoil.

"You are not well, my darling," she said softly. "Please… please let me help you to bed. You must rest."

Elisiana was becoming a little more lucid and along with that lucidity came anger and panic. "Where is Papa?" she demanded. "Where is he?"

"He is—"

She wouldn't let her mother finish. "I want to see him *now!*"

She was practically shouting, and Sybil opened the chamber door, sending a hovering servant running for Adriano. Meanwhile, she tried to keep her daughter calm.

"We have been so terribly worried for you, my darling," she said. "Téo said he found you in a tavern. A *tavern*, Elisiana! What were you doing in a tavern? Is that where you have been all this time?"

Elisiana was starting to feel sick, mingling with her anger. "Téo hit me," she said. "If I ever see that bastard again, I will kill him!"

"You must not say such things!"

"I do not care," Elisiana said. "He hit me. He hurt me! Do you not even care?"

Sybil didn't know what to say. "He was saving you, Lisi!"

"Saving me from *what*?"

"*Mi hija!*" Adriano was suddenly in the doorway. "What happened? Did you fall?"

He rushed toward his daughter with the intent to help her off the floor, but Elisiana began kicking at him, too. He came too close and she smashed him in the shins, causing him to stumble back in pain and confusion.

"What is the matter with you?" he demanded. "Lisi, what is wrong?"

Elisiana exploded. "What is *wrong*?" she cried. "Do you ask that question seriously? What is *wrong* is that I am here and I do not wish to be here. If I wanted to come home, I would have come home by myself! You had no right to bring me here!"

Adriano wasn't sure how to answer. He considered her statement, looking at his wife for support, but she was as fearful and baffled as he was.

"This is your home, Elisiana," he finally said. "This is where you belong."

Elisiana was struggling to her feet, using the wall for support. "I do *not* belong here," she said. "I found a place where I belonged and you sent Téo to brutally rip me from my chosen home."

Adriano wasn't exactly sure what he'd expected when his daughter regained consciousness. Her brother had said she had fought against him and he'd had to knock her on the head, twice he'd said, so she would be no trouble for the ride back to Fremington. Perhaps Adriano had been hoping for a tearful reunion, apologies from his errant daughter, and a genuine desire to do what her parents wished for her to do. He'd expected anything but what he was receiving, and that was a furious daughter who was declaring her hatred for her own home.

He was genuinely shocked.

"Then tell me what is so terrible about this home, *mi hija*," he pleaded. "Tell me why you left us. It has been agonizing not knowing what happened. Were you taken from us? Did you run away? What happened?"

Elisiana had made it to her feet, but she was feeling so horrible that she staggered back over to the bed so she could sit down. "You know what happened," she snapped. "You forced Adolph upon me. You force him down my throat like the most foul-tasting medicine, positive I would simply accept him without question. But he is a vile, mannerless man who asked me to touch his genitals once we were alone. I am certain he did not tell you that."

Sybil gasped in horror as Adriano looked outraged. "He did not," he said. "He said that he was speaking with you in the garden and someone struck him. When he came out of the pond, you were gone. He thought you might have been abducted. Servants saw you in the stable with your horse, alone, but we thought that you were forced to leave us somehow. We did not know."

Elisiana rolled her eyes. "I was not forced to leave you," she said, marginally calmer. "And I am not surprised that Adolph did not tell you the truth. I kicked him and pushed him into the pond, and then I ran. I ran as far and fast as I could because I will not marry the man. I will commit myself to a convent first."

Adriano sighed heavily. "Why could you not have come to tell me all of this?" he asked. "Why did you have to run?"

Now that the rush of fear and anger was draining out of her, Elisiana was feeling nauseated and weak. "Because you would not listen," she said. "You have never listened to me."

"That is not true."

"It is," she insisted. "I could have told you about it, but you would have probably told me to forgive him and make peace with him. Well, I do *not* want to forgive him. I do not want to make peace. Papa, I deserve a husband who respects me and behaves kindly. I do not deserve an animal who asks me to touch his manhood."

Sybil gasped again at the mention of the offense, putting her hand over her mouth in shock as Adriano rubbed his temples. He was starting to get a headache.

"Of course you deserve the best," he said. "I agree with you, *mi hija*. But Adolph... He seemed very concerned that you were gone. Is it possible... possible you misunderstood him?"

Elisiana looked at the man in exasperation. "Of course I did not misunderstand him," she said, growing agitated again. "I am not stupid, Papa. He behaved horribly and I refuse to marry him. If I ever see him again, I will kick him again where I kicked him before. Do *not* send him to me. Is he still here? Never send him to me unless you want a battle."

Adriano held up his hands to ease her. "Ease yourself," he said. "He is not here. He is home near Launceston. After we did not find you right away, he returned home and has been there ever since."

"Good," Elisiana said. "Keep him there. I've no desire to see the man ever again."

Adriano glanced at his wife, who was watching her daughter with sorrow. Everyone was upset so it would do no good to argue with Elisiana tonight, but the truth was that she could not have everything she wanted. She'd been brought home for a reason and whether or not she wanted to marry Adolph was immaterial. She was going to pay the price for Adriano's debt and there was nothing she could do about it.

The sooner she realized this, the better.

"It is late, *mi hija*," he finally said. "Your mother will bring you some food and then you will sleep. We will continue this discussion in the morning."

Elisiana didn't reply immediately, so Adriano turned for the door. He was almost through it when he heard her voice, soft but unmistakable.

"Papa, I was happy where I was," she said. "I do not want to stay here."

He turned to look at her. "We will discuss it tomorrow."

Elisiana turned to look at him. "Nay, we will not," she said. "I will tell you now that you took me away from a place where I felt needed and respected and loved. You took me away from simple people who extended friendship to me in a way no one else ever has. And you took me away from a man I very much want to marry. I am going back to him, just so we understand one another. Neither Adolph nor you will stop me."

Adriano stood in the doorway, his gaze drifting over his daughter, who seemed to have changed a good deal over the past six months. She still looked the same, mostly—her beautiful face, her beautiful hair—but there was something in her voice that suggested maturity. Somehow, she'd grown up a little. But he wasn't hard pressed to admit that he was displeased to hear that his daughter had met a man she wanted to marry.

"If you are married to Adolph, you cannot marry another man," he told her. "You have a betrothal contract with Adolph. You are his, by rights and by law. Who is this man you wish to marry?"

She shook her head. "Someone who is greater than you could possibly imagine," she said. "A descendant of a Bernician princess. A great man who is greatly respected. And he means the world to me."

"Then the refusal to marry Adolph is because of this man?"

"It is because I hate Adolph. He is unworthy."

"He is your uncle's wife's son."

"That does not mean he is worthy, nor does it mean he is family. He is nothing."

Adriano sighed sharply. "Your time away has taught you to be disrespectful to me," he said. "Is that what it has done? Taught you to behave shamefully to your own father?"

"It has taught me to defend myself."

For lack of any real answer to what he considered an exhaustingly ridiculous statement, Adriano shook his head and quit the chamber, heading back down to the hall. That left Sybil still standing at the foot of the bed, watching her daughter with concern.

"I will send for some food, my darling," she said. "Would you like to bathe? I can have a bath brought up right away."

Food and a bath sounded wonderful to Elisiana. She was angry, and stubborn, but that only went so far. Food and a bath were things she very much wanted, something to settle her stomach and something to wash away the dirt of her abduction. Looking down at herself, she saw she was still wearing the lavender dress she'd put on for Sinclair.

Sinclair...

The man had fought to help her but, in the end, he hadn't been able to. She could only imagine the torment he was going through. The uncertainty. In truth, she had enough uncertainty of her own because her relationship with him was so very new. They hardly knew one another, and now this. She wondered if he'd gone back to Blackchurch only to decide she wasn't worth the trouble. That he didn't want to get mixed up with a woman whose father was a Castilian count and his cousin was a pirate.

Sweet, beautiful Sinclair...

She wouldn't have at all blamed him if he decided she was too much trouble, but that didn't mean she didn't plan to somehow win him back. She was going to return to the Black Cock and she was going to work hard to bring him back to her. To hell with her parents.

To hell with Adolph.

Elisiana was already planning her escape. But while she was planning her return to Exebridge, Adriano was in his solar, scratching out a missive to his brother-in-law. He was doing exactly what his daughter didn't want him to do.

Elisiana is home. Send Adolph right away.

The wheels, for both father and daughter, were in motion.

CHAPTER TWELVE

Four Days Later

H E LOOKED LIKE Jesus.

Not that Sinclair had actually ever seen Jesus, but he imagined the man would look a good deal like St. Abelard de Bottreaux, leader of the band of English pirates known as Triton's Hellions. He controlled four main vessels in the *Argos*, the *Mt. Pelion*, the *Pagasa*, and the *Athena*, but he'd also confiscated other ships over the years, some larger and some smaller, including a very large vessel that belonged to the king of France called the *Fountainebleau*. He kept that particular ship moored at Lundy Island, coincidentally about ten miles to the west of Fremington and more than double that distance from where St. Abelard kept his main fleet on the Devon coast. Lundy was, indisputably, St. Abelard's island, and there was even a fortress there that he kept manned with his men. Ten cannons protected the harbor where the *Fountainebleau* was located because he was so damn proud of that vessel that he'd kill anyone who tried to get close to it.

For St. Abelard, it was all about collecting possessions.

And he had many.

It was this man that Sinclair was introduced to when Amir came for him as he was teaching his swordsmanship class on a misty morning. Amir, whose father was a great Egyptian warlord, was intimidated by no one, but even he was a little intimidated by St. Abelard. Sinclair had only ever seen the man at a distance and never truly met him or dined with him, so when he was formally introduced in St. Denis' solar, he could see what had impressed Amir so much.

St. Abelard was positively enormous.

He was as tall as a tree, taller than even Tay, and he had flowing white hair and a black and white beard, with bushy, dark eyebrows over piercing eyes that were the same color as St. Denis'. That was the only family trait that indicated the two of them might be related, but the truth was that their familial connection had been five generations ago. Now, they were merely distant cousins who shared the same name and the same Devon connection. St. Denis received nothing monetarily from Triton's Hellions, however, as all of that belonged to St. Abelard, and St. Abelard received nothing monetarily from St. Denis and Blackchurch. The enterprises were separate.

But the same determined, controlling attitude was not.

"Sit, Sinclair," St. Denis said after he'd introduced them. "I have told my cousin about your troubles. He is willing to speak with you about de Fernandez."

"Aye, de Fernandez," St. Abelard said, lifting one of those bushy eyebrows. "My old friend."

Sinclair cocked his head curiously. "Then he is an ally, my lord?"

St. Abelard snorted ironically, perhaps one of the loudest and most disgusting sounds Sinclair had ever heard. "Of course not," St. Abelard said. "The man is a thorn in my side. But we do have an understanding these days. A truce, if you will. He stays away from Ireland and western England and I stay away from France and the Castilian coast, though France is no great stretch. They are still furious that I have their warship. Ah, the *Fountainebleau*. What a beautiful woman she is. If I were to sail her near France, they would launch everything at me to get her back."

Sinclair eyed St. Denis, unsure how to proceed, so he did carefully. The last thing he wanted to do was anger this mountain of a man who happened to be a deadly pirate.

"Then if Lord Exmoor has explained the situation, you know it is a complicated one," he said. "I would like to speak with de Fernandez under the flag of truce and I would like to tell him that his young cousin is in peril because of this marriage contract. I would like to ask for his help in freeing her from the contract so that I may marry her. Mayhap you can tell me how best to accomplish a parlay with de Fernandez, since you know him. Would you have any advice, my lord?"

St. Abelard rolled his eyes and stood up, all flowing robes and furs, leather breeches, and that long white hair. He went over to a table that held fruit and wine and picked up the wine bottle, drinking from the neck.

"All for a woman, is it?" he finally said.

"Aye, my lord."

He eyed Sinclair. "Would it not be easier to simply find another one?" he said. "You are a handsome man. Surely there are many women who would make you forget this one."

So he's not a sentimentalist, Sinclair thought. That didn't surprise him. In fact, the man seemed callous to the situation, but that was his prerogative. He wasn't involved in any way, so he could afford the unsympathetic attitude.

But it gave Sinclair a clue as to how to deal with him.

"Let me ask you a question, my lord," he said. "Would any other ship replace the one you took from the French? The *Fountainebleau*? Or is there something so special about that vessel that no other ship comes close to it?"

St. Abelard stopped with the wine bottle halfway to his mouth. He stared at Sinclair a moment before breaking down into a grin. "You are a smart man," he said. "You have explained it to me in a way I will understand. Then she means very much to you."

"Very much. And the French have taken her away."

St. Abelard chuckled, bring his bottle back over to the chair and sitting heavily. "And you want her back."

"I do, my lord."

St. Abelard thought on that, taking another swig of wine. "And all you wish for me to do is make it so you can speak with de Fernandez?"

"That is all, my lord, I swear it."

"You do not wish for me to interfere to get your lady returned to you?"

Sinclair shrugged. "I think de Fernandez, being the lady's cousin, would have a better chance," he said. "They might listen to him more than a stranger like you."

St. Abelard's eyebrows flew up. "A stranger?" he exclaimed. "I am not a stranger to anyone in Devon or Cornwall. They will know me and they will know my ships!"

"The lady told me that de Fernandez hides his ships in the River Taw, near Fremington."

St. Abelard calmed down unnaturally quickly. "I know," he said, a twinkle of mirth in his eyes. "He thinks he is so clever, but I know they are there. The *Navia*, which is his prized vessel, is large, and he has trouble tucking it into the mouth of the river, so he has tried to use Lundy Island for his ships, but that is *my* island. He cannot have it."

"Sinclair is one of our finest trainers, Abby," St. Denis interrupted, his tone unusually serious. "This is an important matter to him. I told him that you would not exact a fee for your assistance, but de Fernandez might. He is willing to pay. So am I, if necessary."

Sinclair looked at St. Denis in shock. "*You* pay?" he repeated. "My lord, I will not accept anything from you. This is my fight, not yours. We established that."

St. Denis looked at him. "We did," he said. "But I thought about this all night. What you did for Toxandria was for me as well as for Athdara. Her father was a dear friend and you were all of the help I could give him. Therefore, I owe you a debt, Sin. You may as well accept that."

Before Sinclair could argue, St. Abelard spoke up. "If you are willing to pay, Denis, then I will humbly help this man speak with de Fernandez," he said, drowning out Sinclair's protest. "But you know what I want from you."

St. Denis sighed heavily with displeasure. "What do you want?" he said. "Money? My second-born child?"

"Nay," St. Abelard said as if the man were stupid. "The cog on the lake. I want the big cog."

St. Denis rolled his eyes, shaking his head and burying it in his hands when he realized his cousin had caught him. "God's Bones," he muttered. "Anything but the cog. I need it."

St. Abelard smacked his hand on the table. "*I* need it," he said. "I am taking a fleet south, to Lisbon, in the autumn, and I need that ship!"

"Nobody is taking anyone's ship," Sinclair said loudly, intervening. He looked at St. Abelard. "This is *my* debt, my lord. I will pay you what you wish."

St. Abelard cocked an eyebrow. "Then buy your lord's ship and give it to me."

Christ, Sinclair thought. As he shook his head at the ridiculousness of it all, St. Denis and St. Abelard began to argue over the cog and how St. Abelard would even get it to the coast. St. Denis pointed out that he'd had master ship builders disassemble it, take it to Blackchurch, and then reassemble it over a several-month period, but St. Abelard didn't care about that.

He just wanted the damn ship.

Sinclair sat and watched the cousins argue over the ship, over who was more helpful to whom, and then over something that happened in their childhood that St. Abelard still wasn't over. They were veering off the subject at hand, which didn't sit well with Sinclair.

Finally, he'd had enough.

"For the past three years, I fought a mighty battle in Toxandria," he said loudly enough to shut them both up, which was quite a feat. He looked straight at St. Abelard. "If you do not know where Toxandria is, then I will tell you that it is near Brabant and borders France. I tell you this because one of my rewards for fighting for the rightful heir was a title and lands, which are profitable because they produce grapes and wine. Lord Abelard, I will give you this title and these lands if you will help me find de Fernandez so that I may ask for his help in recovering my lady. They are worth more than the cog in the lake. Do we have a bargain?"

Both St. Denis and St. Abelard were taken aback by not only his tone, but by the offer. In fact, St. Abelard looked at St. Denis even as he pointed to Sinclair.

"Is this man sincere?" he demanded. "Does he think to toy with me? Does he think I am stupid?"

St. Denis held his hand up to calm his cousin. "Sinclair de Reyne does not lie," he said. "He is indeed serious. Aren't you, Sin?"

Sinclair nodded. "Upon my oath, as serious as I have ever been," he said. "I was gifted the title of Lord Brexent. My lands produce a good deal of wine and you would have your own supply of wine should you agree to my offer. I have the documents that give me this title and property. I will hand them over to you if you will only help me find de Fernandez and gain me audience with the man. Please, my lord, I am begging you."

St. Abelard gazed at him, clearly trying to determine if he was, indeed, serious. Since his vocation didn't involve elite knights and men whose word was their bond, he was naturally suspicious of any man. *Every* man. But he knew his cousin put enormous stock in his Blackchurch trainers, of which this man was one. One of his best, St. Denis had said. A trainer who had fallen in love with a woman who was abducted by her own family to marry someone else. It was complicated.

But, then again, so was he.

"I want the cog," he finally said, looking at St. Denis. "If your trainer is serious, then mayhap he'll give you the Brexent lordship in exchange for the cog, which he will then give to me. That is the only offer I make and the only one I will accept."

Sinclair looked at St. Denis. "Of course I will give it to you in exchange for the ship," he said. "The documents are in my cottage. I will retrieve them at this moment."

St. Denis was furious at St. Abelard for driving the bargain. "Sin, I—"

Sinclair cut him off. "Please, my lord," he said. "The property is worth ten times what that ship is worth. You can sell it and buy yourself a new ship."

St. Denis threw up a hand to silence Sinclair, his gaze moving back to St. Abelard. "You are despicable," he muttered, shaking his head in disapproval. "I have asked you to help a man who has served me well and all you can do is taunt him with bargains that involve me."

St. Abelard folded his big arms over his chest. "That is how I get what I want," he said. "Well? When do I get my ship?"

St. Denis cocked his head. "I am not entirely sure," he said. "Mayhap I should visit your wife and ask her. After I tell her how I have been sending eighty pounds a year to a woman you impregnated not once, but twice, and begged me to support the children because your wife sees your ledgers and you did not want her asking questions about it. Now, tell me... *when* do you get your ship?"

St. Abelard's eyes widened. "You would not *dare*."

"Are you willing to wager on that?"

St. Abelard bolted out of his chair furiously. He lifted the wine bottle to smash it against the wall in his rage but realized it still had some wine in it, so he drank it first and then smashed it. He then proceeded to kick over a table, throw a chair, and take every book off a shelf near St Denis' table and throw each one on the ground.

"I want that ship!" he boomed. "Give it to me or I'll not help your man in the least!"

"Help him, give him what he asks for, and I will consider it when this is over."

"I want it now!"

St. Denis scratched his chin thoughtfully. "If I leave today, I will be in Minehead by the morrow," he said. "Sweet Mary will be very glad to see her husband's favorite cousin."

Scowling, St. Abelard picked up the books he'd thrown to the floor and threw them down again. Then he stomped on them. Enough to leave a footprint, but not hard enough to really damage them. The man was throwing an epic temper tantrum as Sinclair tried not to react to it and St. Denis yawned, bored with the scene.

"Well?" St. Denis said. "I do not have all day. Will you help Sinclair or not?"

St. Abelard stomped over to Sinclair and jabbed a finger in the man's face. "I hope Santiago cuts your feet off and forces you to row for eternity!"

Sinclair didn't back down, nor was he afraid. After the tantrum, it was quite honestly difficult to take St. Abelard seriously. "I am not afraid, my lord," he said. "Will you help me?"

St. Abelard huffed and puffed. But he eventually sat down again, refusing to look at either of them.

"We depart at dawn for Minehead, where my ships are docked," he muttered. "If you are not ready at that time, I will leave you here."

"I will be ready, my lord."

"He has just come back from a long time away. He may be too busy to talk."

"I am willing to take that chance, my lord."

With that, he stood up and marched out of the chamber, all flowing robes and flowing hair and a particular hatred for his cousin at the moment. St. Denis and Sinclair watched him go.

"Where is he going?" Sinclair asked.

St. Denis waved a dismissive hand at him. "Probably to look at the cog he wants," he said. "You'd better go and warn Kristian. Abelard may try to take it over and Kristian will have a fight on his hands."

Sinclair nodded and headed toward the door, but before he reached it, he paused and turned to St. Denis.

"I really will give you the Brexent title and lands for the cog," he said. "It seems that Abelard very much wants it, and I do not want to have to face an angry pirate every day until he gets what he wants. He will blame me."

St. Denis grinned. "And that concerns you?"

Sinclair cast him a long look. "I am asking the most feared English pirate who sails to help me parlay with the most feared Castilian pirate who sails," he said. "I am walking on very thin ice, my lord. It would help if one of them was not furious with me."

St. Denis laughed softly. "Do not fear," he said. "I will give him the cog if he wants it that badly, but I will expect you to help me replace it from your Brexent revenue."

Sinclair nodded with relief. "Gladly, my lord," he said. "May I tell St. Abelard?"

"Nay," St. Denis said flatly. "Let him stew for a while. Not everything can be so easy for him."

Sinclair nodded, smirking as he quit the chamber. The relief, the satisfaction he felt, was indescribable. He felt like he'd just been through purgatory with the devil and lived to tell the tale. At least now, there was hope.

He clung to it.

As he headed down to finish his class for the day, he made note to send a servant for Kristian to warn the man about St. Abelard. As soon as he exited the castle, he came across a few soldiers whose duty was to guard the keep and do St. Denis' bidding, and he sent one of those men on the run for Kristian. Sinclair had his own class to attend to, now with the knowledge that he would be leaving in the morning. That meant he wouldn't be here to teach his class for an undetermined amount of time, and he had to make arrangements for that.

Quickly.

Coming down the hill, he could see his class in the distance with Anteaus at the helm. The man had stayed true to Sinclair's teaching, never varying, since Sinclair had returned. He'd been respectful and diligent, the first man to the class in the morning and, other than Sinclair, the last man to leave, and Sinclair knew it was because he was trying to prove his worth. Sinclair hadn't worked with him for any length of time like the others had.

But that, too, was going to have to wait.

Sinclair was going to have to trust his class to someone he didn't really know.

Reaching his class, he stood at the top of the slope and watched the men work on another move that he had introduced yesterday. This was an offensive move, and Anteaus ran them through it for the rest of the day as Sinclair walked among the group and watched men repetitively thrust the sword. If he saw someone not doing it correctly, he helped them.

Over and over again, all afternoon, until the approach of sunset for men who were ready to drop. Arms were aching, backs were aching, and Sinclair finally called a halt to the class. Dismissing them to return to the cloisters, he held Anteaus and Thomas Ram back. Once the class had cleared away, he turned to the pair.

"I have been called away by Abelard de Bottreaux," he said. "If you do not know the name, you should. He is the leader of Triton's Hellions. I do not know how long I will be gone, but I will be entrusting my class to the two of you. Anteaus, you are clearly an excellent swordsman and you have a gift for teaching. You will continue my class until I return and later tonight, after sup, I will go over the moves you will continue with until I return. Is that clear?"

Anteaus nodded, but he appeared puzzled, as Sinclair turned to Thomas.

"And you," Sinclair said to the big farmer. "You do not have the skill that I need to teach, but you have drive and determination and I believe you will be of great help to Anteaus. Listen to him, learn from him, and if he needs you to walk among the ranks and encourage men in the midst of their training, then you will do so. I have seen you with the men. You have a good manner about you and they like you. Will you do this?"

Thomas nodded solemnly. "I will, m'lord," he said. "I'm sorry we are losing you."

"Only temporarily," Sinclair said. "For now, make sure this field is picked up of any weapons left behind, and after sup, you will join Anteaus in my cottage to go over the future lessons."

"Aye, m'lord."

"Be on your way."

Thomas moved away swiftly, heading down the slope to make sure the servants collected all of the weapons.

Sinclair and Anteaus watched him go.

"You," Sinclair finally said to the man. "Walk with me."

"With pleasure, my lord."

Sinclair headed off toward the village with Anteaus walking beside him. Overhead, birds flew in formation toward the west, looking to find shelter for the coming night, and they were loud enough that both Sinclair and Anteaus looked up to watch them go.

It was a still, cool evening.

Peaceful.

Perhaps the last peace for Sinclair for what was to come.

"I'm afraid I've not been here long enough for you to form an opinion about me," Sinclair said. "I spent six long years at Blackchurch before I went to Toxandria, and now it seems I must depart again."

Anteaus looked at him. "That is because your skills are much in demand, my lord," he said. "That is quite admirable."

That wasn't exactly the truth, but Sinclair gave the man a lopsided smile. "Possibly," he said. "But the point is that we've not had much opportunity to truly become acquainted, but I want to compliment you on how you teach the class. Your manner is good, as are your skills."

"Thank you, my lord."

"Do you want to be a Blackchurch trainer?"

Anteaus shrugged. "I did not come here with the intention of being one."

"Why *did* you come here?"

"Because I wanted to accomplish something my brothers have not," he said. "I come from a very old family, my lord. My eldest brother is Sheriff of Westmorland and my middle brother has taken duties from my father due to the weakness of his heart. The physic suggested he was too burdened with overseeing our home, Castle Keld, so my middle brother has taken up the mantle."

"Where is Castle Keld?"

"Very far to the north, near the Scottish marches."

"You must have a good deal of experience fighting Scots."

"More than my share," Anteaus agreed. "For quite some time, I've been splitting my time between Berwick Castle and Pelinom Castle, where my sister is married to Lord Blackadder."

Sinclair thought on those castles because they sounded familiar. "Pelinom," he repeated. "Is that not the demesne of de Velt?"

"Aye," Anteaus said. "My sister married the heir, so they live far to the north, but the Scots still fear the name of de Velt. They avoid Pelinom when they will attack other castles."

"And splitting your time on the Scots marches has afforded you a good deal of practice with your sword," Sinclair said. "It makes sense now why your skills are so polished."

"Mayhap, but a man can always learn more," Anteaus said. Then he cast a glance at Sinclair. "It was an honor fighting alongside you at the Black Cock. I can easily see where you have earned your moniker."

Sinclair sighed faintly. "That was not the norm here at Black-church," he said. "In fact, the past week has not been the norm at all, at least not with me. I'm the man who does his job, goes to bed, and repeats the process the next day. There is nothing much exciting that happens in my life other than teaching recruits. But the past week... it has been different. I hope you will not judge me by it."

Anteaus came to a halt, causing Sinclair to stop as well. When Sinclair looked at him curiously, Anteaus seemed quite serious.

"I am in no position to judge any man, least of all you," he said. "May we be honest, my lord? I know you are suspicious of me, but I swear to you, I do not want your position. I am helping because I have been asked to help, because I am well trained, but usurping you has never been my plan. However, I would like to ask this—if you are truly leaving tomorrow with the pirate, will you consider taking me with you? Creston and Cruz can teach your class again until you return, but I feel as if you and I have not had a chance to get to know one another, and I should like the chance to earn your trust if I am to be part of Blackchurch."

Sinclair's eyebrows lifted. "And you want to earn my trust working alongside me with pirates?"

Anteaus shook his head. "Do not forget that I was in the chamber when you told Lord Exmoor about your plan to seek the pirates to help with the return of the lady," he said. "I heard what you said so I know that is why Lord Abelard is here. He is going to help you rescue the lady."

Sinclair cleared his throat softly, averting his gaze. "He is going to try," he said. "But much depends on Santiago de Fernandez. He is the one whose help I truly want."

"Then please take me," Anteaus said. "I know that a Blackchurch trainer can never take sides in a battle. I heard the arguments about it. I know that the other trainers cannot go with you for fear of losing their positions, but I am only a recruit. I am not employed by Blackchurch, nor am I sworn to Lord Exmoor. You may need help and it seems logical for me to go with you."

Sinclair shook his head. "It is a generous offer, but you should know that Payne has already asked to come," he said. "These are extraordinarily dangerous men, de Bourne."

"I fought with, and for, Ajax de Velt," Anteaus said. "The Dark Lord himself. My sister married his heir. That being the case, I have served with the most dangerous man in a generation, so pirates do not frighten me. Can Payne say the same thing?"

Sinclair could see that the man was serious, but it baffled him. "Payne is one of the most capable knights I've ever seen," he said. "He can handle himself. But you... you would go simply to earn my trust?"

Anteaus nodded. "I can think of no better test. Can you?"

Sinclair couldn't. "I suppose it makes sense if you are to assist me in my duties," he said. "But most assistants remain with the trainer. They do not go through the rest of their classes, meaning your training will stop with me."

Anteaus shrugged. "Strangely, that does not distress me," he said. "I've thought about it. I came to Blackchurch to prove something to myself and mayhap even seek out a new adventure. I had a few reasons, I think. But nearly since I arrived, I've been helping with the swordsmanship class and I like it. There is satisfaction in seeing a man discover his combat talents. Mayhap this is where I belong for now."

"And going with me and the pirates will be quite a new adventure."

Anteaus grinned, giving him a shrug. "Mayhap I'll discover a new love for piracy in the meantime."

"If you fought with de Velt, I think piracy might be too tame for you."

Anteaus laughed softly. "Possibly," he said, sobering. "Will you at least think about allowing me to go with you?"

"I will think on it."

"Thank you."

Sinclair merely nodded, but there was warmth in his eyes that hadn't been there before when dealing with Anteaus. He left the man and headed back to his cottage, amused that first Payne wanted to go with him and then Anteaus. Payne he could understand, because the man still had an emotional attachment to Elisiana. But Anteaus' reason was different—as he'd said, they'd hardly worked together, certainly not enough to build trust, and Anteaus knew he was suspicious of his motives. Sinclair didn't think he'd been that obvious, but he evidently had been. So Anteaus, like any good colleague, wanted to walk through fire with him as a means of building trust. And have an adventure. Sinclair didn't blame him on that account. Life, in and of itself, was an adventure.

This would just be another part of Life.

By morning, Creston had agreed to teach Payne's class and Fox had agreed to teach Sinclair's.

CHAPTER THIRTEEN

Fremington Castle

S HE HAD A guard on her.

Elisiana's parents were so afraid she was going to try to run again that they'd assigned a servant to watch over her, a woman who went everywhere with her and never let her out of her sight. She'd known the woman since childhood and although they'd never been close, they'd had a pleasant relationship.

Not anymore.

It had been days since her return home, and with each passing hour, Elisiana was becoming more and more determined to escape. The only time she was allowed a moment alone was when she bathed or slept. Everything else was monitored. Her mother tried to spend time with her daily, as did her father, but she shut them out. She was miserable, longing for the life she'd built for herself, longing for the man she'd left behind.

She was in turmoil.

But she still had her drawings. Vellum and charcoal were plentiful at Fremington because over the years, she'd managed to acquire quite a supply. Therefore, she took to drawing the lewdest pictures she could conceive of, mostly of women naked above the waist, and passed them out to soldiers and servants. She would leave them in the hall for all to see, including her father, who flew into a frenzy when they first started appearing. He and Aristeo ran all over the castle trying to find them, like hidden gems, until all of them were confiscated, but even then, the soldiers kept them hidden. They were quite beautifully done and very realistic. Considering Elisiana had used her own breasts and torso to draw them, they were quite realistic.

Today, she sat in her mother's garden in the midst of a warm summer's day with her drawing implements at hand, like weapons. Weapons against her parents. She'd had a small table brought out for her and sat on a bench while drawing naked women. Her guard, the female servant, tried to speak to her about them, to tell her to stop, and she'd barked at the woman so viciously that she made her cry. Normally, she would have never done such a thing, but her misery was coming out all over the place. She wanted her parents and everyone else to know just how unhappy she was. If they knew, maybe they'd have more sympathy.

Maybe they'd take her back where they'd found her.

Her latest drawing was the image of a woman from the neck to her breasts, and she was in the process of drawing a man suckling the woman's breasts. She couldn't quite get the lips right, however, so she'd been working on it since morning, carefully sketching, using a small, polished silver mirror to look at her own pursed lips to get it right. She was so intent on the curve of the bottom lip that she failed to notice someone entering the garden. The figure lingered for a few moments, watching her, before speaking.

"Lisi." It was Aristeo. "We must speak."

Since her brother had stayed away from her since her return to Fremington, his appearance was somewhat surprising. Elisiana heard his voice, realized who it was, and then paused in her drawing.

"I have nothing to say to you, Téo," she said. "Go away."

"I will after we speak," he said. "But we must talk. We have always been able to talk. I am sorry if you view me as the enemy, but I was carrying out Papa's orders. You know that, so I do not understand why you are so angry with me."

She stopped drawing and looked at him. "You do not understand?" she said as if he'd just said something ridiculous. "Of course you understand. I explained it to you when you came to the Black Cock. But rather than show compassion to your only sister, you chose violence against me."

Aristeo took a deep breath, averting his gaze. "I am not proud of that," he said. "I would have killed anyone who hurt you as I did. But you gave me no choice. You were trying to hit me with that spiked club."

"I was defending myself!"

"Why are you being so stupid?"

"Me?" she said, aghast. "*I'm* being stupid?"

He nodded. "You are," he insisted. "You seem to think that your desires are the only thing that matter in this world, and that is stupid."

"It is not!"

"You are part of a family, Elisiana," he said angrily. "We all have family obligations that we cannot ignore, yet you run off as if the mere gesture will cause Papa to change his mind and exclude you from the obligations we all have. Just because you do not want to be part of us does mean you *aren't* part of us. You are. And you are teaching Diaz and Esteban to be rebellious and not listen to Papa. Is that what you want to teach them? To be wicked to our parents like you have been?"

Elisiana was taken aback by his passionate scolding. Technically, everything he said was true. But that didn't stop her from feeling so very alone in what she was going through. Maybe she was wrong— maybe she'd been wrong to revolt against her parents from the beginning. But she knew, in her heart, that it wasn't wrong to want to be happy.

"I thought you knew me better than that," she said. "I am not going to justify my actions to you, Téo. You see what you want to see."

"I see a sister who is refusing to honor her parents."

"And I see a brother who has stolen my happiness," she snarled. "I hope you are happy with yourself. I hope it was worth my hatred."

With that, she turned back to her drawing, fighting off the tears. He hoped he would go away, but he didn't. He came closer, to a bench that was a few feet away. She could see him in her periphery, sitting down.

"Téo, I will not tell you again," she said. "Go away. I have nothing more to say to you."

He sighed heavily. "Papa owes Uncle Robert a good deal of money."

"That does not concern me."

"He is paying the debt by marrying you to Adolph."

That brought Elisiana to a halt. She lifted her head, looking at her brother in horror. "And you know this for certain?"

Aristeo nodded. "I do," he said. "He thinks I do not know, but I overheard him speaking with Mama about it."

Elisiana was shocked. "What on earth could he owe Uncle Robert money for?" she said. "What did he do?"

Aristeo shrugged. "The new house that Mama wanted in the country, near Atherington?" he said. "Papa did not have the money to pay for it, so he borrowed it from Uncle Robert. When Uncle Robert demanded payment, Papa did not have all of it, so they discussed your marrying Adolph to keep him away from a merchant's daughter he is fond of. If you want to know my opinion about that, I think it was Uncle Robert's intention all along. Adolph may be a knight for the Earl of Lincoln, but he is not a very good one. He will never be more than he is. A marriage to you would make him the son-in-law, and eventually a brother-in-law, of a count."

Elisiana set her charcoal down. "And I become the sacrificial lamb."

"Exactly."

Elisiana didn't know what to say. So much made sense now, but in that knowledge came new hope.

"But if it is money Papa needs, then I have money," she said. "Mayhap he will take my money and cancel the contract."

Aristeo shook his head. "It cost Papa a good deal of money to build that house," he said, then added bitterly: "A house that Mama does not use. It simply sits, empty, watching the passage of time and probably wondering why no one lives there."

Elisiana wasn't giving up on the buyout subject. "How much did it cost Papa?"

"More than you have."

"I have a good deal."

"Do you have a thousand pounds?"

That question poked holes in her rising hope. "Nay," she said reluctantly. "But I can earn it if Papa would only let me—"

"He will not," Aristeo said, cutting her off. "He has promised you to Adolph to pay off the debt and there is no hope of changing that. Uncle Robert wants you for his wife's son. Papa can do nothing."

Elisiana was trying not to lose hope, but it was difficult. She could feel it slipping away. "Then why did you tell me if nothing can be done?" she asked.

He looked at her. "Because I did not want you to continue acting the fool while Papa has done this because he had no choice," he said. "If you want to be angry with someone, be angry with Uncle Robert. I believe this was his scheme. And Adolph—that idiot—is simply a pawn like you are."

Elisiana sat forward, elbows on her table while she rubbed her forehead as if to wipe away the pain the entire situation was causing her. "I am sorry that Papa has his troubles," she said. "But I should not be the means by which he gets out of those troubles. He is making his trouble *my* trouble, for life. He will not be married to Adolph forever—*I* will."

"I know," Aristeo said in a genuine show of sympathy. "But it is the way of things. Parents have dominion over their children and we must do as they say. I will do it to my children and you will do it to yours."

"I will not make my children miserable," she snapped back softly. "I will listen to them. I will try to understand them. And I will help them where needed."

Aristeo stood up from his seat. "And I am sure you will make a very good mother," he said. "But imagine if you had a daughter and she refused to do what you told her. She ran off and hid for six months. Imagine how much anguish you would feel."

Elisiana turned her head away. "I would never force her to do any-thing that would make her utterly miserable," she said. "Téo, I have met a man I intend to marry. He is wonderful and kind and handsome. Believe me when I tell you that Adolph will *not* be my husband."

Aristeo frowned. "Who is this man?"

She sat back from the table. "You are a knight, are you not?" she said. "You trained at Pevensey while I was there, so you understand how the world of knights work."

"I do."

"What do you know about the Blackchurch Guild?"

His eyebrows lifted. "Blackchurch?" he repeated. "I know they train killers. Men with no feeling, no soul. Warlords pay a high price for the men who do what Blackchurch trains them to do."

"Do you know anyone who has passed their training?"

He shook his head. "Nay," he said. "Why do you ask?"

"Because Blackchurch was in the village where I was living. North of it, anyway," she said. "Did you know that?"

Aristeo had to ponder that. "I think I did," he said. "I knew it was in Devon, somewhere."

Elisiana studied her brother for a moment. Aristeo was a good knight, but a better administrator. He helped their father manage

Fremington quite nicely, which was why she was surprised he'd allowed their father to borrow money for the country home that Sybil wanted, only to let it sit vacant.

But that seemed to be water under the bridge now.

She was to pay the price for her mother's folly.

"I worked as a tavern maid in a tavern that the Blackchurch trainers frequent," she said after a moment. "Men who train those soulless killers. I can say from experience that they were kind, considerate, and brilliant. They are also fiercely loyal to one another."

Aristeo shook his head, a distasteful expression on his features. "Interesting," he said, but he didn't mean it. "Why are you telling me?"

"Because the man I intend to marry is a Blackchurch trainer," she said. "He is also a former master knight of Kenilworth. He is the most accomplished, talented, and kind man that I know. And even now, he is coming for me. I know he is."

Aristeo eyed her seriously. "We have an army to stop him," he said. "If you truly believe that, then you must send him word not to come. Papa will kill him."

Thoughts of Sinclair brought her a warm, comforting feeling. "Not him," she said. "They call him the Swordsman. He will find a way."

Aristeo didn't know what to think. If what she said was true, then perhaps Blackchurch was over the hill, preparing to rain hell down upon Fremington, which hadn't seen a proper siege in decades. They had an army, but not a hugely experienced one, and any defense they every really needed came from Santiago, who moored his ships in their river.

He hoped she wasn't serious.

"Lisi, if Papa does not kill any man trying to take you away, then Santiago will," he said. "If any of this is true, then you would do better to send the Blackchurch man a missive and tell him not to come. Otherwise, he will be walking into his death."

She lifted an eyebrow. "A Blackchurch knight? A former master knight?" She shook her head. "You are fooling yourself if you think so."

"So are you if you think Papa will not do everything he can to stop him."

The conversation was taking a downturn again, and Elisiana didn't want to go down that road. She was already upset with Aristeo for what he'd done, and this conversation hadn't promised to improve things. Picking up her charcoal, she refocused on her drawing.

"Good day to you, Teo," she said as she began to shade the lip again. "I have work to do."

Aristeo watched her return to a drawing that looked like a head. When he peered closer and saw what it was, he hissed with disgust.

"Don't you know that what you are doing is horrifying at best?" he said. "You are putting Papa and Mama in a terrible position. You are embarrassing them!"

"Then mayhap they should not have sent you to brutally take me home."

Aristeo slammed his hand down on her table, snatched the vellum, and began to crumple it. "Mayhap they should not have," he snarled. "But they did. You are not worthy of the de Verra name, Elisiana. You have brought shame to us all with your behavior. I hope your marriage to Adolph punishes you for the rest of your life."

With that, he stormed off, leaving Elisiana pondering his words. She felt a little as if he'd smacked her around, a verbal assault that had been cruel and to the point.

But he wasn't wrong.

Pulling out another piece of vellum, she tried not to let his words bother her. They were wrong, she was right, and nothing was going to change her mind.

Where are you, Sin?

CHAPTER FOURTEEN

Raleigh Park Castle

"WHAT SHOULD WE do?"

Robert de Norbury was looking at the missive in his hand, the one from his brother-in-law, Adriano. The question from his wife was one he'd been asking himself for the better part of the day, ever since a messenger arrived from Fremington Castle informing him that his niece, Elisiana, had been recovered and was currently back home.

What should we do?

Frankly, he had no bloody idea.

What he should have done was tell Adriano the very moment it happened. He should have been forthright and simply told the man, but he couldn't bring himself to do it. Even now, he couldn't bring himself to do it.

But he had to.

"They brought her home," he muttered, still looking at the carefully written message. "He says that Elisiana has been recovered."

His wife was looking between him and the missive nervously. "Does he say where she was found?"

"He does not."

"Nothing about where she was and what she was doing?"

"Nay."

Helena, Lady de Norbury, was as nervous as a cat. "This is terrible," she said, wandering away and wringing her hands. "But this may also be our salvation."

"Why would you think that?"

"Because she may have been with a man for all we know," she said, whirling to face her husband. "She may have returned to them impure. Can they prove that she isn't? We can break the betrothal based on that."

Robert cocked his head thoughtfully. "It is possible," he said. "But you forget that Elisiana is my payment for the money I loaned her father, and I do not want to discount her value so easily. I can sell the betrothal for more than enough money to settle the debt, you know. A rich Frenchman. A titled lord from Saxony. You can write to Adolph's grandfather and tell him of the situation. Mayhap he can find me a buyer."

Helena nodded, though she was still twisting her hands. That was a bad habit she had, one she'd tried to keep from Robert when they were courting because a relatively unattractive widow with bad habits and tics wasn't exactly a desirable marriage prospect. The only thing she had that was worth pursing was her dead husband's fortune—a fortune that was now Robert's, large enough that he could loan money to his brother-in-law.

But that brother-in-law might not be so understanding of the bind they now found themselves in.

"I will try," she said. Then she tugged at her hands, harder, and began to pace. "Oh, Adolph! Why did you have to marry the merchant's daughter? Do you not know what we have to face now with your Uncle Adriano?"

Robert put the missive on the table. "He married her just to spite us," he said. "He says it was love, but it was spite. I know it was spite.

Your son is going to cause me a great deal of trouble, Helena. This is trouble I do not need."

Helena cowered because she was used to cowering from husbands. The last one she had liked to let his open palm fly into her face on occasion. Sometimes he didn't even need a reason. He simply struck her. Robert hadn't yet, but the marriage was relatively new. There was always a first time. Therefore, she stayed clear of Robert as he voiced his displeasure.

"I understand," she said evenly. "Adolph knows that what he did was wrong, but when it involves love, what's a man to do?"

Robert looked at her, frowning. "He does not marry another when he is already betrothed—*that* is what he is to do," he said. "Now I must explain all of this to Adriano and pray he does not become too enraged. But I will assure him that a fine husband will be found for Elisiana. It simply will not be Adolph."

"I hope he is not too disappointed."

Robert sighed, returning his attention to the missive. "He will be," he said. "She is rather old to be a new bride, but I will find her a husband. I want my money."

"Will you tell him this?"

Robert nodded. "This is something I must tell him in person," he said. "I will go. In fact, I will go to Fremington and tell him what I am going to do. I will not argue with him or bargain with him. Elisiana's contract belongs to me and Adriano will know that I hold the power now. Not him."

Helena hesitated. "He may not appreciate it if you are too forceful."

"I do not care," Robert said. "He owes me money and I have every right to sell what belongs to me to regain it."

"Even his daughter?"

"Especially his daughter."

Helena wasn't sure she liked the sound of that, but she didn't argue.

"Do as you must," she said reluctantly. "But make sure to bring Francois. If Adriano becomes angry, you will need protection."

She was speaking of the very expensive French knight that Robert insisted on having. He'd purchased the man's fealty last year on a trip to Paris—a knight who used to be an expert executioner, but Robert wanted him as a sort of bodyguard and protector.

He got what he wanted with Sir Francois de Argentan.

"Good idea," he said. "I do not wish to hurt my sister's husband, but if he becomes enraged over Adolph, I will make sure to have Francois in place. You see? He is worth the money, after all."

Helena had her doubts about that but didn't say so. The knight that Robert had purchased with her dead husband's money. In any case, she quit the chamber without another word as Robert sat down at his desk, preparing to send Adriano a missive.

Coming to Fremington shortly.

Short and to the point. Most importantly, it didn't tip Adriano off. For all he knew, Robert was coming to discuss the betrothal. And that was exactly what he wanted Adriano to think because, in a sense, he *was* going to discuss the betrothal.

And he was fairly certain Adriano wasn't going to like it.

Robert, the French swordsman, and ten men-at-arms departed Raleigh Park at dawn the next day.

CHAPTER FIFTEEN

The Argos

THE SEAS WERE surprisingly calm.

The only instance where Sinclair had spent any time on a vessel was when he sailed to Toxandria and then back again, and that was on a cog crowded with men and animals.

This time, it was much different.

Setting off on a misty morning from Blackchurch with Payne and Anteaus beside him, Sinclair followed St. Abelard and the small escort the man had brought with him north to the rambling seaside village of Minehead. It was less than twenty miles from Blackchurch, which meant the travel took less than a day. They arrived in Minehead with plenty of daylight left and St. Abelard headed straight to his vessels.

It was rather impressive seeing them from the top of the bluffs overlooking the sea. Not strangely, there were several of them, but four larger ones had men all over them. Sinclair could see them even from the distance. All of the ships had sails—the smaller ships with two sails and the largest one with three—but they also had the ability to row them because Sinclair could see oars peeking from holes in the hull of the ship. As the wind blew and the seagulls cried overhead, St. Abelard took Sinclair, Payne, and Anteaus to the largest ship he had.

The *Argos*.

As St. Abelard had explained, the smaller ships dotted around the inlet were ancient ones left to him by predecessors. Some of them seaworthy, some not. Some were so old that they were half sinking into the water and never used. But the larger ships were ones that he'd managed to confiscate over the years, and he was quite proud of that. The *Argos* was a former Grecian vessel that was absolutely magnificent. It had a former name that St. Abelard couldn't pronounce, so he named it the *Argos* in honor of that ancient vessel that carried Argonauts.

When Sinclair boarded it, he had to admit that he felt rather like an argonaut himself.

It was in the spirit of another adventure at sea that St. Abelard and his four largest ships departed the next day for the western Devon coast where Santiago hid his ships—poorly—from his rivals. It took the ships more than half a day to reach the bend in the coast where they began their southerly travels, and the mouth of the River Taw was less than ten miles from that point.

That was when the maneuvers began.

Up until that moment, Abelard had been using his captives to row the ships westward. Because of the flow of the tide, the ships moved rather quickly. But once they reached the curve in the coastline where it started traveling south, St. Abelard sent the smallest ship toward the River Taw under a white flag while he unfurled the sails on the remaining three ships and took them out to sea, about three miles from the mouth of the river. They could see the coastline, and the river from that vantage point, but more importantly, they could be seen. White flags were flapping in the wind.

The white flag of parlay.

"This is where the fun begins." St. Abelard came to stand next to Sinclair, who was watching the coastline from the stern. "As I said, Santiago has been gone for many months, but my spies tell me that he has returned recently. However, he may be too busy to talk, but we shall see. You saw me send the *Athena* into the river to catch de Fernandez's attention. Mayhap we can draw him out."

Over to their right, Payne vomited over the side of the boat, coming up with a smile as he wiped his mouth with his arm. "I'm born tae be a pirate," he declared. "I'll get my sea legs soon enough."

Sinclair started laughing as Payne tried to laugh with him, but he ended up dry heaving instead. Anteaus, standing on his other side, was far gone with giggles as Payne struggled against his seasickness. St. Abelard shook his head in disgust.

"And you are a Blackchurch trainer?" he asked.

Payne nodded, wiping the tears from his eyes caused by the upheaving. "Aye, m'laird."

"What do you teach?"

"How tae fight a man," he said. "How tae assess an enemy and discover his weaknesses. How tae exploit the weaknesses."

"I see," said St. Abelard. "And what are *your* weaknesses?"

"I have none, m'laird."

St. Abelard rolled his eyes. "If this ship were to be boarded at this very minute and we had a fight on our hands, you could not kill a man by vomiting on him," he pointed out. "How do you intend to fight if everything is coming out of your stomach?"

Payne didn't miss a beat. "I'd vomit on the deck and cause him tae slip and hit his head," he said. "When he's down, I kill him."

St. Abelard looked at Sinclair in disbelief, but Sinclair was still chuckling. "And he would do exactly that," he said. "There is no wasted movement with Payne. He would kill him one way or the other."

St. Abelard grunted. "I'd like to see that," he admitted. "And you? How do you feel?"

Sinclair's smile faded. "I feel quite well," he said. "But quite anxious to get on with it. I have no way of knowing if my lady has already been forced to marry. The sooner I can get into Fremington, the better."

"What if she's already married?"

Sinclair sighed heavily as he pondered his answer. "I do not know," he said honestly. "I've tried not to think about it."

St. Abelard's gaze lingered on him for a moment. He seemed to be in a much better humor than he was at Blackchurch, and that was because he'd gotten the cog he wanted. St. Denis had promised to have the thing partially disassembled and sent up to him, so he was eagerly awaiting that delivery. He had shipbuilders that could piece the ship together in a week, and she would be perfectly seaworthy, so he was thrilled about that.

Until that could happen, however, he had a task to perform, and given he was dealing with honorable men in the Blackchurch trainers, he was being true to his word. Since he'd spent a few days with Sinclair already, he was becoming more emotionally invested in the situation more than he should be. Emotionally invested was probably too strong a term—he was interested in the situation, as an outside observer. He could see the expression in Sinclair's face when he spoke of Lady Elisiana, and that fascinated him. He remembered the times in his life when he'd felt that way for a woman. It had been a while, but he remembered.

Sinclair was starting to bring it back.

"You'd better let yourself think about it," St. Abelard said after a moment. "If de Fernandez tells you that she's been married and taken away, do you intend to pursue her?"

Sinclair was watching the coastline. "I know you think this is a foolish endeavor, my lord, and I do not blame you," he said. "Were I not involved, I would probably think so also. But there are situations that arise in a man's life that he knows are worth risking everything for, and this is one of them. If she has married the man and he has taken her away, I will follow. I will not involve you, but I will follow."

"And if you catch up to them? Then what?"

Sinclair shrugged. "The man she was betrothed to is a knight for the Earl of Lincoln," he said. "I will go there and I will claim her. I do not know how, but I will. And then I will take her back to Blackchurch where he can never get at her."

"You will not kill him?"

"If he fights me for her, I will do what I have to do."

St. Abelard turned and leaned against the railing, focused on Sinclair. "I'm fascinated by this," he said. "What is it about this woman that lures you so? It is like the call of the siren, and you are answering."

"True," Sinclair said, smiling weakly. "I am not certain what makes her different from other women, only that she is. The one woman who looks into my soul and makes me feel things I've never felt before. Things I want to feel the rest of my life. Have you not ever felt that way before?"

St. Abelard thought on that, nodding. "Aye," he said. "I married her before anyone else could."

"And you do not regret it?"

St. Abelard cleared his throat softly, looking down at his feet. "Not really," he said. "Mary is my wife. We have been together many years. We have two daughters together, but no sons. I know you heard Denis speak of other children, and I do have others. Two boys from a woman in Minehead, a woman who is kind and understanding. I do not regret them, either. A man must have sons to carry on his name."

"And these boys will take over Triton's Hellions?"

"Already, the eldest says he will be a greater pirate than me," he said. "Remember the name St. John de Bottreaux. He likes to be called Black Jack."

"How old is he?"

"He has seen nine years. He'll be formidable in a few more."

"Given that he is your son, he is probably formidable now."

St. Abelard snorted, lifting his gaze to look at Sinclair. "Do you want some advice from an old man?"

"I would accept your advice regardless."

St. Abelard leaned forward. "No mercy," he muttered. "When it comes to the man the lady is supposed to marry, show no mercy. If you do not kill him, it could have fatal consequences."

A smile played on Sinclair's lips. "You are telling a Blackchurch trainer to show no mercy?" he said. "My lord, that is what we train on. No mercy given, no mercy taken."

"Good," St. Abelard said. "If you like, I can take him on board my ship as a captive. He'll never see land again. It will be the same as being dead."

Sinclair's smile broadened. "I can think of no worse fate for any man," he said. "If you are serious, mayhap I will consider it."

"I never jest."

"I would imagine not, my lord."

St. Abelard chuckled and turned around, looking out at the sea again, the coastline, the sky. Off to their right, Payne was dry heaving over the side of the ship because there was nothing left in his stomach, but he still swore he'd make a fine pirate.

Sinclair had no doubt.

The day turned into night and with still no response from de Fernandez, St. Abelard invited Sinclair and Payne and Anteaus down below deck for supper. They ate and drank long into the night even though Payne could hardly keep any of it down. Still, it was a good night of stories, of bonding, and of planning their next move. When Sinclair retired to bed late that night, sleep came easily with dreams of flying fish and stormy waves.

He was awoken in the morning by a cannonball flying over the bow.

CHAPTER SIXTEEN

The Navia

"*M*E PREGUNTO QUÉ *quiere decir mi viejo amigo?*"

Santiago de Fernandez spoke those words to the man by his side, an older man who was the uncle of one of his officers. Luis Sabio, or Wise Luis, as he was called, was something between an oracle and a sage old grandfather when it came to giving advice, so naturally, Santiago asked him.

But Luis Sabio had no quick answer.

"Who knows what your old friend wants?" he said. "Mayhap he is bored and needs conversation of intelligent men. God only knows he will not find it among his own kind."

Santiago grinned. He wasn't a big man, rather short and round, but very sharp. He had wavy hair that was a mixture of silver and dark, and a beard with a cultivated point on it. But in contrast to St. Abelard's loud mouth, Santiago was soft spoken and smiled a good deal. Hardly the behavior of a man who cut the feet off his captives. Even with his smaller stature and amiable demeanor, he was more than a match for St. Abelard.

De Bottreaux's ship, *Athena*, had come bearing a white flag of parlay and lingered just inside the mouth of the river for most of the day before Santiago sent a boat out to meet it. Of course, it told Santiago that his secret mooring location for his vessels was no longer secret, but that didn't matter. He knew exactly where St. Abelard moored his vessels, too. The *Athena* relayed to Santiago that St. Abelard wanted to parlay, a not-so-unusual request, and it wasn't one that caused Santiago any great distress. He and St. Abelard had a treaty of sorts, but he hadn't seen the man in well over a year. Perhaps things had changed. Whatever the reason, he agreed to see him.

Not that Santiago could avoid the man, considering he knew where Santiago hid his fleet.

Therefore, at dawn the next morning an a particularly clear day, Santiago set out with two ships—the *Navia* and the *Santa Maria*, which had been the most prepared to take to sea—and left the shelter of the River Taw then headed to open sea, where St. Abelard and his four ships were waiting. In the early morning light, Santiago could see the vessels dotting the horizon, and the white flags were reflecting the sunlight like tiny dots against the sky. The smell of the sea was strong, the air damp, and it felt good to be at sea again. The truth was that Santiago had been gone for nearly eight months, having only recently returned to his base in England. He was still offloading booty he'd obtained on his quest into the Mediterranean.

But he was more than curious about a parlay request.

Closing in on St. Abelard's ships, he could see something approaching from the south. It was a foggy further out to sea, so by the time he realized what he was seeing, it was too late. The Irish pirates that clung to the Eire coast, troublemakers more than they were businessmen like Santiago and St. Abelard, were coming up from the Celtic Sea. Santiago saw, quite clearly, when they fired a salvo at St. Abelard's ships, and he saw quite clearly when St. Abelard fired back. In fact, St. Abelard was turning his ships toward the Irish contingent and preparing to engage.

"Ah!" Santiago said with excitement. "The Irish *bastardos* have made this a great day! We will help my old friend!"

Santiago only had two ships, but they were his biggest and he was proud of the cannons he had on board. The wind was picking up, blowing them in the direction of what was already sizing up to be a naval battle. Calling themselves *Clann mhac Fragarach*, or the Sons of Fragarach, which was the sword that the Celtic sea god Manannan wielded in battle, the Irish were a smaller faction but a vicious one. As they closed in on Triton's Hellions, the Demons of the Sea came in on their southern flank.

It was a short battle.

C3

USING A ROPE that had snapped from an overhead sail, Payne went flying overhead, over the gap between the *Argos* and the ship that had attacked them, and landed on the deck of the Irish cog. St. Abelard had managed to damage it with his cannonballs, so the ship was beginning to list slightly and the rudder was smashed. It wasn't going anywhere. Swords and fists were flying as the men from the *Argos* boarded the Irish vessel that had fired on them.

"See?" Payne yelled above the smoke and fighting. "I *do* make a good pirate!"

Sinclair had to laugh at the Scotsman taking down Irish pirates who got in his way. He was heavily armed, dressed in mail though without his helm, and he was having a fine time beating Irish arse. Sinclair came over after him, boarding the Irish ship at St. Abelard's order by leaping from one ship to the other, and was immediately confronted by unhappy Irish sailors.

The Swordsman lived up to his name that day. There were headless bodies everywhere, and by the time more ships got involved, the battle was nearly over. Anteaus, who was the first one to board the Irish ship when it came close, did his own serious damage below decks. Bloodied men were struggling to come up from below, but the sounds of fighting down there were savage. Anteaus finally appeared dragging a man with him, tossing him at St. Abelard's feet once the man boarded the Irish ship.

Anteaus pointed at him.

"He was hiding below, dressed like a lad," he said. "I do believe we have the captain."

St. Abelard glared down at the man at his feet. "You're not Mac-Phee," he said suspiciously. "Who are you?"

A young, pale man lifted his head and pulled off the hood of the cloak he was wearing. "MacPhee is dead," he said, spitting blood and eventually a tooth on the deck. "I'm Berkant."

St. Abelard frowned. "Berkant," he repeated as if it sounded familiar to him. "You're one of his crew, I think. Did I not see you in Dublin once? In that place down by the sea called the Wind and the Woman?"

He was referring to a tavern heavily visited by most of the pirates along the west coast of England, Wales, and Scotland. Somehow, the Wind and the Woman wasn't off-limits for them to visit as long as they spent a good deal of money. Berkant was rubbing his jaw where Anteaus had hit him, shrugging to the question.

"I've seen a lot of people," he said, mostly avoiding giving an answer. "Are you going to kill me now and take my ship?"

St. Abelard turned to look at the *Argos*, which hadn't sustained any real damage other than the sails. Then he looked at the boat they were standing on, stomping on the deck to test the sturdiness of the wood.

"Where *is* MacPhee?" he asked pointedly.

"I told you," Berkant said. "He's dead."

"Did you kill him?"

Berkant looked at him, irritated. "He died a month ago off the coast of Porto," he said. "The fleet is mine now. We fought for it and I won."

"Nay, you did not," St. Abelard said. "*I* did."

"What do you mean?"

"This ship is now mine!"

He motioned for his men to take Berkant and his men away, dragging them over to the *Argos* to meet a captive's fate. The English were swarming on the larger vessel, but St. Abelard had caught sight of other ships to the south during the battle and now could see them clearly. The bright red skeleton against the white sail told him exactly who it was.

"It looks as if the Demons have the other ship," he muttered. "Damn scavengers. This was *my* battle."

Sinclair had no idea what the man meant. He and Anteaus were standing together, trying to figure out what he was referring to, when Payne walked up carrying a sack that was full of something that was quite heavy. It was also making noise, and if Sinclair didn't know better, he would swear it was coin. Payne was pale from having been vomiting since yesterday, but the fight had energized him. So had the bag of coin. Like most warriors, he was happiest in a battle.

"Who are those fools?" he demanded, pointing toward the smaller ship off the stern. "I saw them come in from the east."

"The Demons of the Sea have arrived," St. Abelard muttered, watching the larger of the two Castilian ships approach the vessel they were standing on. Ropes began to fly over to the listing ship so they could come alongside and secure the ships from floating away from one another, but St. Abelard marched over to the starboard side and started shouting to them.

"This is *my* ship!" he boomed. "I'll let you have the smaller one, but this one is mine!"

Some men yelled back, speaking Spanish, and a few of them laughed. Somewhere in the crowd of Castilian pirates, a voice rose.

"I am disappointed that you do not wish to share with me, my old friend," said a man. "After I took care of the second ship attacking you, still, you will not share?"

St. Abelard recognized the voice but couldn't see the man who was calling to him. On his right, Sinclair was standing with his sword ready, and on his left, Payne and Anteaus were prepared to leap across the water and descend on the arrogant men who were evidently laughing at them, but St. Abelard held up a hand to ease them. He knew they wanted to fight, but there was no need now.

The very man he wanted to see had arrived.

"De Fernandez?" he called. "Show yourself!"

A short man with long, wavy black and silver hair came to the railing, waving at St. Abelard with a joyful smile on his face.

"It is good to see you!" he said. "It has been a long time!"

St. Abelard's lips twitched with a smile. "That is because you have been gone a very long time," he said. "Now you are home, and look what I have given you—a new ship to take with you."

He was pointing to the second, smaller Irish cog, and Santiago acknowledged it with a firm nod of his head.

"I accept," he said. "I am coming over to see you!"

St. Abelard shrugged. He supposed one ship was as good as another to meet. He stood back as the Castilian sailors began to use their ropes to pull the ships closer together.

"The devil has appeared, de Reyne," he said in a low voice. "Be prepared to tell the man what you want quickly. Do not waste his time."

Sinclair nodded, watching the Castilians as they began to vault over the side of their ship and onto the Irish cog. St. Abelard ordered his English pirates back onto the *Argos* because whenever two pirate factions were too close to one another, it was inevitable that a fight would break out, and he didn't want that happening. As his men went back about their ship, more Castilians came onto the cog, including Santiago. He went straight to St. Abelard and embraced him like one would a long-lost brother.

"My dear man," Santiago said, patting St. Abelard on the cheek. "You have sent for me and here I am. Did you send for me just to help you with the Irish?"

St. Abelard snorted. "The Irish were most unexpected," he said. "But thank you for your assistance, and you are welcome for your new ship."

Santiago glanced off to the southwest where the ship was bobbing in the current. "Not as grand as this ship, but it will do," he said, returning his attention to St. Abelard. "Now that I have come, tell me what you wish to speak of. How can I be of assistance?"

He was to the point and so was St. Abelard. He pointed to Sinclair. "This man serves my cousin at the Blackchurch Guild," he said. "He is one of their trainers, a man known as the finest swordsman in all of England. He was also a master knight at Kenilworth, so he is highly skilled, highly trained. This man is an elite among elites and from a good family. Now that I have introduced you properly, I will let him tell you why you have been summoned."

All eyes turned to Sinclair as he faced a man who looked more like a merchant or someone's grandfather than a pirate, but here was Santiago de Fernandez in the flesh. This was the moment he'd been waiting for and it had come swiftly.

But he was prepared.

"My lord," he said, dipping his head in a show of respect. "I come on behalf of your cousin, Elisiana de Fernandez y de Verra. She is in distress, my lord. She hoped you could help. *I* hope you can help. That is why I asked Abelard for help securing an audience with you."

The mention of Elisiana changed Santiago's demeanor immediately. He went from smiling at St. Abelard to being instantly concerned with the subject matter. Sinclair could see a deadly flicker in those dark eyes that hadn't been there before, something that hinted at who this man was and what he was capable of.

The Demon of the Sea.

"What's this?" Santiago said. "What has happened to my dear Lisi?"

Before he answered, Sinclair quickly turned to Payne. "Clear every-one off this ship," he muttered. "This is conversation between me and Santiago alone and I may only have one chance, so move everyone. Quickly."

Payne nodded and turned to Anteaus, whispering the orders. They swiftly moved away and began shouting at the men, moving them away from Sinclair and St. Abelard and Santiago. Abruptly, everyone was moving off the ship, heading back where they belonged, and when Sinclair was satisfied, he turned to Santiago.

"Apologies, my lord," he said. "I do not think we need an audience for this."

"*What* has happened to Lisi?" Santiago demanded.

Sinclair could see how anxious the man was. *Good*, he thought. *This may yet go in my favor.*

But he wasn't counting on it.

"If you will allow me to briefly describe the situation first," Sinclair said. "Lisi and I met because she had run away from home. Her father is forcing her to marry a man of his choosing, a man most foul. He has not been respectful or even kind to Elisiana. Because of this, and because of her father's refusal to break the betrothal, Lisi ran away and ended up in Exebridge."

Santiago was frowning. "Adriano is *forcing* her to marry?" he said. "Why is he doing this?"

Sinclair shook his head. "I do not know," he said. "But Elisiana does not like this man. She cannot even tolerate him and, as I said, he has been most crude with her. When I met her, we were friendly at first. Simply polite conversation. But… Well, to explain it concisely, we wish to be married, but her brother found where she had been hiding and took her back to Fremington. Most violently, I might add, because she put up a fight. I have come to you in the hope that you would intercede. Truly, my lord, you are our only hope, and if you believe Elisiana should be married to a man who adores her and who will always be good to her, then I hope you will, indeed, intercede on our behalf. And that is why I have come. Thank you for listening."

There it was, all wrapped up neatly for Santiago to process. But it wasn't the conversation he was expecting, so he appeared a bit baffled at first. He looked between St. Abelard and Sinclair before it finally began to sink in.

"*Who* is this man that has been forced upon *mi corazon*?" he asked.

"His name is Adolph de Rade," Sinclair said. "He is a knight with the Earl of Lincoln, but he is also the stepson of Elisiana's Uncle Robert."

"De Norbury?" Santiago said, aghast. "*That* man?"

"Aye, that man."

Santiago made a face. "I never liked him," he said, rather forcefully. "He is greedy. He sees what his sister has and he covets it. But why should Adriano betroth his daughter to his wife's son? Surely there are far better prospects out there for the daughter of a *conde castellano*."

"I do not know, my lord," Sinclair said. "All I know is that it was so terrible, Elisiana ran away from it. But her brother found her several days ago and had to fight to take her back to Fremington. It was a terrible scene. For all I know, she has already been forced to wed de Rade, so time is of the essence. I pray you consider helping us. Please."

Santiago was already nodding. "*Si*, of course," he said. "But what do you want me to do?"

Sinclair shrugged. "If they are not already married, then convince Adriano to break the betrothal," he said. "I know you do not know me, my lord, but St. Denis de Bottreaux can vouch for my character. So can anyone at Kenilworth Castle. I may not have a great title, or great wealth, but I will be a good husband to Elisiana. She is a very special woman, my lord, although I'm sure I do not have to tell you that."

Santiago's gaze drifted over him. "Special enough that you want to break her betrothal and marry her?"

"Aye, my lord, that is the idea."

"What if they are already married?"

St. Abelard had asked him the same question. Sinclair could do nothing more than shrug. "I do not suppose I could convince you to take him prisoner and drop him in the sea somewhere?" he said. Then he grinned weakly. "I did not mean that. Forgive me."

"That is the greatest thing you have said yet," Santiago said, elbowing St. Abelard. "Take this man and drop him in the sea? I have done more with less provocation. Of course I will rid you of him. I will be happy to."

Sinclair chuckled. "I did not mean to sign the man's death warrant," he said. "All I want is to separate them. What he does with his life does not concern me so long as it does not involve Elisiana. And although I do not have wealth that you are accustomed to, I will pay you for your efforts. Any agreement we can come to will be satisfactory with me."

Santiago looked him up and down. "Payment?" he said, grinning. Then he pointed to the smaller Irish cog. "I have already received my payment. Abelard is giving me this cog for my troubles. But I should have somewhere to keep it. Someplace safe."

St. Abelard snorted. "Take it up the River Taw like you do the rest of your vessels," he said. "You are not so clever that I did not know about your ships, Santiago."

"I was not thinking about the mouth of the river," Santiago said as he turned to him. "I was thinking of Lundy Island."

Immediately, St. Abelard scowled. "That is *my* island."

Santiago shrugged. "You have brought this man to me seeking my help," he said. "And I helped you with the Irish *bastardos*. I would think you would want to show me a measure of friendship and let me take my ships to Lundy Island. The river is so dirty—and the ships drag the bottom at low tide."

Sinclair looked at St. Abelard, trying to keep the pleading expression off his face, but St. Abelard saw it anyway. He clenched his teeth angrily.

"It is *my island*," he repeated.

"I know, *mi amigo*," Santiago said soothingly. He wanted something and knew butting heads with St. Abelard wasn't going to get it, so he was trying to sound sympathetic. "Let me have the western side and I swear I will not bother you. We can both have the island and it will be well protected from those Irish. And also from the French. They are a thorn in my side and I know they want the *Fountainebleau* returned. I will help you protect it."

Those were the magic words for St. Abelard. Someone to help him protect his prize? How could he refuse? "The French are dogs," he said flatly. "I hate every one of them."

"And they hate you," Santiago said, rather dramatically. "Let me help you protect your beautiful French ship. It seems like a small price to pay for me to help your cousin's man, eh?"

St. Abelard was verging on a tantrum again. He looked at Sinclair, jabbing a finger at him. "This is your fault," he said. "You did this!"

Sinclair struggled to keep a straight face. "But think of what you have gotten out of this deal already, my lord," he said. "Not only will Lord Santiago help you protect your island, but Lord Exmoor has given you the cog you very much wanted. It was certainly worth the deal, was it not?"

St. Abelard didn't think so but kept his mouth shut. He was wise enough, and experienced enough, to know how deals were made. He was still shaking his finger at Sinclair, without further berating him, before turning to Santiago.

"There is a big cove on the west side that you may use," he said. "But station no men on the island. And I expect fifty pounds a year in tribute!"

Santiago laughed. "There, you see?" he said. "It was not so painful for you to be friendly. I will give you the first year's tribute today, my greedy friend."

St. Abelard grumbled and stomped away, heading back to his ship, as Santiago continued to laugh at him. As St. Abelard climbed over the railing to the *Argos* and his men prepared to set sail, Santiago called after him.

"Where are you going?" he said.

St. Abelard scowled at him, leaning on the rail. "Home!" he said. "My work here is done. I promised to bring the two of you together and I have done that, so take that ungrateful, lovesick man with you and good riddance to you all!"

Santiago's laughter returned. "Do you not want to come?" he said. "We could work together, you and I!"

St. Abelard waved him off brusquely. "I am going *home!*"

Santiago continued to smile, waving at him as if waving at his best friend in the world. He even blew kisses, clearly making fun of him. The Castilians were having a good laugh at St. Abelard's expense. As the *Argos* began to pull away, heading back to her base near Minehead, Santiago returned his attention to Sinclair.

For a moment, he studied the man, looking him over again, perhaps trying to determine just how sincere he was about Elisiana and the betrothal. But that was a foolish thought because he could see it in the man's eyes.

He was missing something he very much wanted returned to him.

"Now," Santiago said quietly, "come with me, on my ship. We are going back to Fremington. I will see what my cousin has done with my lovely Lisi and why he is forcing her to marry this disgusting man."

Sinclair felt a surge of hope. "Thank you," he said with sincerity. "I shall forever be in your debt."

Santiago looked down at the big hand that was holding the enormous, bloodied sword. He may have presented a jovial, kind appearance, but that was far from the case. He was as sharp as a razor when it came to things he needed or wanted.

And it was possible that he wanted something.

"You are a swordsman, you say?" he said.

"Aye, my lord."

"Then mayhap you will pledge that sword to me to pay that debt."

"If you require it, it shall be yours."

That response made Santiago very happy. With a big smile, he clapped Sinclair on the shoulder and indicated his ship.

"I have a plan to get to Lisi," he said. "Come with me and we shall discuss it."

With Payne and Anteaus in tow, Sinclair became the guest of the Demons of the Sea.

CHAPTER SEVENTEEN

Fremington Castle

SHE STILL HAD the guard.

Trapped in her bedchamber, Elisiana knew the woman who had been guarding her since her return home was just outside the door. She had a stool she sat on simply to watch the door. She wasn't allowed to put her hands on Elisiana to physically prevent her from leaving her chamber, but she was instructed to run straight to Adriano if Elisiana ventured away.

And she'd done that, several times.

But Elisiana pretended the woman wasn't there. This madness had been going on since she returned from Exebridge, days and days of feeling like a captive, trapped in her childhood home that no longer seemed like her home. It felt like a prison. Even the colors of her home were different, dingy and dirty and reeking of mildew and broken dreams.

Her broken dreams, to be exact.

Or perhaps she was really seeing Fremington in its true light for the first time.

Whatever the case, the endless monotony and suspicion was starting to wear on her. She had piles of drawings now, anything to pass the time, anything to upset her father and mother and punish them for the anguish they were causing her. But her father would no longer supply her with vellum, so she had taken to drawing on both sides. Her drawings were circulating furiously through the army and servants of Fremington, and when they were done with them, they were selling them to townsfolk, who were raving about the scandalous sketches.

The wildfire was spreading.

Two days ago, the priest at St. Peter's in the village had gotten hold of some of the drawings and brought them to the castle to complain to Adriano. Furious that the church was now in possession of some of the filthy drawings, Adriano had stood outside of Elisiana's chamber and shouted at her through a closed door. He tried to come in to talk to her, but she had locked him out. The bolt was thrown and it was going to remain thrown. That infuriated the man, and he had spent a solid half-hour shouting at her and telling her how terrible she was behaving and how much she was shaming her family.

That only made Elisiana smile.

As the days passed, a plan had been formulating in her mind. She simply wasn't going to sit by and wait for Adolph to show his face, because she was fairly certain her father had sent word to the man. Knowing he was coming, and knowing her time was limited, had made her step up the timeline of her escape. Her original scheme had been to lull her parents into a false sense of security by behaving herself, and when their guard was down, she would run. Adolph being on his way, however, meant that she couldn't afford the luxury of waiting for her parents to relax.

She was going to have to make the escape sooner rather than later.

But the timing still had to be right.

She'd awoken to those thoughts this morning. Would this be the day she'd see an opportunity to flee? Over the past few days, she'd been waking up every morning with that on her mind. But thoughts of escape meant she needed to do some reconnaissance, and even though she knew her guard was watching her door, she made plans to leave the chamber. Dressed in a pale green garment with a square neck and short sleeves, with her long hair pinned up on the back of her head because the weather had turned sticky, she threw open the door. Armed with little more than her determination, she ignored her guard and headed down to the entry level.

It was still fairly early in the day for her father to be in his solar, so she ventured inside to pilfer vellum from his writing kit. Her guard was following behind her at a safe distance and she knew the woman would tell Adriano that his naughty daughter had stolen vellum. The woman could tell her father anything she wished and Elisiana didn't care a hoot. Leaving her father's solar, she headed for the kitchens.

The old cook was probably the only person Elisiana would speak to with any civility. She had known the woman all her life and had a genuine fondness for her, so she went to the kitchens to see what she could steal for a snack. It made her think of all of the wonderful foods that she had made for the patrons of the Black Cock, of the delicious ginger wafers that Sinclair had been so fond of. She had been looking forward to making him more delicacies, so in a sense, the kitchen brought her some sadness as well as solace.

It reminded her of a life she wanted back.

The cook, a tiny woman with no teeth, greeted her fondly and gave her pieces of apple that had been cooked in honey and allowed to dry out. Elisiana took a handful of them and headed out to the kitchen yard because she wanted to get a look at the postern gate. There were a few servants out in the yard, gathering eggs and other chores, and Elisiana wandered through, stolen vellum under her arm and apple chips in her hand. She was chewing on them, casually glancing at the postern gate tucked back in the yard. Her shadow was behind her, in the kitchen doorway, so she didn't want to pay any more attention to the gate than she already had. She thought she saw a lock on it, probably put there by her father, but she couldn't be sure. She'd have to make another trip out here at some point to see if her observations were correct. If there was a lock on it, she'd have to figure something else out.

"Lisi?"

Looking over her shoulder, she saw her mother standing a few feet away. She hardly gave the woman a glance before she returned her attention to the chicks.

"Mama," she greeted her without warmth.

Sybil watched her daughter with a sad expression. "I thought you would want to know that your Uncle Robert should be here shortly," she said. "Your father is preparing for his visit."

That had Elisiana's attention. Eyes wide, she forgot about the chicks as she faced her mother.

"Is Adolph coming with him?" she demanded.

Sybil shook her head. "I do not know," she said. "Possibly."

Terrified and infuriated, Elisiana marched up to her mother and jabbed a finger at her. "I am *not* marrying him today or any day," she said. "Tell Papa that if he tries to force me, I will jump from the top of the keep. I will kill myself before I marry that dog!"

She ran off before Sybil could stop her, through the kitchens, where she grabbed bread and anything else she could get her hands on, preparing for a long siege with her in her locked chamber and her father on the other side, begging her to open it.

Well, she *wasn't* going to.

The thought of Adolph arriving at Fremington made her feel more fear than she could adequately process. Was she serious about jumping from the window? If her father pressed the issue, she was. She didn't want to, but she didn't want to marry Adolph more.

Now, the situation was about to become critical.

CHAPTER EIGHTEEN

"S ANTIAGO!"

Adriano couldn't have been more astonished to see Santiago ride through his gatehouse with a small contingent of men. He'd been expecting Robert, because the man had sent word ahead that he would be arriving today, but what he hadn't expected was his seafaring cousin.

Santiago was very glad to see him.

"Ah!" he said as he dismounted a gorgeous silver horse he'd stolen along with cargo from Lisbon a couple of years ago. "My favorite cousin, Adriano. How have you been? You are looking well."

Adriano embraced his cousin, who hugged him hard enough to crack his spine. "That is kind," he grunted. "But after that embrace, I am not so certain. I think you nearly squeezed me to death."

Santiago laughed. "Because I am very glad to see you," he said. "Where is your lovely wife? And your lovely daughter?"

"What about my lovely son?"

Santiago continued laughing. "Aristeo is dead to me because he will not join me at sea," he said. "I do not care about him. However, you can tell me anyway, and I will decide if I have an inclination to care about him or not."

Adriano laughed at the man. "You are the same as always, Santi," he said. "Happy and angry. But I am eager to hear about your voyage. We saw your ships return several days ago. You were gone a very long time."

Santiago had his arm around Adriano's shoulders. "My voyage was fruitful," he said. "But I have come to discuss other things. Let us go inside and share some wine and conversation."

"Of course," Adriano said. "I would be honored. Téo and Sybil will be happy to see you also."

Santiago's eyebrows lifted. "And Lisi?" he said. "Will she not be happy to see me also?"

Adriano's smile faltered. "Of course she will," he said. "But you should know that Lisi is very unhappy these days."

"Because you are forcing her to marry your brother-in-law's step-son?"

Adriano's eyes widened. "How would you know this?"

Santiago tapped his head. "I know everything," he said, forcing Adriano to walk toward the great hall because the man seemed to be stumbling. "I have my ways. You will tell me about this betrothal and I want to talk to Lisi about it. You will send for her immediately."

Adriano wasn't terribly compliant. "She is not herself these days," he said. "You have no idea how difficult she has been. How rude she has been to her mother and me."

"Because you are forcing her to marry a man she does not wish to marry?"

Santiago seemed to have all of the answers, and Adriano was grow-ing increasingly puzzled as well as irritated. They ended up in the great hall, at the dais, as Santiago's men lingered back by the big double entry doors that were embedded with the carving of a tree. A strong, immovable tree that was the de Verra family crest.

A tree that seemed to be splintering.

"I will send for Diaz and Esteban," Adriano said, trying to divert the subject. "My parents are also still here, your Uncle Jorge and Aunt

Alicia. Elisiana was named for my mother, you know. Surely you wish to see them?"

"In a moment," Santiago said. "I love Uncle Jorge and Aunt Alicia dearly, but you and I have something to discuss, Adriano. I have been hearing unpleasant things about your treatment of Elisiana. I want you to send for her immediately. I wish to speak with her."

That was the second time he'd asked for Elisiana, and it didn't make Adriano happy in the least. He thought about denying Santiago, but no one denied the man. No one sane, anyway. Somehow, someway, Santiago had been told about the betrothal and now he wanted to interrogate Elisiana about it. That would put Adriano on the defensive because Elisiana would make it sound like her father was condemning her to death by marriage.

Adriano didn't want to be put in a bad light.

But he had no choice. With the greatest reluctance, he sent a servant for his daughter simply to keep the pirate happy. He also ordered food and drink to be brought forth as Santiago went around the table trying to find the most comfortable chair. When he found it, across the table from Adriano, he sat heavily and put his feet up on the table.

"Ah," he said, "much better. Now, while we are waiting for Elisiana, I will tell you a little of my travels. We went to the Great Sea far to the south and sailed the islands near Rome. I have many wonderful things from there."

Adriano wasn't so thrilled with his cousin's visit anymore and even less enthused with the conversation. "You took a chance going so far away," he said. *Too bad someone didn't sink your ship!* "Was it dangerous?"

Adriano shrugged. "Sometimes," he said. "There are primitive people in villages around the Great Sea, but they are fearsome. We traded with some, stole from others. I've brought back spices and other things to sell. You might be interested."

Adriano nodded. "Possibly," he said without much excitement. "Were you able to go to Pontevedra?"

He was speaking of Santiago's home base in Castile and the city that Adriano held dominion over. Santiago nodded to the question.

"I saw my wife and children," he said. "Three of my sons serve with me on my ships, you know. I am very fortunate that they will, but I still think having Aristeo aboard my ships will give him valuable experience."

Adriano snorted. "Experience in what?" he said. "Piracy? Stealing?"

"Battles and warfare."

Adriano waved him off. "Téo can do without that kind of experience."

Santiago cocked an unhappy eyebrow, watching his cousin and wondering why the man seemed so uncomfortable. He could hardly look him in the eye. Servants began to bring out food and drink, distracting Santiago for the moment, but as soon as the wine cups were full and food was in front of him, he was back on the offensive again.

"Your wine is rubbish," he said, smacking his lips after tasting what had been put in front of him. "I have better wine for you."

Adriano frowned. "Better wine that you will charge me for," he said. "This wine is acceptable. I purchase it from France."

"French rubbish wine," Santiago said stubbornly as he set the cup down and went for the bread. "Now, let us discuss Lisi. Why did you pledge her to your brother-in-law's stepson? Does he come with lands and title?"

Adriano wasn't interested in eating. He just wanted the wine to dull the irritation at this conversation. "Aye," he said. "He inherited the title of Lord Wynford from his father."

"Is he rich?"

"He has money."

"But he serves the Earl of Lincoln?"

Adriano sighed sharply. "Who has told you all of this?" he asked. "How do you know so much about my business?"

"Why?" Santiago said. "Are you ashamed of it?"

"Of course not," Adriano snapped. "But who has been telling you such things? Has Lisi written to you? Is that how you know?"

"Nay, I have not written to him." A voice came from the entry. Elisiana was heading toward the dais, her gaze on Santiago. She smiled at the man when their eyes met. "I have not written to him but I am very glad to see him. *Buenas tardes, Tio.*"

She had always called him *Tio*, or uncle, because he was more of an uncle than a cousin. Santiago stood up with a big smile and embraced her.

"Lisi, *mi hija*," he said. "My beautiful girl. I trust you have been in good health?"

Elisiana hugged him in return. "I am very well, considering," she said. "Have you come for a visit?"

Santiago shrugged. "A little," he said, standing back to get a good look at her. "But I mostly came to speak with you."

"Her?" Adriano said with confusion and concern. "What do you want—"

Santiago hissed at him to quiet his question before continuing with Elisiana. "I have heard you are unhappy, *mi hija*," he said, taking her hand and sitting her down next to him. "What is troubling you?"

Elisiana seemed surprised by the question. She glanced at her father, who had a furious expression on his face, which led her to believe she had been the topic of conversation. She'd been quite surprised when the servant who fetched her told her that it was Santiago who had come to visit, not her Uncle Robert. Santiago was an ally and always had been. If Uncle Robert and Adolph did show today, then Santiago would stand against him because he had never liked Robert. With that knowledge, Elisiana had unbolted the door and hastened down to the great hall.

She could hardly believe the luck.

In fact, she was rather speechless at the moment. She didn't know how much Santiago knew, but clearly, he knew something. Someone had told him something, which she assumed to be her father. And there was no telling what spin Adriano had put on the subject, trying to make himself the sympathetic character and his daughter a rebellious ingrate. But, as always, Santiago was her ally, as she'd told Sinclair, so she knew he would listen to her. If anyone had a chance of talking her father out of this betrothal, it was Santiago.

She wasn't going to let this chance slip away.

"I *have* been unhappy, dear *Tio*," she said. "It all started when Papa betrothed me to my Uncle Robert's stepson, a man who is a knight for the Earl of Lincoln."

Santiago was listening patiently. "And you have met this man?" he said. "Was he kind to you?"

Elisiana sighed sharply. "He was polite when we were around others," she said. "But once we were alone, he was lascivious and wanted me to touch his manhood."

Santiago's eyes flew open. "He said this terrible thing to you?"

"He did," Elisiana said. "He was vile and vulgar. I told Papa what he did but Papa has told me I must marry him regardless."

Santiago was still holding her hands, now giving them a gentle squeeze. "That is terrible, indeed," he said. "But is this the only reason you do not wish to marry him?"

Elisiana had nothing to lose by telling him everything. Perhaps if he understood, he would stand with her. He could do more than convince Adriano to break the betrothal. Perhaps he would even threaten him if he didn't.

She had nothing to lose by spilling the truth.

"Six months ago, I ran away," she said. "Did Papa tell you that? I ran away because he was forcing me to marry this lewd man. I found a place, a wonderful place, where I made friends. Where I was respected for being myself. Where I met a man... *Tio*, he is such a wonderful man. We have the most wonderful conversations. He was kind to me and showed me great respect before he even knew of my past. It is he I wish to marry, not this fool Papa has condemned me to. But Papa is being stubborn. He will not even listen to me."

Santiago sighed heavily and cast Adriano a look of great disapproval. "Why are you doing this to her?" he said. "Why sentence my Lisi to a life of unhappiness? What are your reasons?"

Elisiana dared to look at her father, who was so furious that he drained his cup of wine and poured himself another sloppy measure. "He is a knight," he said defensively. "There is nothing wrong with him."

"Except that he thinks I am cheap and common," Elisiana said angrily. "Someone told him about my drawings and about leaving Pevensey because of them, and he thought that made me as bawdy and common as he is. What kind of man asks a woman he has hardly known to touch his manhood? Would you rather that I had done it? Is that what you think of me, too?"

Adriano waved her off. "You make too much of it," he said. "It is not as if the man assaulted you. He did not touch you or strike you."

Elisiana looked at Santiago. "You see?" she said, tears filling his eyes. "He defends him. He defends this vulgar fool!"

"I am not defending anyone," Adriano snapped back.

"That is clear," Elisiana nearly shouted at him. "You certainly have not defended me in any of this. And I know why. You owe Uncle Robert a debt, don't you? And I am to pay it!"

Adriano was startled by the revelation of a secret he thought he'd kept buried. "Who told you that?" he demanded.

"I did."

The words came from the hall entry, and everyone turned to see Aristeo standing there. He'd come to the hall when he heard of Santiago's visit, but he was hanging back when he heard the tone of the conversation. Especially with Elisiana present. No longer able to hold his tongue, he came forward, toward the dais, his focus moving between Santiago and his father, but he ended up holding up a hand of surrender toward Adriano.

"Forgive me, Papa, but I told her," he said. Then he looked at Santiago. "Papa owes Uncle Robert money for the home he built our mother a couple of years ago. It is a goodly sum of money that we cannot repay in full, so Uncle Robert demanded Lisi for his wife's son. Papa felt that he had no choice."

Santiago turned to Adriano. "Is this true?" he said, incredulous. "You owe the man money so you pay him with your daughter?"

Caught in a truth of his own making, Adriano averted his gaze. "It is not as unusual as you make it sound," he said, weakly defending himself. "Such things are done all of the time. This is nothing special."

"Except your daughter is miserable," Santiago said, gesturing emphatically to Elisiana. "Are you truly so stubborn and cruel, Adriano?"

Adriano shrugged. "It is not a matter of being cruel," he said. "Robert loaned me eighty-three pounds for the country house. He wants his money or he wants a bride for his stepson. He assumed that Lisi would be the best candidate because she is his sister's daughter. And she brings a hefty dowry with her, so he would get his money."

"Ah!" Santiago said sharply, pointing at him. "There it is! Lisi's dowry would pay back the debt, not Lisi herself!"

"Papa, I have over fifty pounds that I have earned myself," Elisiana said eagerly. "Tell Uncle Robert you will give him the fifty and I will convince Mama to turn over the rest of it from my dowry. It comes from her, does it not? From her father?"

Another shameful revelation made bare as Adriano closed his eyes and turned away. "Aye, it does," he muttered. "Fremington comes from him. The money comes from him. There is money I cannot touch because he gave it to the bankers in London to hold for your mother and I cannot have it, so ask your mother for it. Shame me more than you already have, Elisiana. Beg your mother for her father's money!"

"I will pay the full amount. I will give it to you today."

Another voice had entered the mix. One of Santiago's men, who had been lingering by the entry door, was suddenly moving out of the shadows, heading for the dais. He was cloaked so that no one could see his face, but as he came closer, he pulled off the hood and Elisiana gasped. No one knew why she suddenly burst into tears. She looked as if she'd seen a ghost.

Perhaps she had.

It was a sight she wasn't sure she would ever see again.

Sinclair had come.

CHAPTER NINETEEN

H E'D HEARD ENOUGH.

It was bad enough that Sinclair couldn't grab Elisiana when she walked past him into the hall. Payne had discreetly stopped him and rightfully so. To have touched her, to have made his presence known so soon, wouldn't have been prudent. So he'd stood back in the shadows and listened to Adriano's reasons for betrothing her to Adolph and so much more.

So very much more.

A great deal had become clear to him, but the truth was that he didn't care about any of that. Elisiana was within his grasp and his arms were fairly aching to hold her.

She was all he wanted.

Now he'd revealed himself, and as Elisiana stood up, weeping, Santiago grasped her so she couldn't run to Sinclair. That was a wise move given the situation, but Elisiana was pulling against her cousin. She wanted to hold Sinclair as badly as he wanted to hold her.

But there was business to attend to first.

He had to get it out before Elisiana came to him and overwhelmed his senses.

"My name is Sinclair de Reyne," he said, addressing Adriano. "I am a trainer at Blackchurch. I have also been a master knight of Kenilworth. I am a trainer of men, my lord, but I have also been a sword for hire. I come with the finest recommendations from men of the highest order. I hold the title Lord Brexent, but I also hold another title, a much older one. My mother was a descendant of the kings of Bernicia and through her, I have inherited the title of Lord Ebchester. I believe that I am an excellent match for your daughter and I can pay your debt to your brother-in-law immediately."

Adriano was greatly confused. "*You?*" he said. "I do not know you. Where did you come from?"

"Blackchurch, my lord," Sinclair said. "When your daughter ran off those months ago, she ended up near Blackchurch. That is how I met her. That is how… how I fell in love with her. You have raised a remarkable woman, my lord. It would be a great honor to be her husband."

"*That!*" Santiago nearly shouted, standing up and pointing at Sinclair. "That is the kind of man Lisi deserves, Adriano. Can you not see that she loves him too?"

To prove his point, Elisiana yanked away from Santiago's grip and raced to Sinclair, throwing herself at him. He swept her up in his powerful embrace, holding her tightly as her father tried to figure out what in the hell was going on. Scowling in confusion, he looked at Aristeo, who was watching his sister with a smile on his face. Realizing he was in the minority of whatever was happening, he began to wave his arms around.

"Wait!" he said. "Lisi, step away from that man. I have questions!"

Elisiana wasn't going to move away from Sinclair. They were holding each other tightly with no intention of letting go. "I will *not* step away, Papa," she said. "You'll have to use a knife to cut me away from him because I am not moving."

Adriano stared at her a moment before turning his attention to Santiago. "Is *that* what you have done?" he asked incredulously as he pointed to Sinclair and Elisiana. "You have brought this... this knight with you? This knight who wants to marry her? I do not even know who he is!"

Santiago shrugged. "He told you who he is," he said. "What part of his explanation did you not understand?"

Santiago was taunting him. Adriano had well understood the words. De Reyne was from Blackchurch. He wanted to marry his daughter. Elisiana clearly knew the man.

But what was he doing here?

"I understand none of it," Adriano said with exasperation. "None of it! *What* is he doing here?"

"You have already answered that question," Santiago said. "I brought him. He came to me and told me what had happened with Lisi, so I had to see for myself, and I see that he was right. You *are* forcing my Lisi into a miserable marriage. Shame on you, Adriano. For shame."

Adriano rolled his eyes. "God's Bloody Bones," he muttered, slapping a palm to his forehead. "This is ridiculous. You had no right to get involved in this, Santi. No right at all."

"But *I* have a right."

Yet one more person entered the hall, and this one brought an armed escort in with him. All eyes turned to see Robert entering the great hall, his focus on Elisiana in the arms of Sinclair. He pointed to her, wagging a finger.

"Get away from that man, Elisiana," he said steadily. "You belong to me. I decide whom you shall wed."

Santiago, Adriano, and Aristeo looked at the man as if he'd lost his mind. "What is the meaning of this, Robert?" Adriano demanded. "Leave your men outside. Weapons are not permitted in my hall."

Robert came to a halt but didn't order his men away. His gaze was still on Elisiana. "Unfortunately, I suspect that I am going to need them, so they will remain," he said. "I've come with news, Adriano. Bad news."

The mood of the hall began to turn into something dark. Robert's appearance wasn't unexpected, but it was strange. *He* seemed strange. Adriano, puzzled and angry, stepped off the dais and headed toward his brother-in-law.

"What news?" he said. "What are you talking about?"

Robert finally looked at him. "I received your missive about Lisi returning home," he said. "The unfortunate truth of the matter is that Adolph would not wait for her. You know he had another woman that he wanted, a woman beneath his station. That is why I pushed for the betrothal with Elisiana in the first place, so that he would not have to marry beneath his station. But with Elisiana running off, Adolph took it upon himself to marry the merchant's daughter. He has been married for months, only I did not tell you because I was certain Elisiana would never return home and the contract would be dissolved, and you needn't know what Adolph had done. But now... now she has returned and we find ourselves in an interesting situation."

Adriano's jaw dropped. "Adolph has already *married*?"

Robert nodded. "He has," he said. "Against my wishes, of course. But he did."

Adriano's jaw closed as the news began to settle. "Then there is no more contract," he said. "Adolph saw to that."

Robert lifted a finger. "Untrue," he said. "You still owe me money. Even though Adolph married another, the contract still belongs to me because it is for a debt. And I intend to collect that debt."

"And I will pay," Sinclair said, even as Adriano tried to silence him. "Whatever the debt is, I will pay it, my lord."

Robert looked at him with some disdain. "You cannot pay what I am asking," he said. "Release her. I will not tell you again."

Sinclair didn't move. "What are you asking?"

"I will not discuss this with you."

"You will have to because I intend to marry Elisiana. Whether or not your debt is paid, she belongs to me."

"You are taking your life in your hands, sir," Robert said. "I suggest you do as I say."

Sinclair shook his head. "I will not."

"Then I will force you to."

"You can try."

Robert didn't say a word. He motioned to the man next to him, a tall and willowy fellow, who tossed back his cloak and produced an enormous broadsword. When Robert pointed toward Sinclair, the command was obvious.

Kill him.

Shocked, everyone began to shuffle away from the tall man with the big sword. Everyone but Sinclair, that was. He was forced to push Elisiana away from him and unsheathe his own broadsword, a wicked-looking thing that reflected the light of the great hall.

"Robert!" Adriano said. "What is the meaning of this?"

Robert was watching his swordsman advance on Sinclair. "I should think that would be obvious," he said. "I came here to collect payment for my debt. I will not let anyone stand in my way."

Adriano was nearly beside himself. "This is my home," he said. "I forbid you to violate my hall like this. Get out and take your men with you!"

"Not without my prize."

"There *is* no prize!"

Robert didn't respond, and Adriano began looking around desperately for a servant to send after his soldiers. He needed help with whatever was happening.

But help was already here.

Back by the entry door, Payne and Anteaus swooped in on Robert's escort and did away with five of them before the rest could even unsheathe their weapons. It was chaos back by the door as Robert realized his men were being set upon. Anteaus had managed to get the attention of some of Adriano's men out in the bailey, and they came running. Soon, soldiers were flooding in through the main entry door, dragging Robert's men out and kicking bodies to the ground.

As this was going on, Adriano managed to get hold of his daughter and pull her back toward the dais, away from the fighting. Santiago, always armed, unsheathed his own weapon, a smaller and more elegant piece, and pointed it at Robert.

"Call off your knight or you will be the next to die," he declared in a voice that didn't sound anything like the congenial pirate he was known to be. "You know who I am, de Norbury. Unless you want all of your properties burned to the ground, you will surrender your claim to Lisi and leave. I will not tell you again."

Robert, who had so recently been in control, now found himself in a bad position. He was without his armed escort thanks to the men in the back of the hall and how his French swordman was advancing on the man who had offered for Elisiana.

He was on his own.

"She belongs to me," he said, fear in his voice. "You cannot harass me, de Fernandez. I have a bigger army than you do!"

Santiago began to laugh as if he'd just heard something incredibly funny. "You think so, do you?" he said. "Well, you shall find out. And just so your defeat will be complete, I suggest you let your knight engage the man who wants very much to marry Elisiana. That way, the matter shall be decided decisively."

Robert's nervous gaze moved between Santiago and his French swordsman. "I should warn you that he is a specially trained swordsman from France," he said. "If you want him to fight the man who wishes to marry Elisiana, so be it. And when he wins, you will regret your words. Lisi will be mine."

Santiago's laughter faded and his dark eyes took on a deadly gleam. "I will not regret anything," he said. "But *you* will because the man your knight is about to attack is a Blackchurch trainer. He was also a master knight at Kenilworth Castle. He trained men like your Frenchman, so I think this will be a lesson to you, *mi amigo*. A lesson in losing."

That seemed to wipe some of the confidence off Robert's face. By the time he returned his attention to his Frenchman, the fight had already started.

And, quite possibly, was already lost.

CHAPTER TWENTY

A FRENCH SWORDSMAN.

Sinclair was looking forward to the challenge. It wasn't often that he had the opportunity to fight someone who was specifically trained only with the sword in mind, so he was ready for it. He was eager for it.

The fight, from the start, was violent.

The Frenchman used a longsword, made from steel, that was heavy and sharp and deadly. Sinclair assessed it the moment he unsheathed it. But Sinclair was carrying his personal sword, the one forged in Spain with a textured hilt, a wider hand guard, and a serrated edge. It was a beast of a sword, surprisingly lightweight, but it could carve through a man's body cleanly in one stroke if delivered with enough force.

And Sinclair had done it, time and time again.

The Frenchman came at him first and Sinclair simply stepped aside, letting the man's momentum take him right past. The Frenchman had more to prove, and it was clear from the start that he believed himself superior to anything Sinclair could do.

That was where Sinclair was going to defeat him.

But he had to shut everything out. The noise, the surroundings. Mostly, he was shutting out Elisiana, whom he could hear weeping off to his left. He had to reduce his fighting stage to his own little world, where only his opponent was visible, and that was exactly what he did. More than that, the Frenchman's initial offensive would be his last because Sinclair intended to end the fight quickly. He didn't have time for a prolonged battle. Once the Frenchman stumbled past him, it was his turn to attack.

And he did, ably.

With a heavy arc of his sword, he caught the Frenchman on the left side of his torso, carving into his back because the man hadn't had the opportunity to turn around and face him again. It was a deep cut, a bloody cut, and one that put the Frenchman at long odds from the start. After that, Sinclair charged him like an enraged bull, throwing his weight and skill at the Frenchman, who was already in a difficult position. At first, he was able to fight back and drive Sinclair back a little, but he was bleeding heavily from the gash that had driven mail, leather, and fabric into his torso and kidneys. In a short amount of time, there were bloody footprints all around him as he bled down his leg and onto his shoe.

But Sinclair showed no mercy.

No mercy!

The fight moved across the great hall floor, which was stone because Sybil didn't like a dirt floor. But that also meant the blood dripping down the Frenchman's left leg was making it slippery, and more than once, he slipped in his own blood. But Sinclair didn't let up. He swung at the man so hard, and so swiftly, that sparks flew when their blades came together, and the Frenchman, for all his skill, was being beaten into the ground by a man who had far more to lose than he did.

But the fight went on.

At one point, they reached the dais and the Frenchman got a hold of one of the pitchers of wine and hurled it at Sinclair, who was able to turn his head in time so he wasn't hit in the eyes. That simply enraged him, so he leapt over the table and tackled the Frenchman, shoving him to the ground and landing on top of him. The Frenchman tried to fight back, but Sinclair was on top of him, bringing his blade around to cut his head off. The Frenchman managed to move his head, and his body, which threw off Sinclair's aim. His sword ended up hitting the stone and bouncing back up again, only to embed itself in a chair. It was enough of a diversion to give the Frenchman the opportunity to throw a punch into Sinclair's face that sent him tumbling backward.

The Frenchman was on his feet now, staggering away from the dais, practically dragging his sword because his blood loss was so great. He teetered in Santiago's direction and the pirate king gave him a big kick, sending him sideways and onto his knees. As Sinclair finally managed to yank his sword from where it had been wedged into the wood, Aristeo appeared from behind his uncle.

And he was armed.

Sinclair leapt over the feasting table again, hunting the injured Frenchman, but Aristeo was hunting him as well. For his sister, for the anguish she'd been through, it was an apology as only a brother could give. He came up behind the Frenchman and rammed his broadsword into the man's back, effectively ending the fight. Before Sinclair could reach him and finish the job, the French swordsman bled out all over Lady Sybil's stone floor.

The battle was over.

Realizing this, Sinclair simply stood over the man, watching him breathe his last. It was a sobering thing watching a man die, especially when it did not have to happen. Winded, Sinclair finally moved his gaze to Robert.

"I will pay you what you are owed," he said in a voice that was not meant to be countermanded. "You no longer own any betrothal contract. Agree with me at this moment that Elisiana is free to wed whomever she chooses or I swear I will take your Frenchman's sword and ram it down your throat. Is this in any way unclear?"

Robert, eyes wide, tried to back away, but Payne and Anteaus were there. He had nowhere to go. Cornered, and frightened, he simply nodded. Once.

But it was enough.

Thank God, it was enough.

Now that the situation was acknowledged, Sinclair heaved a sigh of relief and returned his attention Aristeo. He studied him for a moment before speaking.

"I have seen you before," he said. "The night Lisi was taken from the Black Cock. You were the one who took her."

Aristeo nodded. "I did," he said evenly. "But you understand I was under orders."

"I know."

Aristeo shook his head after a moment, pointing his bloodied sword at the Frenchman. "No more orders," he said. "At least, none that I am going to follow where it pertains to my sister. This situation is finished."

He smiled faintly, and Sinclair's features reflected the expression. With a nod of his head in silent thanks to Aristeo for assisting him with the Frenchman, Sinclair turned to Adriano.

He was standing with his arm around Elisiana, his pale eyes fixed on Sinclair. Before Sinclair could say a word to him, Adriano looked at his daughter.

"This is the man you want?" he asked quietly.

Elisiana, who was still somewhat in shock over the fight she had just witnessed and the magnificence of Sinclair's skill, nodded eagerly.

"Aye, Papa," she said. "*Please.*"

There was such pleading in her tone that Adriano knew he had no choice. "If I denied you, we would never know a moment's peace, would we?"

"Nay."

Adriano nodded as if his suspicions had been confirmed. With a grunt of resignation, he turned to Sinclair. "I hope you know what you are asking," he said. "Dirty drawings and all. I have no sympathy for you."

Sinclair laughed softly. "I am not asking for your sympathy, my lord," he said. "But I am asking for permission to marry your daughter."

Adriano looked between his daughter and the man who had vied for her hand. More than that, he'd killed for it. But Adriano still really had no idea who the man was other than what had been told to him in the heat of an argument, and he started to laugh at the ridiculousness of everything. As he put his hands over his face, perhaps to reconcile himself to what was coming, Elisiana left her father and rushed to Sinclair, throwing her arms around him.

"Are you well?" she asked. "Did he hurt you?"

Sinclair shook his head. "Of course not," he said. "Why? Did it look like he hurt me?"

"He was very skilled."

He poked her nose affectionately. "But I was better."

She nodded, laying her head against his chest and hugging him tightly again. Sinclair kissed the top of her head, letting her work through her fear of just having seen him participate in a deadly fight, as Santiago made his way over to them.

"Lisi," he said, putting his hand on her back. "Is marrying this man what will make you happy, *mi hija*?"

Elisiana was still clinging to Sinclair, unwilling to let him go, fearful that Santiago might try to separate them even though she knew he wouldn't. Still, after what she had just witnessed, and after everything she had been through with her father and brother and even her Uncle Robert, she wasn't convinced that someone wasn't going to try to take her away from Sinclair again. She wondered if she'd ever get over that fear. But for now, it seemed that everything was as she'd prayed it would be.

The man she wanted was here.

Adolph was already married.

There was nothing more to say.

"Aye," she said to Santiago. "This is what will make me happy. *He* is what will make me happy. And you brought him here. He was with you all the time?"

It was more a statement than a question. She had figured out that Sinclair had come in Santiago's escort, and Santiago nodded.

"I brought him," he said. "He is a determined man, Lisi. He came to me for help and I am glad he did."

Elisiana turned her adoring face up to Sinclair. "So am I," she said. "I do not know how any of this came about, but I suppose there will be plenty of time to explain it. All that matters is that you are here. I can still hardly believe it."

Sinclair smiled at her. "It took some doing," he said. "You told me that Lord Santiago was sympathetic toward you and I had to take the chance that he would care about this betrothal enough to do something about it. It was really the only chance I had to break your betrothal. Thank God it worked."

He kissed her on the forehead, in full view of her father and brother, who did not protest. Aristeo was not displeased at the prospect of having a new brother-in-law who was a Blackchurch trainer, and Adriano was simply resigned to the fact that his daughter would get what she wanted in the end.

But there was still the matter of Robert.

He was still standing back with Payne and Anteaus, who hadn't let him move except to check on his French swordsman. Santiago had been eyeing him since the fight ended, and even now, as he stood with

253

Elisiana and Sinclair, he continued to eye Robert. After a moment, he turned to Sinclair.

"Do you remember when we were on board my ship and you told me that you would be in my debt for helping you with Lisi?" he asked.

Sinclair's demeanor suggested that he was leery of where the conversation was going. "I did, my lord," he said. "That has not changed."

Santiago indicated the great hall with its broken chairs and blood all over the floor. "I have seen many swordsmen in my life," he said. "But I have never seen one with your skill. The Frenchman never stood a chance against you."

"Thank you, my lord."

"I told you that I may want that sword arm someday in payment of your debt to me."

Sinclair sighed faintly. "And you have it, my lord," he said. "But may I at least marry Elisiana first? That way, you and I shall be kin. And I am always happy to lend my skill to my kin."

Santiago looked at him in surprise. "You would not be ashamed of having a pirate as a relative?"

Sinclair chuckled. "I would be honored," he said. "Also, I think having you as a cousin will greatly irritate Abelard."

Santiago burst out laughing. "And I am always looking for the opportunity to do that to him," he said. "My old, dear, and irritable friend Abelard. I like you, Swordsman. You think like I do."

Sinclair chuckled, glancing at Elisiana, who was laughing along with them even though she'd not met St. Abelard. Still, she knew enough about Santiago to imagine what St. Abelard must be like.

"I will take that as a compliment, my lord," Sinclair said. "But if you want my sword, when will you want it? You've not been clear."

He was back to business because there was no telling what Santiago would want, or how long he would want it. Santiago's focus lingered on him, and Elisiana began to fear that her cousin would want him indefinitely.

"*Tio*," she said softly, "please… do you truly need him now? May we not marry first?"

Santiago looked at her and a gleam came to his eye. After a moment, he turned to look at Robert, across the hall, and pointed to him.

"You," he said. "You tried to harm my Lisi and I cannot tolerate this. You told me that you have a bigger army than I do, but I have something you do not."

Robert, unable to move because of Payne and Anteaus, eyed Santiago with some fear. "What is that?"

"*Demonios del mar*," Santiago said, his dark eyes glittering. "I have a new ship and she needs men to take care of her. Someone to scrub her decks and ensure her sails are always prepared to fly. Come with me, de Norbury. I shall make a man out of you."

Robert looked at him in horror. "I will *not* go with you," he said flatly. "I am not a seaman."

"You are not a decent man, either," Santiago said. "You would be perfect amongst my fellow pirates. You are underhanded and unforgiving, and you also make light of a man's life like you tried to make light of Lisi's. In fact, there are chains in the hold with your name on them. For trying to ruin my Lisi's life, you deserve nothing less."

He looked at Payne and Anteaus, nodding his head in the direction of the bailey, and they took the hint. They proceeded to take Robert by the arms and began dragging him toward the entry door.

"You cannot do this!" Robert cried, panicking. "Stop this instant! Adriano, tell him to stop!"

Adriano and Aristeo were watching the man being dragged away. So were Sinclair and Elisiana, all of them with hardly a flicker of emotion in their expression.

Adriano shrugged.

"I will pay you the money I owe you when you return," he said, lifting a hand to bid farewell as if the man was taking a pleasure trip. "I will tell your wife that you chose to sail with Santiago de Fernandez, the most feared pirate in the world. You are off on a new adventure, Robert, that you very much deserve."

Robert started to dig his feet in, refusing to be dragged. "I will not go," he said. "You cannot force me!"

"Ah, that is where you would be wrong," Santiago said. "I *can* force you. And I shall. Take your punishment like a man, de Norbury. And know that if you try to run, I will cut your feet off and put you in my hold for the rest of your miserable life."

With that, he pointed to the bailey where the rest of his pirate escort was currently gathering. Sinclair took Elisiana by the hand and they walked to the door, watching Robert as he was tied up and tossed onto the back of a horse. Santiago had a brief conversation with Payne and Anteaus before turning to bid Sinclair and Elisiana farewell. He blew kisses at them, waving happily, before mounting the silver horse that he was so proud of.

As Santiago and his men began to move out with their unhappy captive, Payne and Anteaus returned to Sinclair.

"Do you want us to clean up the Frenchman, Sin?" Anteaus asked, nodding his head in the direction of the cooling corpse. "We can send him to the nearest church."

Sinclair nodded back, turning to look at the crumpled figure. "He was very good," he said. "His death is… unfortunate."

"Better him that you," Elisiana said seriously. "It makes me ill to think that I might have lost you when you were just within my grasp."

Sinclair smiled. "Never," he said. "I had to sell my soul to pirates to get you back, Lisi. No French swordsman was going to stop me."

"You dinna sell yer soul, Sin," Payne said. "But I did."

Sinclair looked at him in surprise. "What do you mean?"

Payne grinned, throwing a thumb in the direction of Santiago's departing party. "I mean that Santiago did indeed want yer sword," he said. "But I offered mine instead and he agreed. It seems as if I'll be a sea devil for the next year."

Sinclair didn't like the sound of that. "*You* are paying my debt to him?" he said, shocked. "Payne, I cannot ask that of you. I will speak with Santiago."

"Save yer breath," Payne said. "Ye have a new wife tae consider, or at least, ye will. I dunna have a wife. Or anyone. It makes more sense that I should go, so let me do this for ye. Ye've been a good friend tae me, Sin. And Lisi... this is my wedding gift tae ye, lass. A husband who will stay by yer side and not be out tae sea."

Elisiana had both worry and gratitude in her eyes. "Are you certain of this, Payne?" she said. "This will be a big change for you."

"Of course," he said. "As I said... I *will* be a pirate, and a damn good one!"

Sinclair put hand on his forehead in disbelief. "You vomited the entire time you were at sea," he pointed out. "Payne, this is *not* a good idea."

Payne grinned. "I'll get used tae it," he said. "Ye must let me do this, Sin. I want tae."

Sinclair tried one last time. "What will your mother say?"

"We're going tae Scotland, so she can join us!"

With that, he leaned over and kissed Elisiana on the cheek before rushing out to find the de Fernandez horse he'd come to Fremington on. Sinclair and Elisiana watched him ride off, following Santiago's party, before Sinclair shook his head in awe.

"That is quite a sacrifice he's made," he said. "You should have seen him shipboard. Every time we found him, he was leaning over the rail, spilling up the contents of his stomach. Therefore, to do this on my behalf—knowing how sick he becomes at sea—all I can say is that the man is a true friend."

Elisiana smiled. "He is," she said. "But isn't it somewhat like the sacrifice you made for Tay? The one that took you to Toxandria for a few years?"

He nodded. "I suppose," he said. "I'll have to explain it to Denis, however. I hope he understands."

"Hopefully he will be accepting when I tell him that I have volunteered to take Payne's class," Anteaus said. "I told Payne that I would. With your help, of course."

Sinclair looked at the man. "He told you of his plans?"

"He did," he said. "I think the truth is that he really does want to be a pirate. He loved it. This was just an excuse."

Sinclair grinned. "I would not be surprised," he said. "I think he'll make a fine pirate, also. As for you, Anteaus… You told me once that coming to help me reclaim Elisiana was a way of building trust between us. I am pleased to say that you have built that trust. You have proven yourself a more-than-worthy man in my eyes. And I shall support you as Payne's temporary replacement."

Anteaus dipped his head in thanks. "That is good to hear, Sinclair," he said, addressing him informally for the first time. "I'm very glad this has ended well for everyone."

With that, he turned back into the hall, where Aristeo and Adriano were trying to figure out what to do with the Frenchman. Anteaus told them that he would wrap the body up and take him to the church, and they were grateful. Adriano had two younger boys that he didn't want viewing a bloody body in his great hall and a wife who would have probably fainted at the sight, so he left Aristeo and Anteaus to clean up the mess while he made his way over to Sinclair and Elisiana.

They were standing in the doorway, wrapped in each other's arms. Adriano watched them for a moment before speaking. He felt as if he was intruding on a very private moment, but it was necessary. Now that the frenzy had died down and the situation was settling, there were a few things he had to say.

To both of them.

"Elisiana," he said, watching both her and Sinclair turn toward him. "I hope you understand that I was not being cruel to hurt you. I had made a bargain and I was determined to stay to it. It was a contract and nothing more. It was never designed to hurt you."

Now that Elisiana had what she wanted, it was easier for her to be forgiving. "I understand, Papa," she said. "But you must understand that even if Sinclair was not involved in the situation, I still would have found a way not to marry Adolph. I am sorry you could not listen to my concerns and take them seriously."

Adriano sighed heavily. "I suppose we will not agree on this," he said. "As my daughter, it is your duty to do as you are told. As your father, my duty is to ensure you are married and have a secure future. A daughter's feelings on the matter do not normally affect that decision."

Elisiana looked at the man who was struggling with his pride, with his control of his family. A rebellious daughter had shaken his foundation badly, and she knew it. She let go of Sinclair long enough to grasp her father's hands.

"I do not want to argue with you," she said, softly but sincerely. "You are my father and I love you. I am sorry we have had this disagreement. But everyone thought you were wrong but you. Even Santiago thought you were wrong. Yet I will not linger on this. In the end, I have what I want and I do not feel the need to discuss this any longer. I do believe Sinclair asked for your permission to marry me, Papa. I did not hear your clear answer."

"I thought I gave it."

"Look him in the eye and tell him, Papa," she murmured. "*Please.*"

Adriano looked at the man with the pale green eyes, the one who had so ably fought the French swordsman. Truly, it had been something to witness. After a moment, he snorted softly.

"You have my permission, de Reyne," he said. "But you are going to need that sword and every bit of your Blackchurch experience to manage this woman you wish to marry. She is headstrong and stubborn and, as I said earlier, you deserve what you wish for. Lewd pictures and all. You have my blessing, *mi hijo*, because you are surely going to need it."

Elisiana was fighting off a smile but couldn't quite manage it. She looked at Sinclair to see that he was grinning, too. With a laugh, she threw herself into his arms as he lifted her off the ground, spinning her around in their delirium. Adriano shook his head at them both, the joyful pair, and headed off to tell his wife what had become of her brother.

Well, maybe not.

As Adriano departed the great hall, Sinclair and Elisiana stood in the doorway, embracing one another in a way that suggested gratitude was the greatest feeling of all at the moment. Hope was paramount, of course, but the only thing ahead of them was life, love, and piles of ginger wafers.

For the Swordsman and the tavern wench, their joy could not have been more profound.

Or a blooming love more solid.

EPILOGUE

Five years later
Blackchurch Guild

ASTRIDE HIM AS he lay on his back, their naked bodies already joined, Elisiana grabbed her husband's hands and pressed them against her bare breasts.

"This way, Sin," she whispered. "Love me this way."

What little control Sinclair had when making love to his wife was gone with those quietly uttered words. Her soft breasts against the flesh of his hands undid him.

With a groan, he fondled one breast as he pulled her down to him, kissing her deeply until she was gasping for air as she rode his manhood, coming down on him again and again. He pinched her nipples until they were hard pellets, and Elisiana's moans were muted against his fevered lips until he sat up and his mouth took possession of a taut nipple. He suckled her hard, from one breast to the other, and Elisiana's hands were in his hair, tugging.

The harder she pulled, the more he liked it.

In a flash, he flipped her onto her back, being very careful not to put any weight on her swollen belly. At nearly eight months pregnant with their third child, she was at the point where she had to make love to her husband every night and sometimes even during the day. Not that

Sinclair minded, but sometimes she was so demanding that he'd had to set some boundaries for her. For example, not during his classes. Not when they were with their friends at the Black Cock.

But anywhere else was fair game.

Carefully, he lay beside her, lifting her legs up and entering her from behind. Elisiana groaned softly with pleasure as he not only fondled her breasts, but her belly as well. He found his pregnant wife to be wildly arousing, this glorious creature who had given birth to two children so far, a son and a daughter, with a body that was made only for him. Since the day they were married, it seemed that all they did was make love, even after five glorious years.

And Sinclair had loved every single one of them.

"You are so beautiful," he whispered, kissing her hand and wrist. "God, I love you."

His kisses were sweet and tender now, his hands roaming her soft body. Elisiana writhed beside him, her legs instinctively parting even though he was lying beside her with his pelvis against her bottom as he thrust into her. His hands began to rove between her legs, stroking the pink folds. She was unbelievably hot and wet, a safe and satisfying haven for a manhood that could not be satisfied. He withdrew from her for a moment, slipping his finger into her sheath and feeling the familiar pleasure of it. Her tight passage contracted about his finger, pulling at him.

It was all he could do not to spill himself at that moment.

Removing his finger quickly, he thrust into her again, and she immediately climaxed as he filled her with his body. Just as he found his release, he could hear someone knocking on the front door of their cottage. He knew their children were with Marina, who tended the children of the trainers by keeping them busy, feeding them, and taking them to their lessons with St. Denis, so he couldn't imagine who was at their door.

Elisiana had heard the knocking, too.

"Whoever it is, I am going to murder them with my bare hands," she said, frustrated and unhappy. "We hardly have any time alone. Who in the world would violate that?"

Sinclair shifted so he could kiss her on the mouth before pushing himself out of the bed. "You will not have to kill them," he said, heading over to the window naked and in a state of semi-arousal. "*I* will do it and take pleasure in it."

"Sin!" Elisiana hissed. "Get away from that window."

"Why?"

"Because the sill is below your waist!" she said, getting out of bed as quickly as she could and pulling the shift that had been bunched up around her shoulders all the way down to her ankles. "Get back, do you hear?"

He paused in the middle of the floor, giving her a lazy smirk. "Why?" he said. "You do not want the other women to see the size of your husband's manhood? They will be quite jealous of you."

She slapped him on the bottom as she walked past him, heading to the window. "You are very naughty," she said, struggling not to grin at him. "Go put some clothing on."

He laughed softly at her, heading off to find his breeches as Elisiana made it to the window and opened it. Their chamber was directly above the front door so she could look down and see who it was.

"Lady de Reyne," Axton Summerlin greeted her politely. "I am sorry to disturb you, but I am looking for your husband. Might you know where he is?"

Elisiana forced a smile and nodded. "Just a moment, Axton," she said. "I will send him to you."

Shutting the window, she came back in and found her husband sitting on the bed, pulling his boots on.

"Axton is waiting for you," she said.

He nodded. "I heard."

As he pulled the other boot on, she found the tunic he'd yanked off in the heat of passion and handed it to him. Finished with his shoes, he pulled the tunic over his head and stood up. Elisiana helped him straighten it.

"I am making meat pies for supper," she said. "Can we eat together tonight? Just the four of us? You and me and Cristofer and Bethania?"

Sinclair nodded. "Of course," he said. "You do not want to eat with Tay and Fox?"

She shook her head, turning away to hunt for her comb. "I love our friends, but there are so many children now," she said. "Eating with Tay and Fox and all of their children is like eating in the middle of a cattle herd sometimes. I just want a little peace and quiet tonight."

As she ran the comb through her hair, he came up behind her and put his arms around her, his hands inevitably falling on her big belly. "Whatever you wish," he said. "Do you feel well?"

"Aye," she said, giving in to his hug for a moment. "I feel perfectly well. But I would just like to eat with my husband and children tonight."

He kissed her on the side of the head. "I would like that, too," he said as he released her. "I will see you later on."

"You certainly will."

Leaving his wife to finish her hair and dress, Sinclair came downstairs only to be greeted with vellum drawings that had blown off the table near the hearth. Elisiana was still drawing these days, though far less titillating pictures. These days, her focus had switched to drawings of animals and fae for all of the children at Blackchurch, and she even sold some in the village. That was the extent of her rebellion these days, but the picture she'd once drawn of him was nailed to the wall in their bedroom. Every time he looked at it, it reminded him of her, and every time she looked at it, it reminded her of him.

Putting the drawings back on the table, Sinclair opened the door.

"Axton," he greeted the man on his stoop. "What are you doing here? Today is a rest day. I thought you would be in town, at the very least. I hear the weekly market has grown quite large."

Axton smiled weakly. "I have gatehouse duty today," he said. "In fact, that is why I came. Santiago de Fernandez is here. He asked for your wife, but she is in a delicate condition, so I wanted to tell you first and let you decide to tell her or not."

Sinclair frowned. "Santiago is here?" he said. "Why on earth is he at Blackchurch?"

"He would not tell me," Axton said. "He wants to speak with you. But he has a woman with him. I thought you would want to find out his purpose first."

That seemed very puzzling to Sinclair. With a shrug, he and Axton headed back to the main gatehouse of Blackchurch. It was nearing the nooning hour on a cool autumn day and the leaves were turning colors all around them. There was one rest day a month for the Blackchurch recruits and their trainers, and it happened to be this day. Sinclair had big plans of inspecting practice weapons and other things alongside Anteaus, but he'd slept past dawn that morning and languished around the cottage, so he truly had no idea where Anteaus even was. But seeing Santiago first was going to have to take precedence over locating Anteaus.

He was more than curious about the man's appearance.

In the five years since his marriage to Elisiana, not much had changed, except Santiago and even St. Abelard seemed to be more frequent guests at Blackchurch—St. Abelard because he felt as if he had more of a right to come after he'd helped Sinclair and Santiago because Elisiana was there. The first time he'd come to Blackchurch, he'd tried to buy the new Portuguese-built cog that St. Denis purchased to replace the one St. Abelard had demanded, but St. Denis wouldn't budge on it.

That had become a running joke between the pair, so Sinclair wondered if that was why Santiago had come—to try to negotiate a boat away from St. Denis again.

He would find out soon enough.

The enormous southern gatehouse of Blackchurch loomed ahead and Sinclair headed for the guard room that was inside the gatehouse itself. It was where visitors usually waited, although he knew that Santiago would be upset because he'd not been allowed to wander into the trainer's village. In fact, even as he approached the gatehouse, he could see a horde of Santiago's men lingering outside. He picked up his pace until he hit the guard room.

Inside, it was relatively comfortable but dark except for a barred window. He immediately spied Santiago standing next to a small woman seated in a chair. She was wrapped in a cloak and next to her stood a boy about fourteen or fifteen years of age. When Santiago saw Sinclair enter the room, he rushed in his direction and practically shoved him back outside.

"Greetings, *mi hijo*," he said. "It has been a long time. But where is my Lisi? I wanted to see her."

Sinclair smiled at the man he'd genuinely come to like. "She is heavy with child now," he said. "She is back at our cottage. Axton said you had asked for her, but I have come to make sure you are not bringing any upsetting news that I must help you deliver to her. I do not want to upset her right now."

Santiago looked stricken. "When have I ever upset her?"

Sinclair waved his hands to ease the man. "I did not mean it the way it sounded," he said. "But your visit is unexpected. I just wanted to make sure it was not a visit that will distress her."

That didn't help Santiago's sense of outrage. "How have I ever distressed her?"

Sinclair cocked an eyebrow. "Then you've not come to tell her anyone has died?"

"Nay!"

"That her father has fallen from his horse?"

"Nay!"

"That her Uncle Robert has returned home?"

Santiago snorted. "He lives aboard the *Navia* and tends the galley," he said. "He will continue to do so until I decide he has been punished enough."

Sinclair breathed a sigh of relief. "Good," he said. "Then you've not come to tell her anything at all?"

"Nay, *mi hijo*, I swear it."

"Then why *have* you come?"

Santiago eyed him as he scratched his beard. "I've come because..." He trailed off before starting again. "I've come because she has asked something of me and I've come to tell her that I found it."

Sinclair's brow furrowed. "Found what?"

"You cannot become angry with her."

"Why would I become angry with her?"

Santiago grabbed his arm and began to walk him out of the gatehouse, away from nosy gate guards. "Listen to me, Sin," he said. "You know I love Lisi as if she were my own daughter."

"I know."

"You know I would do anything she asked."

"I know."

"Then you should know that she has expressed concern to me about your lack of family," he said. "I know that Lisi and the children are your family, as am I, as are Adriano and Sybil and Aristeo. She means *your* family. Your mother and father and siblings."

Sinclair came to a halt. "She has expressed that to you?"

Santiago nodded. "She has."

Sinclair rubbed his chin for a moment before shrugging. "It seems to bother her much more than it bothers me," he said. "I cannot miss what I never really had."

"I understand," Santiago said. "But she asked me some time ago if I could discover what became of your mother and your sisters, and I told her that I would do my best, though I did not know what I could truly do."

"What *did* you do?" Sinclair said. "And why would you do it without speaking to me first?"

"Because she did not want me to," Santiago stressed. "If my search did not turn up anything, she did not want you to be disappointed."

Sinclair was starting to become irritated. "That's ridiculous," he said. "*Tio*, I appreciate that you wanted to do this for her, and that she wanted to do it for me, but there is really no need. My family is here, at Blackchurch. It is at Fremington. It is even on the *Navia* and, oddly enough, on the *Argos*. I do not need to look anywhere else."

"Then should I tell your sister to go home?"

That wasn't something Sinclair had been expecting. His eyes widened. "You found my sister?"

Santiago held up a finger to beg for patience. "It was Abelard who found her," he said. "He knows England much better than I do. I told him Elisiana's request and he went to Kenilworth. Did you know they have an enormous lake there? With ships? Anyway, he went to see if he could find out what happened to Eloise de Reyne and Ophelia de Reyne. They do keep records of the people who have passed through their halls."

Sinclair nodded quickly. "I know they do," he said. "I suppose I should have asked years ago, but I never did. I went on with my life and assumed they went on with theirs. What did he discover?"

Santiago put his hands on Sinclair's arms. "He sent men out to trace them, including your mother," he said. "I am sorry to say that your mother passed away long ago at Coldingham Priory, and your sister

Eloise married an Eynsford living near Canterbury, but she has also since passed away. However, your other sister, Ophelia, married a man from York. She was found there, living in poverty with her son. She has nothing, Sin. They found her working as a seamstress. Abelard's men brought her back and turned her over to me, though Abelard demanded a cache of weapons before he would give her to me. I paid the greedy man and have brought your sister and her son here."

Sinclair was so stunned that a gust of wind could have knocked him over. "Ophelia," he said weakly. "*Here?*"

Santiago nodded. "I was going to tell your wife so that she could break the news to you, but you did not give me the chance," he said. "Would you like to meet her?"

Sinclair could only nod. Santiago led him back to the guard room and ordered the two guards inside to step out. They did, leaving room for Santiago and Sinclair to enter.

"My lady?" Santiago said kindly. "This is your brother, Sinclair."

The woman turned to him, sharply, and Sinclair could immediately see that it was, indeed, his youngest sister. He would know that face anywhere, even though she was a grown woman. She bolted to her feet, her eyes wide with shock and perhaps a bit of fear.

"My God… Sinclair," she breathed in a small, delicate voice. "It has been a very long time since we last saw one another. Do you remember me?"

When Sinclair looked at her, he saw his mother. She looked just like her. Small, fair, and with the same pale green eyes that he had. Ophelia was into her thirtieth year, at least, but she looked young and lovely.

And very, very thin.

"Of course I remember you," he said, reaching out to take her hand. "The question should be, do you remember *me?*"

Ophelia nodded, but the tears came. "Of course I do," she whispered tightly. "My big brother, whom I never really knew. But look at you… A Blackchurch trainer? You have done so well for yourself, Sinclair. I am so very happy for you."

Sinclair grinned. "I can hardly believe this," he said. "I've thought about you and Eloise over the years, but I never… I never thought to reach out to you, Ophelia. I am so sorry I never discovered what became of you after you left Kenilworth. I assumed you married well and were living a good life. Forgive me if that was not the case."

She was shaking her head before he even finished. "We were never close," she said. "You have nothing to apologize for. I assumed your life took you elsewhere and we all simply drifted apart. Sometimes that happens."

Sinclair was studying her, taking a good, long look at the little sister he never really knew. It was overwhelming, truly. He could still hardly believe it. But he noticed the boy standing next to her, and when Ophelia saw where his attention was, she pulled the boy forward.

"This is my son," she said. "I named him Rhodes, after our father. My husband and his father, Albus St. James, was a knight with the Earl of Howsham, but an injury forced him to retire. Drink eventually killed him. But Rhodes is a good lad, a hard worker. He has been an immense comfort to me."

Sinclair looked at the lad as he removed his cloak respectfully. He was tall and lanky, fair and handsome, but like his mother, he was far too thin. A lad that age should have been filling out, building muscle to last a lifetime.

She was found living in poverty.

Santiago's words came back to him, and Sinclair could see that right away. He also realized that standing before him were people who were in desperate need of help. Even Abelard's man, who had found them, must have seen that. So, they'd come south to meet a long-lost brother and hopefully find a better life than the one they'd had.

He realized that he was very glad to see them.

"I am happy you have come," he said to both his sister and nephew. "I must say this is quite a shock, however. But a good one."

Ophelia nodded quickly. "I realize that," she said. "We will not be a burden, Sinclair. But I was told that you were looking for me, so we decided to come. Mayhap we will find a home closer to you, and to Blackchurch, so that we may keep in contact with one another. If you will allow it, of course. I just wanted you to know that I was, indeed, alive and am sorry we never had the opportunity to be closer than we were."

Sinclair shook his head. "You will not find a home closer to Black-church," he said frankly. "You are going to live here, with me, for now. I will find you work, and Rhodes… You look like a strong lad. I can find work for you, too, if you are willing."

Rhodes looked at his mother in surprise before answering. "I am strong, my lord," he said in his newly minted man voice. "I learn quickly."

"Where did you foster?" Sinclair asked.

Some enthusiasm drained out of Rhodes. "I have not had the opportunity to do so, my lord," he said. "My father died before he could secure a position for me in a good house."

He was well spoken, with intelligent eyes, and Sinclair put his hand on the young man's shoulder. "Not to worry," he said. "You can foster at Blackchurch with your uncle and his friends. There will be no finer education in the world."

Rhodes' eyes widened and he looked at his mother, who was in a flood of tears.

"Truly, Sinclair?" she said. "It will not be too much trouble for you to foster Rhodes? I do not care about myself, of course, but if you could only help my son… give him the education he deserves… that is all I would ever ask for."

"But what about me?" Santiago spoke up, looking at the boy.

"Would you rather come to sea with me and learn the ways of warriors upon the water?"

Sinclair rolled his eyes and put himself between Santiago and his nephew. "He does *not* want to become a pirate, *Tio*," he said, pulling the boy out of the guard room as his mother followed. "Your offer is very generous, but let him learn to be a knight first. If he wants to be a pirate once he has been properly educated, then that is his choice."

Santiago smiled joyfully, as he always did, but he put himself between Sinclair and Rhodes, putting an arm around the boy's shoulders and pulling him away from Sinclair and his mother. As he headed into the compound of Blackchurch, Sinclair could see that the old man was keeping up a running conversation with the youth.

Probably trying to talk him into becoming a pirate.

Exasperated, Sinclair shook his head.

"He is going to try to lure him into a life of theft for profit," he said to his sister. "I'm surprised he hasn't done it already."

Ophelia smiled as she watched her son walk away. "I do not know that much about Lord Santiago, truthfully," she said. "We were taken from York to Hull, where we took a ship all the way around England to Fremington, I believe. At Fremington, we were met by Lord Santiago. And he brought us here."

"So you do not know who he is?"

She shook her head. "He has been very kind to us," she said. "The man who brought us from Hull to Fremington was also very kind. Lord Abelard?"

Sinclair snorted at the ridiculousness of the situation. "You do realize that you have been transported by two of the most feared pirates in the known world, don't you?" he said. "Abelard de Bottreaux is the leader of a band of pirates called Triton's Hellions and Santiago is the leader of a group called the Demons of the Sea. They are vicious, deadly men, but somehow, they seem to become decent when it comes to my wife and me. All Elisiana has to do is lift her finger and Santiago comes running."

"Elisiana is your wife?"

Sinclair nodded. "My wife," he said, looking at her. "My love. My everything."

Ophelia laughed softly. "That is good to hear," she said. "I am so glad that you are happy, Sinclair, truly. I have often thought about you often over the years and wondered how you were. Did you ever return home, to Ebchester?"

Sinclair nodded. "Once," he said. "About three years ago, after my son was born. It occurred to me that Ebchester was his legacy, too, so I made the trip."

"What did you find?"

"A small manor inhabited by the remnants of the servants our parents left behind," he said. "The land is rich, but it has not been managed well. I finally hired a man who used to work here, at Blackchurch, to go north and begin seeing to the land and the villeins. Mayhap someday I will want to live there, so it is time to restore the lands of our ancestors. Ebchester is our legacy, after all. I have neglected it for too long."

Ophelia smiled. "I am glad you did that," she said. "Showing respect for our forefathers and for the title that has become yours."

Sinclair held out his elbow, which she gratefully took. "I am sorry to say that along with tending our ancestral lands, I should have paid more attention to where you were and your living situation," he said. "I have been a terrible brother, Ophelia. Santiago said you were found living in poverty."

Her smile faded, but her expression was brave. "You were not a terrible brother," she said. "How could you have known? Sometimes life is not always kind. I will admit that I was hoping to start a new life, living closer to you, for Rhodes' sake. He's such a good lad, Sinclair. He deserves so much more than I can provide, and when the man told me that you were looking for me, I thought... I had hoped..."

She faded off and Sinclair patted her hand. He knew what she meant. "I promise you that Rhodes will be trained as a knight, as he should be," he said. "And you... I will find you work here at Blackchurch. You'll never have to worry over food or money or safety again. You are home, lass. We'll make sure you are taken care of."

Ophelia was tearing up again, but they were tears of joy. "I will admit that I did not know how you would react to seeing me again," she said. "The last time I saw you, you barely looked at me. I always thought you did not want to be troubled with me, so I was afraid to come."

He smiled. "I hope you are fearful no more."

"No more, I promise."

"Good," he said. "This is a joyful day, Ophelia. I get to introduce you to my wife. She is heavy with child, as you will see, and is very emotional these days, so if she cries all over you, please do not judge her harshly."

"Never," Ophelia said. "As I understand it, she has made this possible. I am very grateful to her."

Sinclair could see his cottage in the distance, thinking of the woman who meant everything to him and always would.

"As am I," he said quietly. "Truly... as am I. For everything."

With that, Sinclair took Ophelia to his cottage, where Elisiana did, indeed, greet the woman with tears. So many tears. But tears of great joy and of great anticipation for the future that awaited them all.

And what a future it was.

From Rhodes' fostering to the son born to Sinclair and Elisiana the following month, and to Ophelia and one of the Blackchurch trainers falling in love, life was meant to be full of joy, anticipation, and most of all, family.

Family by blood.

Family by friendship.

Sinclair and Elisiana had, indeed, found their paradise.

CB THE END CD

Children of Sinclair and Elisiana

Cristofer

Bethania

Santiago

Gerardo

Michael

Matias

Rafael

Tadeo

Desdra

Gabriela

AUTHOR'S AFTERWORD

One last thing!

This is the image that Elisiana drew of Sinclair. It's charcoal on vellum, which means it smears and it's not as clear as it should be, but you will note that she did not draw it in the Medieval style of art. Medieval artists had a very specific style when painting or drawing and we've all seen it on tapestries, Bibles, etc. It's a stylistic choice based on what's popular at the time (much as the Egyptians drew stylized pictures and images). Medieval portraits are referred to as traditional static depictions, but around the fourteenth century, they started producing more realistic artwork. Elisiana, as skilled as she is, is simply a little ahead of her time with a realistic drawing of Sinclair.

I love how she saw him.

KATHRYN LE VEQUE NOVELS

Medieval Romance:

De Wolfe Pack Series:
Warwolfe
The Wolfe
Nighthawk
ShadowWolfe
DarkWolfe
A Joyous de Wolfe Christmas
BlackWolfe
Serpent
A Wolfe Among Dragons
Scorpion
StormWolfe
Dark Destroyer
The Lion of the North
Walls of Babylon
The Best Is Yet To Be
BattleWolfe
Castle of Bones

De Wolfe Pack Generations:
WolfeHeart
WolfeStrike
WolfeSword
WolfeBlade
WolfeLord
WolfeShield
Nevermore
WolfeAx
WolfeBorn

The Executioner Knights:
By the Unholy Hand

The Mountain Dark
Starless
A Time of End
Winter of Solace
Lord of the Sky
The Splendid Hour
The Whispering Night
Netherworld
Lord of the Shadows
Of Mortal Fury
'Twas the Executioner Knight Before
Christmas
Crimson Shield
The Black Dragon

The de Russe Legacy:
The Falls of Erith
Lord of War: Black Angel
The Iron Knight
Beast
The Dark One: Dark Knight
The White Lord of Wellesbourne
Dark Moon
Dark Steel
A de Russe Christmas Miracle
Dark Warrior

The de Lohr Dynasty:
While Angels Slept
Rise of the Defender
Steelheart
Shadowmoor
Silversword
Spectre of the Sword
Unending Love

Archangel
A Blessed de Lohr Christmas
Lion of Twilight
Lion of War
Lion of Hearts
Lion of Steel

The Brothers de Lohr:
The Earl in Winter

Lords of East Anglia:
While Angels Slept
Godspeed
Age of Gods and Mortals

Great Lords of le Bec:
Great Protector

House of de Royans:
Lord of Winter
To the Lady Born
The Centurion

Lords of Eire:
Echoes of Ancient Dreams
Lord of Black Castle
The Darkland

Ancient Kings of Anglecynn:
The Whispering Night
Netherworld

Battle Lords of de Velt:
The Dark Lord
Devil's Dominion
Bay of Fear
The Dark Lord's First Christmas
The Dark Spawn
The Dark Conqueror
The Dark Angel

Reign of the House of de Winter:

Lespada
Swords and Shields

De Reyne Domination:
Guardian of Darkness
The Black Storm
A Cold Wynter's Knight
With Dreams
Master of the Dawn
One Wylde Knight

House of d'Vant:
Tender is the Knight (House of d'Vant)
The Red Fury (House of d'Vant)

The Dragonblade Series:
Fragments of Grace
Dragonblade
Island of Glass
The Savage Curtain
The Fallen One
The Phantom Bride

Great Marcher Lords of de Lara
Lord of the Shadows
Dragonblade

House of St. Hever
Fragments of Grace
Island of Glass
Queen of Lost Stars

Lords of Pembury:
The Savage Curtain

Lords of Thunder: The de Shera Brotherhood Trilogy
The Thunder Lord
The Thunder Warrior
The Thunder Knight

The Great Knights of de Moray:

Pirates of Britannia Series (with Eliza Knight):

Savage of the Sea by Eliza Knight

Leader of Titans by Kathryn Le Veque

The Sea Devil by Eliza Knight

Sea Wolfe by Kathryn Le Veque

<u>Note:</u> All Kathryn's novels are designed to be read as stand-alones, although many have cross-over characters or cross-over family groups. Novels that are grouped together have related characters or family groups. You will notice that some series have the same books; that is because they are cross-overs. A hero in one book may be the secondary character in another.

There is NO reading order except by chronology, but even in that case, you can still read the books as stand-alones. No novel is connected to another by a cliff hanger, and every book has an HEA.

Series are clearly marked. All series contain the same characters or family groups except the American Heroes Series, which is an anthology with unrelated characters.

For more information, find it in **A Reader's Guide to the Medieval World of Le Veque.**

About Kathryn Le Veque

Bringing the Medieval to Romance

KATHRYN LE VEQUE is a critically acclaimed, multiple USA TODAY Bestselling author, an Indie Reader bestseller, a charter Amazon All-Star author, and a #1 bestselling, award-winning, multi-published author in Medieval Historical Romance with over 100 published novels.

Kathryn is a multiple award nominee and winner, including the winner of Uncaged Book Reviews Magazine 2017 and 2018 "Raven Award" for Favorite Medieval Romance. Kathryn is also a multiple RONE nominee (InD'Tale Magazine), holding a record for the number of nominations. In 2018, her novel WARWOLFE was the winner in the Romance category of the Book Excellence Award and in 2019, her novel A WOLFE AMONG DRAGONS won the prestigious RONE award for best pre-16th century romance.

Kathryn is considered one of the top Indie authors in the world with over 2M copies in circulation, and her novels have been translated into several languages. Kathryn recently signed with Sourcebooks

Casablanca for a Medieval Fight Club series, first published in 2020.

In addition to her own published works, Kathryn is also the President/CEO of Dragonblade Publishing, a boutique publishing house specializing in Historical Romance. Dragonblade's success has seen it rise in the ranks to become Amazon's #1 e-book publisher of Historical Romance (K-Lytics report July 2020).

Kathryn loves to hear from her readers. Please find Kathryn on Facebook at Kathryn Le Veque, Author, or join her on Twitter @kathrynleveque. Sign up for Kathryn's blog at www.kathryn leveque.com for the latest news and sales.

Made in the USA
Middletown, DE
30 August 2024

60003864R00169